One year ago, we started a wild ride together. Six Minutes the eBook experience became available in over 51 countries on April 8ᵗʰ, 2016. Since then, the journey has been incredible. Shirts, the ultra popular hats, and the people I have had the opportunity to meet along the way is such a blessing I will forever be grateful for. But there were two questions that I found always being asked. Brandon, when does Seven Minutes come out (get it?), and when does the paperback come out? I am so proud to finally give you Six Minutes, revamped with some special tweaks, in paperback. Much love, and thank you for your support.

-Brandon

A lot of times, we get stuck in this mindset that this is life, and this is how we have to live it. We lose our sense of identity, and go on living in a way someone else told us to. There is nothing as sad as someone who did not follow their passion in life. No matter how fast the walls seem to be closing on us, remember that we always have a choice. It is never too late for us to change our universe, find our true purpose, and be great!

For Dad
For Bianca
For Mom
And for you
Looking to the Stars

Brandon Mattinen

SIX MINUTES

BRANDON MATTINEN

Part ONE

1 The Boy with a Heart

Sweat poured down his brow, stinging Tyler Mason's pupils. The vibrations from the roaring crowd bounced off his headgear as he reached out to grip his opponent's forearms but his fingers slid off like they went down a slip and slide.

"It's definitely a hot night tonight, and you can see it on these two stellar athletes. They are absolutely drenched in sweat!" Showman and announcer Zeus Clementine shouted from the edge of his seat, as he looked on at the two athletes suspended from a hovering stage in the middle of the arena above the crowd.

"You're not kidding, Zeus. They look like they have just taken a shower!" His fellow reporter, Daniel Louis joked. "It's just incredible that the match has gone on this long already. Mason should have never made it this far!"

"That's right, Daniel. Caleb, ranked number two in the world, has just two minutes and twenty seconds of this six minute match remaining to break the tie and punch his ticket to the championship this Friday." Zeus said as he ran his hand through his slicked back orange hair and adjusted his blue suit.

"And Tyler Mason, crowd favorite, has two minutes and twenty seconds left to become the youngest championship finalist ever!" Daniel added.

"Playing devil's advocate, I see." Zeus countered.

"Perhaps." Daniel replied bluntly. " Or maybe I am just rooting for the underdog, because someone has to. It's a cut throat business on the world's biggest athletic stage!"

"Well Daniel…I admire your intentions and more importantly your optimism, applaud you for it even, but I don't believe in fairytales." Zeus chuckled, shaking his head.

Caleb's leg was just in reach— Tyler Mason lunged in for a takedown! If he could finish this he would score and lock in a nice two point lead to give him a cushion for the third and final period. His fingertips brushed Caleb's sweat drenched calf, he rapidly threw his arm around to hook it when he felt his right foot suddenly slipped like it was on ice.

He crashed to both knees, barely catching his momentum with his elbows.

Like a bull out of a china closet Caleb rushed around him to gain control and two points, throwing his arms under his armpits.

"TWO!" The referee shouted as he lobbed up two fingers. The screams of the crowd thundered around the inside of Tyler's headgear.

The buzzer only added to the chaos, its screech signaling the end of the second period. He looked down to see the pool of sweat that had caused his fall, and silently cursed to himself. Caleb shoved him back to the ground as he triumphantly paraded back to his coaches.

"Tyler Mason what the hell are you doing? What the *hell* are you doing?"

Tyler looked up to see his own disgruntled looking coaches as they zoomed over on their hover pad.

Smirking, he got to his feet and for the first time tonight, took a moment to take everything in.

Energy.

That was the one word that kept popping up in his head.

The stage they were wrestling on drifted in the middle of a tremendous outdoor arena, and the encircling crowd watched them in seats that towered so high they seemed to be trying to touch the stars.

He could make out a man in the front row with a huge green 'C' painted on his face who looked as though he was going to pass out as he hollered at the top of his lungs, spilling his drink on the woman next to him. Many of them in the crowd had painted their faces, bodies, and shirts with the colors of their country, while others had the colors of their athletes. The Tournament of Champions was just as much about fashion as it was sport.

For a second, Tyler almost forgot he was in the middle of the most important wrestling match of his life.

"Tyler?"

He turned to see Jason and Monty, who now hovered next to him.

"Oh good, you're back to the Earth with the rest of us. Do you want to tell me what *the hell* that was?" Jason probed as he stopped waving his hand across Tyler's face. "Thirteen seconds left and you take a shot like that?" Jason moaned as discreetly as possible, despite the fact that if he did yell no one would hear over the thunder of the crowd.

Jason Teach. He couldn't say that name without a cluster of different feelings bubbling to the surface. Jason was the only recruiter who ignored the ugly zero percent chance he would become anything—and gifted him with an opportunity. Over their last year and a half together, Tyler had become accustomed to seeing him flustered when matches were close, but never like this!

"Tyler...Tyler...TYLER!"

"What—oh— sorry!"

"Can you just bare with me here for two little minutes? Let's win the biggest match of your life now, and daydream later. Hell, I'll even daydream with you! Now back to that shot—"

"It wasn't a bad shot, Jason, I had it! It was the puddle of sweat that took away my balance!" He pointed to it just as a few maintenance men with mops arrived to dry it up per instruction of the referee.

"Alright kid," Lester Monty, his 'comic relief' coach and assistant to Jason said as he hopped off the coaches hover pad onto the big one (which was not allowed), drying him off with a towel. "Are you going to let the puddle of sweat beat you this match?"

"Absolutely not!"

"Forget it, then. You're doing great! You've got everyone scratching their heads right now because this should have been him polishing the floors with you. Keep doing what you're doing. Stay calm and stay collected. We are *going* to make it to Friday."

"Sir if you don't get off the mat right now I am going to—

"Sorry about that, bro! I slipped!" Monty said as he hopped back on to the coaches' pad, chomping at his gum like a mad man.

The referee glared at them in annoyance.

"Lets get back to the center now. I am ready to start the third period." He said as he walked away from them.

"Nice going, Monty." Tyler said with a wink.

"Shut up, kid." Monty laughed.

"Enough children," Jason smirked. He grabbed Tyler's shoulders and was back to absolute seriousness. "Tyler, listen to me now. Focus on me and only me. This match is everything you have *ever* worked for. You have done beautifully. I will love you no matter if you win or lose, but lets leave here as winners, alright?"

"Let's do it!" Tyler smiled.

"Mr. Mason, I don't want to have to ask you again. Get to the center of the mat now or there will be consequences." The referee snarled as he pulled up his pants, looking more and more like he was starting to dislike them.

Jason didn't let him go. "What are we going to do, Ty?"

"Control our destiny."

"That's right. Be calm. Be precise. Be great!"

With that Jason let him go, slapping his back as he ran back to the center.

"I am curious to know what was said to each wrestler in their corners?" Zeus questioned.

"I would imagine it was serious in both. There is a lot at stake here, on top of the mountain of pressure that comes with a wrestling match. It's hard to understand unless you've wrestled before." Daniel said.

"Yes, that is what I have been told in the past. Seeing how the second period ended, I am not as confident for your boy, Daniel."

"Just keep an open mind, Zeus, the match isn't over till it's over."

"I see myself as more of a director rather than a directed. Perhaps I will take your open mind offer another day." Zeus smiled.

"No open mind today?" Daniel asked. "In that bright blue suit you better be open minded."

"Ha. Ha. Ha."

"It was Mr. Caleb who had choice last period. That makes it your turn this period, Mr. Mason. What would you like?" The referee asked flatly. The expression of total boredom never left his face.

"I choose…" The crowd began to mum as it eagerly awaited his decision. He turned to Jason and Monty. They nodded at him reassuringly. They trusted him to make this choice. He took a deep breath to keep himself calm while his brain scrambled, trying to think on command.

"Which is it, Mr. Mason? Neutral, starting on your feet? Bottom, starting on all fours with him covering? Or do you want to be gone, kicked out of my arena for wasting my time?"

"Neutral." Tyler snapped with a sharp glare. Glaring back disapprovingly for a few seconds, the referee than signaled to the audience that Tyler had chosen neutral.

"Ready?" He asked as Tyler and Caleb got down into their stances. Tyler stared right through Caleb's arrogant smirk, into his heart. Somewhere in there was a misplaced ideal of being better than everyone else, and he was going to remove that right now. His skin tingled with adrenaline as he impatiently waited for the referee to begin the final period.

"Wrestle!" The referee shouted.

Befitting to his nickname, the 'raging bull', Caleb rushed Tyler using the great brute strength of his massive physical frame to try and out muscle his smaller opponent to the ground. Large new beads of sweat rolled down Tyler's face as he used all of his remaining strength and spirit to resist the onslaught.

He felt himself being thrown to the ground with tremendous force. *Roll, Tyler roll!*

He rolled through the attack to his knees, and dove at Caleb's ankles for a takedown. Caleb quickly tap danced out of the way.

Jumping to his feet, Tyler took another lunge, trying to take the powerful legs out from underneath the bull and get his two he should've gotten last time.

But that first missed take down had given Caleb too much conf—

Immense force began to suffocate him, crushing down on his lungs, it felt like his chest was being crushed as Caleb used Tyler's momentum against him. The crowd awed over Caleb's strength, as he threw Tyler right over his head like a rag doll. Tyler scrambled to get off of his back and into a more stable wrestling position, but the onslaught continued. Was it humanly possible to go at this pace after four minutes of hard wrestling already?

"It doesn't look good for the 'boy with a heart' Tyler Mason as we enter the final minute of the match." Zeus Clementine declared flashing his million-dollar smile to go with his million-dollar suit.

"Zeus, I am telling you, this kid has made it this far. You just can not count him out yet!" Daniel again pleaded his case to his co-worker.

"LETS GO, TYLER!" *Pop! Pop! Pop! Pop! Pop!* "LETS GO, TYLER!" *Pop! Pop! Pop! Pop! Pop!* The crowd cheered.

"We love you, Ty!"

"You got this! He's getting tired, go for the five pointer if you have to!"

The crowd put something back in Tyler he was losing fast— hope. He struggled on to repel the bull as the human was lost in rage as Caleb carried on, trying to beat Tyler's head off. Tyler felt himself getting extremely close to the edge of the mat, and even more important— the *edge* of the hover pad.

Caleb wasn't stopping, and Tyler wasn't about to find out if the electromagnetic beams were working today. He glanced to see the ground under his feet coming to an end, and using Caleb's momentum swung him out of bounds and off the hover pad...where Tyler would have been if he had waited half a second longer. Caleb hollered for his life. Out of nowhere, jets of blue light appeared to catch him.

Electromagnetic beam safety measure working? Check.

Caleb was brought back to the mat safely, though he was looking frazzled and lost.

"Well Zeus, looks like the bull has just been bullied!" Daniel laughed, the camera panning in on the unpleasant frown forming on Zeus's face.

Looking into the audience, Tyler locked eyes with his unhappy looking girlfriend.

What the hell are you doing? She mouthed to him. With her dirty blonde hair and red dress Cailey Lopezzi was not one to be easily missed. With an innocent look on his face, Tyler threw his hands up with a smile.

"Through it all, Tyler still finds it in him to smile! Caleb still looks like he is lost, Zeus!" Daniel snickered.

"That should be a penalty point Daniel, throwing him off the hover pad like that."

"Now you are reaching, Zeus!"

Cailey pointed over at the score and gave Tyler a stern look.

All right, all right. He mouthed as he headed back to the center of the mat.

"That kind of behavior is not tolerated in my arena, Mr. Mason. One point goes to Caleb!" the referee signaled.

"With one minute left that has got to hurt!" Zeus perked up again.

"Are you actually serious?" Tyler groaned under his breath.

"Another word and I will kick you out." The referee growled, still looking very much uninterested in the entire situation. Glancing behind him he saw a smile form across Caleb's face. Did the bull plan this? A hidden rage of his own began heating up somewhere deep inside. He peered over to Jason and Monty, who signaled him to shrug it off.

"Fifty seven seconds left in the match and he's down by three. I'm sorry Daniel, but it looks like the underdog will stay the underdog." Zeus declared.

"Wrestlers ready? Wrestle!" The referee shouted. Charging Caleb as he had done to him moments before, Tyler pounded on the kid with a ferocity that even he hadn't known he was capable of.

Seemingly out of his bull-like energy, Caleb began doing everything he could to stall, trying to keep Tyler from scoring by doing absolutely nothing… except shuffling away from him. He grabbed Tyler's fingers as tight as he could and continued backing away. But Tyler refused to let the puddle of sweat defeat him. He was going to win this match.

"Thirty seconds left in the match!" Zeus proclaimed. The anticipation could be felt throughout the arena, as it grew even more thunderous second by second. TV cameras panned everywhere, broadcasting the event all around the world.

Tyler could feel himself starting to become panicked, and there was no better way for him to lose the match than to get flustered. He took a moment to pause, and relax his mind.

"I don't know what he is doing, but there are only twenty seconds left in the match and he is letting up!" Zeus continued, glancing over at Daniel.

Caleb laughed as he backed away from Tyler, shrugging it off as a sign of victory for himself.

After what felt like only a few seconds Tyler found his cool again. He glanced at the clock, only *seventeen* seconds to spare. As if sensing this, Caleb went on the super defensive. Leg shots were nigh impossible now. *What could he do?*

Wait a second. No one had ever dared attack the bull with an upper body move. He was just too strong. Tyler found his strategy.

"Ten seconds, if he doesn't do something fast then the match will be over before he has even made a final move!" Zeus yelled.

Tyler faked a shot on Caleb's left leg, brought himself up at an angle to the right and slugged his arm around Caleb's neck like he was going to go for a headlock. He felt Caleb's arms come up in a frantic panic!

"Eight seconds!" Zeus yelled as everyone stared down below with unflinching intensity.

"No one has attempted an upper body move on the bull in over two years!" Daniel shouted.

Caught off guard, Caleb did everything he could do to hit, push, or punch Tyler off of him. Abruptly, Tyler let go of his head and swiftly crouched down and saw his wide open target, Caleb's completely defenseless legs. Like a springboard, he launched himself at them.

Caleb wheezed as the wind was pulverized out of his lungs and he was blasted onto his back by the sheer force of Tyler's momentum.

"THE CROWD IS GOING WILD! IF HE KEEPS HIM THERE THAT IS BACK POINTS, AND THE MATCH IS OVER!" Daniel yelled as he jumped up and down. Zeus rose to his feet as the referee counted with a motion of his arm.

"ONE," The crowd counted with the referee. "TWO!" Tyler fought with everything he had to keep the bull down as he roared. "THREE!" The sound of the buzzer ricocheted off of the inside of Tyler's head gear as the referee held up the point count.

He saw two fingers in the air.

"We have two for takedown," The referee announced.

Tyler's heart sank. He really thought he had this won.

Caleb jumped up yelling and thrashing in celebration. He was so close to the finals he could feel them in his bones.

The puddle of sweat had beaten him.

"I am NOT finished yet, Mr. Caleb!" The referee bellowed.

"We have two for near fall, Caleb was on his back for three seconds that is TWO!" The referee yelled as he jumped in the air. Tyler had to do a double take to make sure he believed his eyes; the referee's facial expression had just changed for the first time all night.

He jumped in the air with the referee. He did it! He actually *did it!*

"The crowd is going absolutely bonkers! It's an incredible feeling here! Tyler Mason has just made history tonight!" Daniel shouted as the crowd jumped up on to his hover pad and ran up to the camera.

Panning back to Zeus who was still sitting at his desk, the camera began a slow ascent toward him. "Tonight, we have witnessed history as Tyler Mason has become the youngest athlete ever to make it to the Championship, at 18 years old." Zeus declared as though he had never doubted these events would take place.

"He has just beaten out the previous record of 19 by Champion, Alfredo Lopezzi! Now he takes on Dei Jie, the most feared wrestler in the entire east, starting here live at 7pm Friday! Don't miss my exclusive one on one sit-down with Tyler and Dei on Thursday evening at 6pm! This is the biggest week of the year folks! Thank you for joining, have a fine Sunday evening, and BE GREAT!" Zeus wrapped up the broadcast with a shining smile.

Tyler could barely make his way to the locker room as the reporters and fans alike ambushed him. Monty and Jason did their best to help, but they were short on security. The crowds had broken down the barrier on the east side of the arena and were in a mad rush to see him.

Or trample him. He couldn't tell.

Despite the chaos, he felt like he was floating with every step he took. He could finally see everything he dreamed meshing with reality.

"Mr. Mason, how do you feel right now?"

"Tyler, can you stop and give me a moment of your time please?"

"Have you seen Cailey yet?"

Tyler used his hand as a shade his eyes as the flashes blinded him.

"TYLER! TYLER?" A familiar voice cut through the rest. He stopped and turned to see where it was coming from. He could see the army of people behind them parting as a large group of men in black suits parted the masses.

The men immediately surrounded him, Jason, and Monty. "Contender secure." One said into his earpiece. "Escorting them to Sector A now."

"Sector A?" Monty asked, as he ran his fingers through his graying black hair to make sure it was still slicked back perfectly. It wasn't. A few pieces shot skyward. But Tyler would leave him to his own assumptions.

"The locker room, sir." The man answered.

"TYLER!" Cailey jumped into his arms, squeezing him tighter than ever before as she planted a large kiss on his lips. "You did great, Ty! You did great!"

16

"I know this is going to sound so cliché, but do you know how long I have dreamed about this?" He whispered as if it was just the two of them.

"I do." She whispered back. "I do."

"Okay, so I don't want to be *that* guy, but we do have about a million people all trying to take a piece of you home with them tonight, Tyler. Can we please get a room?" Jason asked, throwing in a rather large smile.

"Absolutely." Cailey said jumping down and walking ahead of them. "Waiting on you now, boys."

Monty and Jason exchanged humored looks, and their procession battled on with a little more ease to the locker room.

Once the locker room door shut, the world suddenly seemed to go quiet again. Away from the chaos and the spotlight, Tyler could hear his own thoughts again.

After talking for a few minutes, Cailey kissed him goodbye, and headed to meet her father at the press conference where Tyler would join her shortly. She had mentioned something about lunch with her father on her way out, but not this week right? It was too busy, heck too big of a week for him to be able to focus on anything else but this.

Maybe next week once his life returned to normal.

"How are you feeling, champ?" Jason asked as he slapped his hand on Tyler's shoulder. "Bring it in for a hug buddy, come on!" He said grabbing him.

"Words just don't do it justice, do they?" Monty asked. "That was great back there kid. I thought we were goners for a minute there."

"I'll admit that I…. was never nervous!" Tyler stated as seriously as he could.

"Ha!" Jason laughed as Monty began pretending to wrestle him.

"But seriously, not only did you get yourself one step closer to achieving your goal, you got us one step closer to our goal." Jason added as his voice became slightly more serious.

Tyler had almost forgotten about their deal. It had been the deciding factor in him being recruited by Jason over anyone else. The people competing with him for the spot had been way more qualified. But Jason told him he had something none of the others had. He hadn't elaborated on exact terms of what Tyler would do other than use what ever it was that separated him from the pack for a cause 'more pure than any other.' Neither had expected the success story that had followed, with Tyler now one of the most recognized faces in the world.

"I can't wait to help, Jason. You've done so much for me and we've come so far. When do you want to talk specifics?"

"Later." Jason said. "It's been a great day. Let's enjoy the moment."

Tyler had a weird feeling about this in his gut, but Jason was right. Why not enjoy this day before it was over. It's not everyday things like this happen, after all.

"You're right. Promise me we will though, alright?"

"Believe me Ty, it won't be too much longer." Jason reassured him with a look that made Tyler trust the man with his career, his future, maybe even his life.

"Alright, I am going to shower now, gentleman." Tyler said. "And I would prefer to do it without ice this time." He joked, referencing the time Jason and Monty decided to ice him in shower last week.

"Well, I guess we could give you a pass today." Jason said with a wink.

"Oh one more thing, Tyler," Monty chimed in before he had gotten into the bathroom. "A friend of mine says she could help you out with your request?"

Tyler's heart skipped a beat. "Serious?"

"Serious." Monty said.

"Life, life's going to be a lot different after this week isn't it?" Tyler asked, as he couldn't shake the feeling.

"What makes you say that?" Jason asked.

"Oh, I don't know. I just have had this funny feeling that I can't shake since the match."

Jason smiled. "Yes, Tyler. I suppose life may be a little different."

2 Treachery or Triumph

Luck, plain and simple.

That's all Casper Lanstark could think of to describe his current predicament, as he replayed it over and over in his head. How they'd managed to get *so* close to stopping him *this* close to the end caused him to feel something in his ambitious heart he seldom felt: fear.

He remembered the final lesson his father had taught him, which was to block the feeling out. Fear, after all, clouds one's judgment. And his line of work could not afford any blunders, especially now that he could taste the sweet flavor of victory, so close.

Yet so far.

Casper and his people knew the feeling only too well. As he stared down into the night skyline of his city, he felt anger fizzing out of his skin, but toward no one but himself. He should have foreseen something like this. Perhaps this had worked out for the better now. He never believed in luck before.

He certainly did now.

His vision for the future had been in motion for almost twenty-three years now. It was ironic really, because the entire plan had been a last minute shot in the dark.

Casper Lanstark remembered that blazingly hot summer day in the bustling streets of New York City twenty-three years ago. The world had almost ended. The streets were filled with people rejoicing that it *hadn't* ended that day

One was not.

Obviously he did not want the world to end, just come pretty close. It was all part of the plan. As those first few nuclear missiles took flight, he really thought his dreams would merge with reality. But, one thing he had learned quickly in life was that nothing is ever what it seems.

Using the Olympic games, his organization ignited the already searing tensions between the U.S. and China, the world's two superpowers, and finally a war as big as they had

19

hoped began. Within days the domino effect had taken its toll, as did the war. Whole countries were obliterated in hours. These were just casualties, however. What his organization really needed was the two superpowers to knock each other out of the game. Then, with their money and influence, they would freely assume control of the world and finally establish the vision they were so painstakingly working for.

A better world.

So what caused their massive defeat? The will of a single man.

On the eve of the massive Chinese invasion of the mainland United States, and the U.S.'s own space fleet weapons attack over China, the President of the United States stood against the war cries from around the world, and his own people.

"The suffering by the people of Earth," he said. "Has been worse than ever seen in history in the first few weeks of this conflict alone. The suffering of our fellow human beings brought on by fellow human beings is truly shameful to our species. Therefore, effective immediately, I am ordering all U.S. forces around the world to cease fighting, immediately. To our allies around the world, whether you consider this country a friend or foe, I ask you this, at what cost are you finally going to say enough? Look at your family sitting next to you. Tomorrow they will be gone. Gone. Unless you make the decision to look deep inside of yourself right now, and do what you know is right— stop this fighting."

And amazingly, impossibly, unbelievably, it worked. Literally overnight, on the verge of utter and total victory, it was over.

As peace talks began, his organization, which had flourished since the beginning of man, crumbled. Members were leaving in droves. The bank accounts were being cleaned out. And in contrast to the boundless feelings of the thousands on the streets, he had never felt so crushed. His dream of leaving his mark on the world was still very much that, a dream.

At the time, he had been undercover as a diplomat in the U.S. State Department. There he sat in his $4,000 suit, a broken man as peace was made before his very eyes. Delegates from every country signed the peace treaty on large mahogany desks as cameras flashed. Casper Lanstark never quit anything, from his days as a star athlete to crushing friends or foes. But maybe it was time.

A little part of him died at the thought.

He could easily withdrawal the millions left in the accounts and take off as had most of the others. He could live the 'ideal life' everyone thinks is so grand. But would that really make him happy?

As the weeks passed, the countries of the world all agreed that there needed to be something to give humanity somewhere else to channel it's focus other than war. The only problem was, they couldn't figure out what. The Olympics, its reputation tarnished thanks to Casper and his people, could no longer be used. As arguments were made, an idea, as unlikely as it was, began to form in his head. Excitement was growing in him so much he had to excuse himself from his meeting to take a walk around New York City.

The next day, as the towel had been thrown in on a viable replacement, he got up from the chair in the back of the room. Ignoring those who mocked him to sit back down, he walked straight to the center of the room.

That would be the last day he sat in the back of the room.

It was on this day that a young Casper Lanstark rose from a confident, but still unproven young man to a lion. His seemingly common sense proposal, which called for another worldwide sporting event in place of the Olympics, coined the Tournament of Champions, passed overnight.

They even agreed to let him spearhead the project - and gave him $50 billion to do it.

The TOC's popularity spawned the globe. He became an international hero, billionaire, and virtual titan in just five years. Unbeknownst to all, Casper was not as he seemed. His enemies had all fallen deep into his traps, and today he stood on the brink of total victory.

"Argh!" Like an explosion of bubbling lava his anger escaped him as he swung his arm knocking the glasses off the table, sending them crashing to the floor.

"Sir?" The familiar voice of Alfredo Lopezzi echoed throughout the penthouse.

"Twenty years of patience, Alfredo. Twenty years!" He roared. The boom of the oblivious celebrating crowd below seemed to break the seriousness of the moment. Casper couldn't help but smirk.

"With all due respect sir, he is an eighteen year old boy all by himself against *us*." Unlike his colleague, Casper had not forgotten who had stopped them before- a single person. He was President of the United States, so that may have helped a little. But...

"Alfredo, let me ask you, what did the kid do tonight?"

"He...won?"

"So what does that mean?"

"He is going to the championship...but I am not sure I follow where you're going with this."

"He is going to the championship in the biggest phenomenon the world has ever seen perhaps since the smartphone! The kid has gone from celebrity to megastar in the past few hours." And that means that all the people who followed this kid, supported him, and believed in him would listen to him.

It was smart. He had to give his old pal that. Using his own event against him to make a name for the people to rally behind.

He motioned for Alfredo to follow. As quickly and as quietly as they could, stewards appeared to clean the glass off the floor, before disappearing back into the shadows once they were done.

As they walked, Casper gazed out the window at the city named after him.

Lanstark City was a miracle of modern science, with every top dollar luxury possible stuffed into the 14 and a half-mile man made island city. Lanstark's penthouse was no exception. As the two men navigated the hallways on the perfectly polished floors, they passed priceless items of both today and yesterday.

"We can try and buy him sir?"

The thought had crossed his mind.

After the long trip through the dark hallways of his palatial lair, they arrived to a room on the other side of the floor. This was a part of the floor a very select few had ever ventured into, and even fewer had been inside the room they were about to enter. Two massive armed guards stood at the door, clad in black armor with the bright golden TOC eagle on their chest. They shrank in the presence of their leader, nodding at him as the doors parted ways for their exclusive occupants.

"I will say this, the luck of us finding the connection is incredible given they only had to stay invisible for five more days."

Very few people in the world would even dare to breathe, let alone speak in the presence of the world's most powerful man. But Alfredo Lopezzi was the exception, having earned himself the spot below Casper Lanstark in the Venom chain of command.

With a few flicks of his finger on a tablet, Alfredo brought up multiple videos, pictures, interviews, phone calls, Internet searches, and movements of their new eighteen-year-old friend. Casper took a seat, studying everything about this new inconvenience. Yesterday he had no idea who the kid was, and today he was looking up everything there was to know about him.

Now that he saw the pictures, he did recognize him somewhat. He was a complete statistic anomaly; he wasn't even supposed to make it out of the first round of the tournament. And yet here he was.

It killed him to admit it, but he liked the kid already.

"What do we know about him?" Lanstark asked.

"His fans are true diehards. They live and breathe for this kid." Alfredo's voice suggested a hint of humor at the notion. Casper felt the same— until he saw pulled up some of the videos and pictures he was now. People clung to this kid like a child does to a teddy bear. And not just teens, people of all ages too.

This unsettled the world's most powerful man.

"There is also the matter of our old friends, who have been guiding him along the way." Alfredo brought up their pictures on the screen.

"Even in death you are still trying to haunt me, Michael?" Casper smirked. "We will do nothing for now. Let's keep them in the dark about our findings."

Alfredo nodded in agreement. "That leaves the boy."

Plenty of scenarios entered his head, but all of them were failures. The eyes of the world were watching to see the young man in the championships. The boy's distinctive body shape and face also ruled out replacing him with an actor, and once the wrestling started any makeup or fake facial features would be rendered useless.

Again, the videos of the people's affection for the boy on the screen caught his attention. There was something about this kid, something in his gut that bothered him. Goosebumps tried to etch their way up on his skin, and for the first time in thirteen years, his absolute confidence briefly deserted him. No matter how brief of a period it was, it was not a feeling he was used to.

Surprisingly, steam did not begin to rise out of his ears as the wheels in the complex mind of Casper Lanstark began to turn faster. His thoughts again took him back in time; back to the last time he thought he was this close to victory. Back to the last time their enemies were on the run. Back to the last time he had seen people flank to someone like this. The thoughts hatched painful memories in his head.

It was by design that this boy was here.

To the world, Michael had been a symbol. To Casper, he was the greatest threat to his dreams yet. The man had an unbelievable ability to rally people. The day he died it actually saddened him, even if it was by his own hand.

However, the odds were in *his* favor this time. He had discovered this little plan. And unlike the mistakes of the past, he now knew this was coming, and would put an end to it.

"I know exactly how we are going to handle the boy." Casper stated as a smile began to form across his face.

"As it so happens, Alfredo, the boy will be very useful to us."

"How is that exactly, Casper?" Alfredo grumbled, as if he were missing something.

"He's a symbol."

"A symbol?"

"To appear to the common mind of the masses is a task few individuals are able to accomplish without doing it through their wallet or through the media. Fewer are able to make this connection at all while missing only one of those means. Even fewer are able to cross that line of trust to the level where they become a *symbol*. You see, Alfredo, these people are the few throughout history who have moved entire populations to revolution, conquest, peace, and destruction. This young man, as impossible as it seems, has transcended all barriers and became exactly that: a symbol."

"So what does this mean for us? We can't do anything to him." Alfredo complained.

"My friend, it's not what we are going to do *to* him. It's what we are going to do *with* him."

It suddenly occurred to Casper that he did not know the name of his new ace in the hole. He typed a few things onto the screen on the arm of his chair. A file whizzed up on one of the monitors.

"Well look at that, he comes from Michigan same as me." Alfredo remarked.

"Small world." Casper laughed.

A video of the press conference from a few hours earlier popped up on the screen.

"Tyler, congrats on your big night. You've made history here, and went from being a self described nobody to a global phenomenon. Now that you have this enormous platform, what are you going to do with it?"

"You know, that's a great question Carol, and I can honestly tell you it is a bit overwhelming. But I have the best team behind me, I owe much of my success to them and I can't wait to get out there and make history on Friday."

The reply fascinated Casper. He paused the screen.

"You will make history, Tyler Mason. That much I can promise you."

3 **Purpose**

He pushed down even harder on the gas pedal.

The wind began to lash at his cheeks with even more fury.

The car sprang forward, burying him back into the seat. He whizzed past a few lights.

Should I do it? He pondered. After all, it was against the law. But when would be the next time he would get the opportunity to drive one of these?

He lunged the wheel forward, yelling with excitement as the car began closing in on the towering skyscrapers of Lanstark City. The Dragon Fly X was everything he had ever heard it would be and more. As the world's fastest, most versatile flying car it could easily be navigated around city skies by an experienced driver, something Tyler was not.

"Wooooooooohhhooooooooo!" He bellowed as he weaved around the corner of a building. Pure adrenaline pumped through his veins as he swung the car right to head downtown. He checked the speedometer; he was going 102, now 104, did that really say 115?

If Jason saw you right now…

He would be in deep doo doo.

His reflection smiled back at him as he pulled alongside the towering mirrored skyscrapers. Waving to himself, he lunged the Dragon Fly even further down toward Gross Pointe Avenue, the street below. It was always littered with sports cars. Imagine if they saw an even better one right above their heads…

He swung the wheel left and flew the bright red marvel above some shorter buildings to get to the next block. Already, he could see all the topless sports cars racing back and forth. Perfect! He jerked the wheel down as his descent provoked the screams of some of the partiers below, probably thinking a crazy drunk was about to crash.

Right as he was going to plow into the line of cars he pulled up, and turned on the bottom cameras of his flashy ride.

He watched as the hair of the woman in the car below thrashed every which way as he zoomed right over all their heads.

"Just what do you think you're doing, kid! Do you know *who* I am?"

He cruised down the line getting similar threats from everyone. One of them was bound to call the island police. With that thought, he swung the wheel, throwing the car right.

"WOAH!" He dabbed left, narrowly avoiding a small collision with a building. No dent. Phew!

He pulled up to a safe distance above the gleaming skyscrapers, and put the gears in full throttle to get back to the hotel. This city was truly the nicest place he had ever been able to call home. Tyler's thoughts drifted to the road ahead after this. He would be able to purchase a house of his own, among other things he had always dreamed of having as a child.

Tyler smiled at the thought. It was odd, really- that he hadn't been pulled over by island security. He hadn't flown in the designated areas at all. Shrugging it off as the hotel came into view, he arched the beautiful machine up to the very top floor where its owner currently resided.

He took a last minute swing through some clouds before bringing the car down to the landing pad where he could make out the silhouette of a man. Switching autopilot back on, the car did all the landing work for him.

He hopped out of the Dragon Fly X to greet his visitor.

"Do you know how many things I want to say to you right now?" Jason sighed.

"Look it could have been worse. I didn't even get a ticket!" Tyler smirked.

"That is because I had to call in every favor I had for them not to detain you, the car, and plaster it all over the news." Jason scolded as he ripped the shades off of Tyler's face.

"Oh…well maybe I could have slowed down a little."

"A little? You flew this car *inches* over the heads of some of the richest, most egotistical individuals on the planet. You didn't think there would be any blowback from that?"

"Jason it was just a bit of fun. Can we please not dwell? I am in the finals! We're almost home."

"We aren't home *yet,* Tyler. You would be wise to remember that."

"Look, I appreciate what you've done for me Jason, but sometimes I just need my space."

"Right over here, Angelica." Monty arrived with who had to be the owner of the penthouse, and the Dragon Fly X.

"Thank you, Lester. Jason." She nodded before circling Tyler, inspecting him up and down as her high heels announced her every step with a *click. click. click.*

"You must be the famous Tyler Mason." Her accent made added so much gravity to his name he loved it.

He cleared his throat. "To who do I owe the pleasure?" He said with a smile.

"Tyler, this is Angelica Musk. She is a very big friend of ours, and one of the most successful in her field of business." Monty said as he gave Tyler the look of *'behave or I'll kick your ass.'*

"One of the most beautiful, too." Tyler winked.

"So, you're reputation proceeds you, Mr. Mason. Good. The world needs a little more color, anyway." Angelica said as she gave peculiar glances to Jason and Monty.

A man dressed in blue came and whispered in her ear before running off.

"As much as I wish I could stay longer I have to be on my way, gentlemen. It was a pleasure making your acquaintance, Tyler." She said walking away before pausing. "One more thing." She walked within a breaths distance from Tyler, and stuck her hand in his pocket.

She pulled out the Dragon Fly X keys.

"I hope you enjoyed your ride."

"Believe me I did." Tyler smiled. "Maybe next time you could come along?"

"Maybe," She nodded, walking away. "But I don't go for younger men. Good day, gentlemen. Tyler, I am sure I will be seeing you again soon."

Tyler couldn't help but laugh to himself as they headed down to his suite. There was something about that woman. He couldn't quite put his finger on it, but there was something. He continued to drown out the complaints of Jason and Monty as they walked on. Didn't they realize he was only joking with his so-called flirtations? So he had a little bit of fun? He deserved it.

He loved Cailey, and he was seeing her this afternoon.

"Tyler, when I told you a friend of mine was allowing you to take a Dragon Fly X for a test drive, I didn't think you would interpret that as a pass to flirt with her." Monty said with an annoyed expression on his face as he closed the door to Tyler's suite.

"Monty, it was just a bit of fun! I didn't mean anything by it." Tyler insisted.

"Which is all good fun, unless you're in a relationship that the public closely follows. Can you imagine the repercussions if the cameras were around?" Jason chimed in, also looking rather irritated.

"We are now less than five days out from the end of this, Tyler. Can you please just hold out a little longer?" Jason pleaded.

"Oh right, I forgot, our deal. The deal we made in order for you to represent me, out here. The deal that I still know zero about!" Tyler found frustration inflating like a balloon in his stomach.

"We haven't told you the specifics yet because we want this experience to be incredible for you. And that can't be if you're ground down in the things that we have to handle everyday." Monty said, as he put his hand on Jason's shoulder before taking a step toward Tyler. "Now, let us do what we have to, and if we need to fill you in on something, we will. For now, we want you to focus."

"Focus?" Tyler frowned.

"On you're wrestling, on the people who support you. Be you. Be the boy with a heart." Jason replied.

"Is that what this is about? You both are going to exploit the position I am in soon like the rest of them?" Tyler fired.

30

"Tyler, we are on *your* side. Please remember that." Jason said.

"My side huh? Because as of right now it looks like the both of you are no different than anyone else keeping things from me and trying to further your own agenda by associating with me!" As soon as the words left his mouth he regretted them.

"It would be wise of you to remember *who* it was that got you to where you stand today!" Monty bellowed.

"*Monty...*" Jason said as the emotions in the room began to boil

"You know what..." Tyler began. "I am going to shower, and get ready for this afternoon. I will see you guys later." With that, he went into his room and shut the door behind him.

Tyler had realized early on that even though Monty was the older one, it was Jason who kept things running smoothly. Monty was usually the one to lose his cool first, with his face turning bright red, a feature that would become even more obvious due to his salt and pepper hair.

But Monty had never lost his temper like that before. Something was different this week, with everyone. He just couldn't put his finger on it. It felt like everyone knew something he didn't, and despite his many 'friends' he had now more than ever, the eerie feeling of loneliness continued to creep up on him.

He flipped on the holoTV just for background noise. They were analyzing every little detail of a suit he had worn the previous week. It was difficult enough to prepare for a wrestling match. It was just you and your opponent out there. This meant that there was no one else you could fend the blame on, other than yourself if something went wrong.

Add on having the world looking at you through a microscope and you really have a stressful situation.

As he prepped to shower and get ready for lunch, he began to think back to the days when he first met Jason and Monty, back when he was invisible. He was an average wrestler, nothing earth shattering. Like many average wrestlers he was a yoyo dieter, often cutting ten pounds a week. Due to his sometimes-quiet nature, he was one of the people most of the kids at Grandville High School ignored.

He was an avid reader of the *Wrestler's Weekly*, and dreamed of one day becoming the next champ of the TOC. That life brought fame, fortune, and everything else to have the perfect life. It awaited the next favorite star of the TOC. But it wouldn't just provide riches to the athlete. No, it would also provide huge rewards to those who represented the athlete and coached them to get on to their countries' competition team. Agents of the TOC came for one week, once a year to take a look at all the talked about athletes of a school, as Tyler's high school was one of the most prestigious in the country. If the agents found candidates from their school that they liked, then they would represent those athletes to Team USA. Then the board would evaluate everything about the athlete. And they really mean everything. From attitude, to perspective, how they treat their fellow man, favorite TV show, least favorite ice cream flavor and finally their athletic ability. If all went well, then those athletes would represent the United States in the Tournament of Champions the following year.

Naturally almost everyone tried to get signed up. The odds of making it were worse than those of winning the lottery. But if Tyler Mason was one thing, he was an optimist.

He remembered his excitement, the first year that the agents were coming. He told Nana, the most courageous woman he knew, that today was a huge day and to wake him up an hour earlier.

"For what, Tyler?" She asked.

"Well Nana, there's a chance we could become famous tomorrow." Tyler beamed.

"My sweet, sweet boy." She laughed. "And how are we going to do that?"

Looking back at it now she had to have realized just how far fetched it was for him to be chosen.

She took his hands and said, "Tyler, you go in there and show them just what kind of boy, what kind of man, you are. Alright?" She smiled.

The next morning, Tyler put on his suit, looked up how to tie the perfect tie, and combed his rebellious hair as perfect as he could get it while giving himself a pep talk. "Today is your day, Tyler. Today you're going to show them who you are."

He got his lunch, gave Nana a kiss goodbye, and headed to school. In first period, he passed his all time crush, Cailey Lopezzi. As expected she didn't even look at him, but once one of the agents chose him, he would talk to her.

The day seemed to be a blur, and then finally it was his turn.

"Next." The cold voice of the sifter commanded.

"Hi, uh Tyler."

"Tyler who?" She glared through her half moon glasses that rested upon her nose.

"Tyler Mason." He said with a big smile.

She swiped around on her tablet.

"Mm, room nine."

"Thanks!" He said. He walked down to classroom nine, took a deep breath, and knocked.

"Hello...Tyler." The man said as he swiped around on his tablet.

"Hi."

"Sit down."

"Oh...okay."

"So, why is it that you believe I should represent you?"

"Well sir, I know on paper I don't look that impressive. But I can tell you that if you just gave me a chance and some one on one training to go to Lanstark City, would be..." His throat went numb, and his palms began to sweat.

"I...I can offer...I...am hardworking..."

"Look son, let me help you out. I know you may think your special some how. That's what everybody's parents say these days. But you're not. Your record is 17-12. Good, but not good enough. I can't waste my time with you when teammates of yours like Mat Hooradian are 29-0. Have a good day."

In the rest of his classes, he went through the motions of what he had to do, but mentally, he was not there.

That night, Nana asked him how it went.

"Not good." He moped.

"What did you say, Tyler?" She asked.

"It doesn't matter." He grumbled. "They can't waste their time with me anyway."

"Hey, don't you talk like that." She said as she stopped putting the food on the table.

"Your parents wouldn't have wanted their son going into life with an attitude like that, and you sure won't do it with me either."

Nana sat down and took his hands.

"Tyler, there are always going to be people like the man you met today. They will always try and tell you that you are not good enough. That is just a fact of life. You can't control that. But what you can control is yourself. You need to let that man know just who you are. Make sure he never forgets you."

She wiped the tears off his cheeks.

"But who am I, Nana?"

"Tyler, my baby. Everyone knows who you are, whether you do or not! And no matter what happens to you, you've always kept true to yourself. You're the —

Tyler stopped his thought as he dried his face and began to comb his hair. He felt guilty to think about it after his behavior this morning.

The following year, it was Nana who knew the date the agents were coming. It was Nana who woke him up an hour early, and it was Nana who dressed him in his suit. Again, he came home that night believing himself to be a failure, and again Nana lifted him back up.

His junior year rolled around, and again, it was Nana who pushed Tyler to go.

"Nana, half the school doesn't even go anymore. Only the studs."

"You don't get anything out of doing nothing, Ty. You're going."

He sighed.

But from the moment he walked in, something was different.

The extremely unpleasant sifter was gone. In her place was a normal person who smiled at you out of common courtesy, not because it hurt.

"Room nine, Mr. Mason."

The number hit a sore spot somewhere in his memory, but he went to the room, expecting the worse as he approached. He knocked on the door.

"Come in, Tyler."

He paused. Bob never called him by name at the beginning of the session. Then again, that wasn't Bob's voice either.

Butterflies immediately ramped up in his stomach as he opened to door to see a young man with dark brown hair combed perfectly smiling at him. The entire situation, from beginning to right now, was completely different than how Bob conducted business.

"Hello..."

"Jason Teach." The man said as he held out his hand. "Firm handshake you got there."

"Thank you." Tyler said as he and Jason sat down. He cleared his throat. "So, I hope I don't sound rude here, but I was just wondering what happened to Bob?"

"We received complaints about Bob for the last two years out of this district so we decided to move him out of here for a year to see if we could find the problem." Jason replied calmly. He looked at Tyler as though he was searching him for something.

"Oh." Tyler said. "Thank you."

"Of course." Jason nodded. "Now, Tyler, it says here your record is 28-10 right now, that's sixty three percent better than last year, and astoundingly better than your freshman year."

"Thank you, sir."

"Absolutely. Now Tyler, tell me, why is it that you want to be in the Tournament of Champions? What is, or what would be your purpose?"

"Well Jason, I used to think I was in love with what I would potentially receive from the Tournament. Money, a big house, maybe even a Dragon Fly X. But recently, with my

Nana getting sick and all, I have realized that's not what excites me. What I really am excited for is the *way* the tournament would change my life."

"How do you mean?" Jason asked.

"Well, I've realized over the years that I don't always remember who, what, or when. But I always remember the way I felt about something. The Champions of the tournament have an incredible platform. They could use it for…something more than getting bigger houses and buying more cars."

"What, exactly, would you have in mind, Tyler?"

"Sometimes, people just need a little bit of hope in their lives, a nice message to get them through the day. I think that is what I would want to give the world. Something to believe in."

Jason smiled. "Tyler, I couldn't agree more."

The buzzing tap of his watch broke his thoughts. He hit the answer button.

"Tyler, where are you? We are late! Can you please get down here?" Cailey moaned.

Crap. "I'll be right down, love!"

He took one last look in the mirror. What happened to that Tyler? Was he still inside of there? Was he still the…

He shook his head, his thoughts returning to a very specific moment with Nana.

She wiped the tears off his cheeks.

"But who am I, Nana?"

"Tyler, my baby. Everyone knows who you are, whether you do or not! And no matter what happens to you, you've always kept true to yourself. You're the boy with a heart."

4 **A Lunch with Lions**

"Welcome to the Lobby, Valet, and Common Room. Please enjoy your day. We hope to see you tonight." A female computer voice informed Tyler from the speaker in the ceiling as the Hovervator's doors flashed open.

"Do you think I am dying or something tonight?" Tyler decided to test the humor of his…friend.

"Of course not, sir. Perhaps I will reconfigure my greetings."

Tyler smirked. "Yeah you do that, Cheryl."

"My name is Nancy, sir."

"Oh." Even elevators were getting attitudes these days. He peaked out into the room ahead.

The lobby of The Silas Luxury Hotel was the busiest Tyler had seen it yet, though up until a few moments ago he had not thought it was possible. A long looping line stretched from the ridiculously curvy front desk. Men in black suits and sunglasses escorted VIPs with pink dogs to their cars parked in the drive while tourists and employees alike crammed around each other as they saw fit, yelling in unison at a rather distressed looking doorman thinking they were being understood. All the while a live band blared in the background as vendors tried to sell Tournament merchandise to everyone in sight. Tyler was weary to step off the hovervator, as he feared his sighting might cause a slight hassle.

"We've reached your floor sir, please step off so I may accommodate other guests."

"One second Cheryl, I am trying to think of a plan." One of the many wonders of Lanstark City: Tyler couldn't bring to memory the last time an elevator had talked, let alone told someone to get going, no matter how polite. Last night replayed in Tyler's head. He had gone out in public without Monty or any security team at all. The minute he was spotted, he was mobbed for everything imaginable. He shuddered at the thought of it happening today. He was on a date today, which after glancing at his watch, he happened to be very late for. Suddenly a light bulb went off in his head. He frantically rummaged through his pockets. He could have swore he brought…ah… here they are…

"We've reached your floor sir, please step off so I may accommodate other guests." Though it was the same message, it felt as though it was slightly more hostile than the first. Tyler slid on his dark black-framed aviators. These should help. He felt his phone begin to vibrate in his pocket. Both Nancy and him knew who it was.

"We've reached your floor sir, please step off so I may accommodate other guests. This is not efficient use of my time." Nancy said, sounding like she was going to come out of the computer and kill him. "Alright! Alright! Chill!" Tyler grumbled as he stepped out of the elevator.

"Good luck getting a date with that kind of attitude, Cheryl."

"My name is Nancy." With that, the hovervator's doors slammed shut and it sped up to another floor.

He had only taken a couple steps when he accidentally bumped into someone. "Watch where you're going buffoon! Do you know who *I* am? And there's no sun in here, take off those glasses! Ha! You must think you're the next Tyler Mason! What a joke!" The woman cackled before returning to her phone call, where she began babbling on about a pet tiger…

Tyler weaved his way through the mass of people with 007 like effectiveness. He tried to be polite at first, "excuse me miss" "pardon me sir" but he soon found out no one was in a courteous mood.

I guess that means doing it the more effective way.

"I say dear boy!" "Hey watch it!"

Shoving his way through, his phone again began to vibrate in his pocket, but the cluster of people around him was so tight he didn't give it a single thought of retrieval. He walked past a girl who was rambling on about a bet she made on the championships, and was a bit nervous he had been recognized as she began staring at him intensely. Instinctively he raised his hand and acted like he was fixing his hair to cover the side of his face.

"What? You're joking!"

"No! I swear that looked like just him!"

"Looked like who?"

"Tyler Mason!"

"TYLER MASON?"

Tyler walked as quickly as he could without breaking into a sprint as panic began to set in; he was so close to the doors! A trio of black SUV's were parked in the front, most likely Cailey's, as her father did not permit her to travel 'unprotected.' Tyler pressed past the last group of people and ran outside.

"Cailey? Cailey!" He called! The SUV's did not look inviting!

"Tyler!" One of the black doors of the middle vehicle opened. A girl in a marvelous pink dress with flowing dirty blonde hair and an air of all things sweet stepped out. Since the day he had laid eyes on her in fourth grade, Tyler had crushed on her. Even today, it didn't seem real to be dating Cailey Lopezzi.

"Boy am I glad to see you." Tyler said, his tone a mixture of affection and relief. Slowly, he took off his sunglasses, trying to act as cool as possible, though he couldn't help his excitment.

"I think wh—

"OH MY LORD! YOU SEE, IT IS TYLER MASON! WHERE'S MOM? GET A VIDEO!"

The girl was back, and she wasn't alone. Behind her was what seemed to be the *entire* lobby, their pace slowly quickening like a lion about to pounce on his prey. It seemed the end was near when, as quick as a flash a wall of black suited men from the other SUV's blocked him from the crowd as another shuffled him into the car and slammed the door. Without hesitation the driver stepped on the gas pedal, and within seconds the Silas Luxury Hotel was getting ever farther away in the distance as they joined midday traffic.

He faced Cailey, who was giving him a stern look.

"You're late." She scolded. And just like that, almost effortlessly with nothing more than a look, she shot a knife to his heart.

"Well it...I-I was...it wasn't my...I mean...you saw what happened back there!" He stammered, realizing he really didn't have a good reason other than the fact that he got dressed really slowly this morning. And he may have taken a Dragon Fly X out for a spin over Gross Pointe Avenue.

Cailey frowned at his excuse. "Fame is not an excuse, Ty. Seriously I told you we had to be on time today because," She stopped, examining his face closely. "Oh no, you forgot didn't you?"

Forgot? What could he have possibly forgotten?

Oh no.

They weren't just sight seeing today. Tyler searched his memory as it stubbornly began to recall what they were doing...next week...right? Tyler's heart felt as though, for a mere second, it stopped beating. Amidst everything that had been going on and all the events that would be happening in the next few days, it had completely escaped his conscious mind that...

"We're meeting my father today!" Cailey's voice broke his thoughts.

"Yes of course!" Tyler said trying to look as calm as possible while his insides slowly melted. "Why do you think I dressed up?" He said holding out his dress shirt.

The fib seemed to satisfy Cailey, whether she believed him or not. She leaned into him so that her perfume scent was the only thing Tyler smelled and kissed him on the cheek, than began talking about the things she wanted to see today, after lunch of course. But Tyler had trouble listening, as the butterflies in his stomach continued swarming faster and faster with every passing second.

It's only natural for any person in any relationship to get nervous when meeting the parents of their spouse, but generally the person does not get so nervous that he begins to sweat in a fully air conditioned car, right? Yet here he was. However, in all fairness to him, many teenage boyfriends do not have the added pressure of their girlfriend's father being a multi record holder of the same sport they are competing in, a titan of an industry, and billionaire on the side. Mr. Lopezzi was indeed all of the above— and more.

A former wrestling Champion of the Tournament, Lopezzi was the most famous Champion of all. None had come close to matching his charm, let alone his skill. None until just recently. In fact, it was said by many in the media that Tyler would *surpass* Mr. Lopezzi if he pulled a win on Friday night, while other analysts argued he had already exceeded him.

Despite all the chatter about him, he felt himself shrinking into his seat as he rode to meet this man.

For an unknown reason, thoughts of grade school with Cailey flooded his brain. Every jock wanted to go out with Cailey Lopezzi just because of her dad, and this continued into high school. She graduated this year however, and was now moving onto life in the 'family business.' Some accused Tyler of going out with her only for the fame, which may have had some grounds, had more recent events not taken place.

Truthfully, Tyler had no idea who Cailey's father really was until a month ago at the start of the Tournament. He always guessed he was someone important because of the men in suits that escorted his daughter. But he never made the connection, nor did he sum up the courage to talk to her...for most of the time they 'knew' each other.

"Are you nervous at all, Tyler?" He heard Cailey ask. He had forgotten they were in the middle of a conversation, with feelings of guilt rising inside of him. He hadn't been listening the entire time, and he made a mental note to *not* make a habit of this. Of course since he hadn't been listening, he had no idea what she was referring to, and though he assumed it was lunch, he wanted to be sure.

"Nervous...yeah...nervous for?"

"Friday..." Cailey said gently, like she was walking on eggshells with the subject.

Though it should have been an obvious topic of conversation, the question caught Tyler completely off guard. Although, how they finally met also caught him completely off guard.

"I...I am." Tyler stuttered, embarrassed. "I, well my critics say I am not even supposed to be there, you know?" His opponent, Dei Jie of China, was not only much more physically intimidating than him. He had won his first Eastern Hemisphere's Championship belt at the age of six, and by the age of 12 they were predicting he would win the TOC when he came of age. His story was legend in East, as he had trained all his life for this one goal to make his native country proud. Dei also hated Tyler's guts because he didn't like those who took the spotlight away from him, and on top of that Tyler was American.

"But you *are* here." Cailey whispered soothingly as she took his hand and squeezed it. "If that really was your attitude you wouldn't even be in this car with me now would you? If I recall we wouldn't even have met if we hadn't *ran* into each other."

He would never forget it. It was the most he had been out of his comfort zone his entire life… up to that point, anyway. He had always tried to, and always chickened out of talking to her. This day was no different.

Tyler had accepted a dare from his all-knowing friends to talk to her, as Cailey was shockingly sitting alone. But his overbearing uneasiness had caused him to take more time to walk the twenty feet to the table than it would to run a triathlon. He was within five feet from her when her posse arrived out of nowhere. Defeated, Tyler turned on his heel, angling his path of travel out to the hall and into the bathroom with echoes of his friends' laughter racing after him.

After mentally beating himself up for quite sometime, he realized he was late for class. He scrambled into the hall, rounding the corner in a flash and…

BAM!

He collided with someone walking equally as fast, and the resulting impact had sent both of their books flying like frightened birds. A sharp pain went through his behind as he landed on it with *thud*. He looked up at the person, ready to rip into him….he was actually a she.

Slowly, he began to observe the she. The girl had long, flowing dirty blonde hair, and the most beautiful oceanic blue eyes. It began to occur to him that this wasn't a dream…

"Oh my— Cailey I am *so* sorry!" He choked as he quickly got to his knees and began gathering her scattered books from the ground. He felt the blood rushing to his face; it was probably redder than a cherry at this point. He had to get out of here. As soon as possible! He prepared himself for the barrage of insults undoubtedly about to come for running into her. However, her response surprised him… and maybe even her too?

"Oh no it's okay!" Cailey said as she slid onto her knees to join him on the floor. "It wasn't just *your* fault. It was mine too." She smiled.

Tyler remembered pinching himself, just to be absolutely positive that he really *was* awake. The *one* time he had rounded up the courage to smile at her he had received a glaring set of eyes. In no way was he expecting this.

"Sooo…are you okay?" Cailey smiled as normal as possible. Tyler realized he was staring at her, and the situation felt as though it had moved to a whole another level of awkward.

"Huh? Me? Oh yes, I'm fine I just, you know?" Tyler mumbled as he slowly stood up, her books under his arm. *This is your chance! Tyler I swear if you do nothing we are never speaking again! SHUT UP ME!*

He cleared his throat.

"Would you uh…" Nothing was coming out. Panic began to set in. As if reflexes decided to take over, his hand slowly reached out to offer Cailey help up. Would she take it? He wasn't sure. But, for the second time that day, he was very much surprised. A very warm palm touched his. Carefully, he helped Cailey to her feet. He was generally good at reading people, but the look on her face was one he couldn't get anything from.

Nervously he handed her back her books.

"Thank you." She said softly.

"No problem, thank you." He said as he accepted his own back. *Walk away! Walk away before someone sees.* He was about to step away when, for the third time that day, things did not at all go the way Tyler Mason had expected them too.

"You're Tyler, right?" She asked.

She knows my name?

"What? Me? Oh…yeah that's me." Tyler laughed.

Cailey giggled. "Well, I'm Cailey, Cailey Lopezzi?"

"Nice to finally meet you, Cailey." He said triumphantly as cries of joy rang out in his head.

"I never noticed you had brown eyes before?" She smiled.

He moved his mouth but no words were coming out. Seconds that felt like years passed.

"Well, if that's all I guess I will…see you around?" She said as she began to walk away. Again he blew his chances. Again he was going to spend days beating himself up. *You were right there Tyler!*

"Actually, there is something."

They paused, perhaps both shocked he had managed the words.

"Yes?" She turned around with a smile.

"…well…you...I was uh, wondering if you might uh…coffee, join coffee for me er join…me for um some coffee—

"Tomorrow morning. Coffee Beans. Seven sharp. *Don't* be late." She said with walking by him with a smile.

He wasn't late. That day, despite his embarrassment, had become one of his most cherished memories in a life that had offered him so few.

"You were so nervous you couldn't even formulate words." Tyler smiled as Cailey's face contorted into a mixture of a smile and outrage.

"*Me* the one who couldn't talk? Mister I uh join coffee!"

"I'm only joking." He winked.

"Honestly, I'd do it all over again, because I am so happy that I happened to *bump* into you that day, Cailey Lopezzi."

"I know. I'm just the best girlfriend ever, aren't I?" She gleamed, a devious expression settling on her face.

"Yeah, hopefully your father thinks I am the best boyfriend ever." Tyler gulped, once again remembering the real reason he was riding in a train of black SUV's. "Where exactly are we going for lunch anyway?"

"It's a surprise." Cailey said. "But knowing you, you'll love it. Fred," She called to the driver as she hit a button, rolling down the window separating them from the front seat. "How far are we?"

"E.T.A. five minutes." Fred sounded as excited to be there as a child who wakes on a Monday morning bright and early, loathing that they have to go to school.

Tyler peered out the window. Even with the shading black tint, he could still see the sun shining bright as ever. Amongst the masses of shiny silver buildings, Tyler could see one in particular that caught his eye. Unlike all the other shiny silver buildings, this one had three long glowing lines running up it. Even with the vivid sun light, the glowing was very much noticeable, its color changing every few seconds.

As they got closer, it became apparent that the drive in front of the place was a huge cluster of jumbled and angry drivers. Other black SUV's, sports cars, and limos filled one half of the drive while camera-wielding paparazzi filled the other half, snapping pictures of the people walking both in and out. But why would they take pictures of random people? Then Tyler saw it, blazing ever so brightly above the entrance:

The Common Club

Now please, don't allow the name to deceive you as intended. If you have never heard of *The Common Club* you'd most likely pay it no thought because it sounds so, well, common. However, if you had heard about it like all the paparazzi in the front of the franchise's newest location, you would know that there is actually nothing common about the place at all. It is where all the major power players, celebrities, leaders, and organizers meet for a private non-recorded meal with maximum security and most of all, maximum privacy. If you wished to be a member, you had to be invited. Or you could buy your way in, though the price is ghastly for the first month alone. Tyler had never even thought of stepping foot in one.

"Cailey," He began, as the SUV leading their motorcade turned into the drive.

"Cailey, I, I don't have a membership here. I haven't been invited." Tyler said sheepishly. How could she expect that he would have a membership in the first place?

"Yes you do." Cailey replied nonchalantly as the SUV stopped in front of the entrance. One of the black suited men opened the car door and yanked Tyler out while Cailey followed behind. Three more formed a wall in front of them as a swarm of paparazzi brought on a blinding barrage of flashing light as their cameras clicked.

While they struggled through the clutter of the crowd, an increasing sense of panic began to run through Tyler. He did *not* have a membership. He would never make it past the security checkpoint. How in heaven's name did she think he would ever get clearance? He imagined himself being escorted out of the building once they realized he didn't have a membership in front of all these cameras. Chills went down his spine. If this was some kind of joke…

"Cailey," He struggled as one of the men shoved him to walk faster. "I don't have a membership! This isn't funny!"

"Tyler—

"Tyler! Cailey! Is Tailey still a thing?" A giant man with a camera yelled. The mess of thirty people saying thirty things at once drowned out Cailey's reply.

"Is it true you guys are taking the next step in your relationship?"

"Tyler what do you have to say about Dei's latest statements?"

"Is it true you fainted the other afternoon?"

"What if you lose?"

"Are you—

Click. The black doors sealed shut behind them. Tyler turned to Cailey. They had to leave before he was kicked out in front of the entire world!

"What on Earth would make you think that I could have a membership here? We have to go before we get kicked out!"

"Tyler, I *know* you have a membership here."

"How?"

"Father owns the Club."

Cailey led the way forward, but there wasn't much to see except a doorway and what appeared to be a very large black wall. Was *this* really the infamous Common Club?

A balding man in a purple suit jacket with black trousers seemingly appeared out of the dark.

"Good day Ms. Lopezzi. Your father is expecting you." He than turned to Tyler, observing him from head to toe as if pondering his worthiness to enter the premises.

He thanked his lucky stars he brought the suit jacket.

"You must be Mr. Tyler Mason. Welcome. Please follow me. We must verify your membership before I permit your entry."

The man clapped his hands twice. Out of the floor sprang a tablet from which a mass of holograms emerged. As the man shuffled through them, a glowing little black chip hovered toward Tyler.

"Thumb please." The man said.

Hesitating for a few seconds, Tyler cautiously pressed his thumb onto the little black circle, and his picture popped up on one of the holograms.

"Ah wonderful, you're not an imposter. It has been a real problem this week. Welcome to the Common Club. We like to do the uncommon here." The man said, directing them through the doorway. As Tyler passed through, he realized the 'black wall' was no more than some sort of hologram. In front of him was a palace even Casper Lanstark would envy.

Compared to the bustling, overcrowded streets and buildings of Lanstark city, the Common Club was very comfortable. Large glass walls reached for the sky illuminated from the bottom by a variety of different colored lights. As you looked higher, the lights grew dimmer. All around them waiters and waitresses in purple suit jackets attended to all the high profile hierarchy scattered throughout the rooms. Similarly to the lights in the walls, lights in the floor where everywhere as well, slithering like snakes in grass. Hovering about here and there were what looked like silver rulers. Tyler opened his mouth to ask what they were when he noticed a sitting woman take ahold of one. At her touch, a hologram showing her the lunch menu appeared, and as she swiped it horizontally, a variety of other images and news were displayed. As they continued walking, Tyler couldn't help but think this was all some how…a dream. It was truly *insane.*

"Cailey, all of this is insane."

"You have no idea."

"So, where's your father?"

"Up." She replied.

Up?

"You know Cailey that's not fun—

Then he saw it. Up ahead was a breakthrough in the purple-lit wall, and long narrow steal beams, looking like the shell of a building that was about to be built towered above them. It looked as though they were supposed to be elevators… how old fashioned for this place. Tyler watched as the party ahead of them stepped forward and pressed their thumbs on the glowing screen. Out of the ground came a square silver platform that looked like it was plucked strait from a chessboard. They stepped on the platform and, staying in the middle of the four narrow beams, it began to rise.

"They are called hoverpads." Cailey said, as if reading his thoughts. "They run off of magnetism, and they are *a lot* faster than hoverators."

"How about *a lot* cooler!" Tyler admired. However, as he wiped the sweat off his palms, he was secretly a little nervous. The walls in hoverators don't just block your view, they protect you from falling out. What would protect you from falling off a hoverpad?

Come on, Tyler. He drove a flying car around the city, why would this scare him?

Seemingly out of nowhere, again, appeared a small woman in a purple suit coat.

"Welcome. The access code for your destination?"

One of the bodyguards marched ahead of them pulling up his suit jacket sleeve. He revealed a glowing band on his arm with a tiny circle engraved in the middle. He held it out for the woman, who scanned it with a tiny machine. A hologram of their identities popped up, and the woman briefly frisked through them before nodding them ahead.

Following Cailey's lead, Tyler nervously stepped onto the silver platform. In the front of Cailey was a tiny hole in the floor. A hologram ignited from it displaying all the floors of the club. It looked as though the wheel of destinations was designed for them to be able to choose their destination, however, right now it was locked on one place in particular that caught Tyler's eye: The Lion's Den.

Tyler had heard stories of the 'Lion's Den' before. There is one in every club, and it gets it's name because everyone who eats there generally is there for one reason: to make some kind of deal, legal or not. Tyler jolted a bit as he realized they had already began their ascent, the ride was so smooth he hadn't even noticed the start. The floors they were passing were some of the most curious he had ever seen. Behind the glass walls on one floor, it looked as though you literally stepped *into* an aquarium, with fish of all shapes, sizes, and colors darting around. Another floor had holograms of famous cities floating over what looked like little bird feeders. Tyler watched as a little boy went over to one, grabbed it, and clapped his hands, enhancing it. The entire city was sprawled out in a hologram across the floor. Tyler could see the little cars turning all over the illuminated streets.

Tyler turned to ask Cailey a question, but caught his tongue when he noticed the look on her face. Was she nervous about seeing her father? Was she nervous about *him* seeing her father? Or was it something else?

"Cailey...are you alright?" Tyler asked softly in hopes the guards would not hear.

"Oh yes, I'm fine!" She said quickly.

Tyler's gut told him differently though. That look worried him. Something was definitely up, but under the circumstances, he would have to let it go for now.

The hoverpad came to a stop at two clear doors, which parted ways as they stepped off onto a balcony. Tyler didn't know what was more impressive: the balcony itself, the view, or the people that were on the balcony. To start, the balcony was absolutely stunning. Shaped like a giant teardrop, it sat high above many of the buildings in Lanstark City. Its white marble floor was perfectly polished, the mahogany dining tables all around had very detailed cloth decorating them, and even the china was a sight to behold. And the view, oh the view of Lanstark City's impressive skyline was something Tyler would add to the unforgettable memories he had made in the mere month he had been here. In the distance he could make out a flying car run way, and the floating street lights, changing red and green on this picturesque sunny day. Champion's Plaza across the way promised glory or defeat, and the massive advertisement holograms looked a little small from all the way up here. Finally, the people present on the balcony in the Common Club, much like everything else in the place, were not common at all. Tyler recognized many famous people, and for a moment, he felt very small compared to the group he was walking in on.

As Tyler stepped into sight of everyone on the balcony the talking and dinging of forks on plates completely stopped.

Everyone stared.

Tyler felt himself freeze in place. He was already nervous, what was all this? He was *starting* to get used to people staring at him, but not *these* people, who were what he considered to be some of the most intimidating on the planet.

"Tyler? Tyler!" Tyler suddenly felt himself plucked from his trance. Cailey stood in front of him, her hand held out. "Come on."

Tyler hesitated.

Was she okay with her father and everyone else seeing this? "Trust me." Cailey said. Tyler took her hand, and she led him on as the talking slowly resumed, though Tyler couldn't shake the feeling that everyone here knew something he didn't.

Almost instantly, however, Tyler forgot about any of his previous toils as he took into notice the man sitting at the table near the end of the teardrop.

The man looked as though he had spent months in California with his perfect golden-brown tan. His lightly graying dark hair was combed back with the utmost perfection. His teeth were pearly white. Between his suit and diamond watch the man looked like nine million dollars. Tyler didn't have to guess, he knew exactly who this was. But, as he observed him; he realized he had seen him before today. He used to watch all of his press conferences as a young child, admiring the speed, ferocity, and skill of the most successful TOC wrestling Champion in history. He was considered the best wrestler to walk the planet, and his fame had not been rivaled since the earliest days of the tournament. As they moved closer, Tyler noticed that another, very peculiar figure occupied one of the two shiny mahogany chairs perched on the opposite side of the table. The man's back was to them, and Tyler couldn't help himself as he questioned his eyes.

"I do not agree with any of it. He is destroying everything I built! If I had it my way you all would be—

Alfredo Lopezzi over exaggeratingly cleared his throat, pointing with his eyes toward the newly arrived guests.

"We can come back, father." Cailey quickly said.

"No, don't bother." Her father's voice was definitely one made for speaking. It was as loud and clear as they come. "Silas was just *leaving.*" His dark eyes narrowed at the man across from him. There was no sign of friendliness in them.

"You'll regret this. *Mark my words.* You both will!" The man said with daggers in his voice. With that, he rose and faced them.

"Tyler Mason." Exclaimed an old, tired voice that still had a hint of rebellion in it. "I must say you're a bit...shorter than I expected." The man's gray eyes narrowed as he inspected Tyler from head to toe. Now that he was standing, Tyler couldn't help but do the same to him. The man stuck out like a robber in a police station. It looked as though he had been transported from medieval Europe and landed here.

Compared to all the nine million dollar suits in the building, the man was… somewhat old fashioned.

That was putting it nicely.

Dressed in long, cranberry colored robes with a diamond encrusted pattern dotting across them, he also wore what looked to be a Santa hat. Except far longer as it touched his shoulder. On every finger, the man had different rings of all shapes and sizes, but what stuck out most was the broach that hung from the chain around the man's neck. It was the planet Earth, but a vicious serpent was ensnaring it, its mouth wide open revealing its devastating teeth.

Tyler, still observing the man's dated attire, was unsure if the man's statement was an insult or just a thought aloud. "A person's appearance or height does not define what he or she is capable of…*sir.*" Tyler said, not rudely, but not cordially.

The man raised his eyebrows with a chuckle. "The *famous* Boy with a Heart has some game. Forgive me, but I do believe you are a bit overrated. You have limped on by nothing but *luck* and *luck alone.*" The man croaked as his gray eyes locked with Tyler's.

He turned to Cailey.

"Ah, Ms. Lopezzi can't say hi to an old friend?" Cailey knew this joker? "Look at you all dressed up. Did daddy put you up to romancing this brash young man?"

Plates rattled on the table as Alfredo Lopezzi jolted to his feet. Tyler could swear steam was coming out of his ears. "Get. Out. *Now.* Or I will have you removed from *my* building."

Looking resistant but defeated, the man began to walk away, but as he did so he leaned in so close to Tyler that he could smell the cappuccino on his breath.

"Enjoy your time in the sun, Mr. Mason. Soon we shall see if you really are all that you are said to be." Tyler felt a shiver across his body.

The man than turned to Cailey and her father. "Good day. Enjoy your building, Al." He mocked before strutting off the balcony.

"Who was that?" Tyler asked, not directly asking Cailey or her father.

"Silas Marshall. Don't listen to anything he says."

"Dad is right. He's a loony." Cailey agreed. It wasn't as easy as she made it out to be, but, seeing the tension between them, it was probably the best thing to do for now.

"Yes. Don't fret over him Tyler. Allow me to introduce myself. My name is Alfredo Lopezzi, you may have heard of me." Alfredo held out a tan hand for Tyler to shake. Tyler took it as he peered deep into the dark eyes of the man he looked up to as a child, always thinking of him as humble, pure, and the definition of honor.

"Heard of you? Sir you're the most famous wrestler on the planet. You inspired me to want to be here." Tyler said as all the memories of the action figures and posters continued to flood his head.

"Well Tyler, rumor has it you're almost as famous as me these days!" Alfredo's lips twitched as he said this. Tyler laughed and looked at Cailey, hoping she would say something.

"Dad, I'm sure you can tell Tyler some stories later. He was just telling me he was hoping to hear the story of when you beat the Frenchman."

"Is that so?" Alfredo said. "Please, sit down." He gestured for them to take their seats as he sat down. He snapped his fingers, and immediately waiters brought each of them *three* beverages. Yes you read that right. Tyler knew the first was water, but he wasn't quite sure what the red or blue liquids in the smaller glasses were.

"Now, Tyler, feel free to peruse the menu, there are many exquisite items to choose from. I made sure if it. I would recommend my personal favorite, the charred sirloin." Alfredo said as he studied Tyler from across the top of his black menu.

"Thank you, sir." Tyler said as calmly as he could. Who was he fooling? The sweat on his palms wasn't stopping. He found the grilled sirloin, $150.

"Please accept my apologies for Silas once again. He is getting old, and is stuck in the past." Alfredo said rather flatly. "Now, you of course are today's news! If you don't mind my asking Tyler, why did you attempt to join the Tournament? What motivated you with odds so…steep like that?"

"Well," Tyler began. "It was always a dream of mine really, but I never gave it much thought until a few years ago when I decided I would just go for it. I asked myself, what's the worse that could happen? If I don't make it, I don't make it. At least I will be at peace for trying."

"He makes it sound like he did nothing! Trust me dad, he trained non stop everyday, especially when it came time for the State tournament."

"So how on Earth were you able to get yourself registered? I've been there before and if I hadn't hired my Recruiter than—

"Oh no I didn't do all that stuff, I was actually recruited by my current manager, Jason. Do you know him?"

It was as though Tyler had insulted him, Alfredo's nostrils flared as a nasty expression began to form on his face, but only briefly before his returning back to it's usual media friendly state. "Yes, we've been briefly acquainted, once before…"

As if sensing an awkward part of the conversation had appeared, the waiter arrived out of nowhere. "Have we all decided on something we may want?"

Whilst they ordered, Tyler carefully observed Alfredo Lopezzi as he ordered his charred sirloin, searching for any sign of the face he had seen moments ago. It was gone. Not wanting to be rude and order something expensive, Tyler decided on pasta.

He was underweight at the moment anyway.

Why would Alfredo Lopezzi be talking to a character like Silas Marshall anyway?

"Tyler knows that's my favorite dish. In fact, one night he invited me over and cooked some himself, didn't you Ty?"

"Wha— oh yes. I'm really not the greatest cook!" He said as he blushed a little. He was here for Cailey, so he might as well do his best to act, right?

"Well, it's the thought that counts." Alfredo commented.

After that bit of awkwardness, things seemed to go well. Cailey was smiling and laughing while Tyler told wrestling war stories of late. Alfredo did end up telling the story of how he beat the Frenchman in the finals some years ago. At the time, he had been twenty-seven, very old for a Champion. Most people who compete in the Tournament were around twenty-one. There was no official age maximum, though the minimum was seventeen, but no one had ever dared compete so young.

It was just not possible with the level of competition.

At the age of eighteen, Tyler was the youngest person to ever compete in the TOC. His critics questioned all the time whether someone was helping him on or paying someone off, while his supporters attributed it to something deeper. Hence the Boy with a Heart was formed.

"So Tyler tell me," Alfredo began, for a moment sounding like the famed TOC show host Zeus Clementine peppering someone with a question. "Why this year? What made this year so important that you, at the young age of eighteen decided you would compete? I mean you are facing kids who are three, four years older than you?"

"Well sir, I suppose it's not so different than you competing at twenty-seven really. I mean sure it's not easy, but the best things in life are the hardest to get." He said, putting his hand on Cailey's.

"Oh please don't take it like I'm trying to discredit you, Mason. I only am curious as to what made *this* year so special? Of course the Tournament taking place here was a factor, but there has to be something more? Something deeper, with your reputation and all."

As Tyler sat and considered the question, he realized he really didn't have an answer. *Why* had he chosen this year? One of the first conversations he had had with Jason came to mind; it was when Jason was officially recruiting him. They met one terribly cold winter night in Glory Park. It was there Jason had insisted the importance that it be this year. At the time, Tyler hadn't really asked questions. He had been too deep in a state of shock for it to bother him. His life's dream was coming true, why on Earth would he ask why they had to do it this year?

What difference would it make?

"Tyler...are you okay?" Cailey asked, grabbing his arm.

"Yes." He said as he came back to reality. He looked back up at Alfredo, who was examining him carefully as if looking for something while he patiently waited for Tyler's reply. "Well...I...uh, actually decided with Jason to have a go at it this year." Tyler stammered as he racked his brain for anything he could throw in as a reason why. Then he remembered... "With the growing tension between the U.S. and China we decided...maybe try this year incase the U.S. didn't compete next year perhaps."

Alfredo raised an eyebrow. He wasn't buying it.

"I understand Tyler, no need to continue."

Thank God he dropped it. Tyler let out a silent breath of relief.

"Tyler,"

Tyler felt his stomach tighten as if prepping for another blow.

"Given the fact that until just recently you were, forgive me for lack of a better phrase, a no one, what do you think made Jason risk his entire career on you? How could he possibly foresee you making it this far?"

Tyler felt blood rushing to his face. He had never really thought about it, now that the question was asked aloud. He liked to think it was because Jason saw something in him. But why did it concern Alfredo Lopezzi? He wasn't a reporter, and Tyler was beginning to get the impression he wasn't the biggest fan.

"*Dad,*" Cailey said in a bit of a hushed tone.

"No, it's okay Cailey. To be honest Mr. Lopezzi, I really don't know the answer to that question. You would have to ask Jason yourself."

As would he.

Alfredo's face coiled in annoyance; clearly he wasn't satisfied with the answer. He began to open his mouth again, probably to pose another question when one of the black suited men who escorted them up here whispered in his ear.

"Is something wrong?" Cailey asked.

"No, just a last minute meeting down at Headquarters. I'm afraid I have to say my goodbyes." Alfredo rose to his feet. Relieved, Tyler followed, grasping the tan hand once more.

"It was good meeting you, sir." He said.

"You as well, Tyler."

He came around the table and gave Cailey a brief hug before approaching Tyler again.

"Amusing, your story. Good luck on Friday. Your opponent is a formidable one but given your recent upsets, it should be a good match I presume?"

Tyler nodded. "Absolutely."

"Excellent." Alfredo smiled. "I would hate for such a story to come to an unpleasant ending." Tyler felt the daggers of words in his gut one by one. With that, Lopezzi paraded off the balcony and out of sight.

"What did he say?" Cailey asked coming to his side.

"Oh he just wanted to wish me luck for Friday."

"Ah. Well I hope your okay. I didn't realize Silas would be here, or that dad would be such a pest. He's just used to dealing with lions every time he eats here."

"You're not kidding."

He was pretty sure her dad *was* the lion.

As they headed home, Tyler could not stop thinking about one peculiar thing. During the entirety of the lunch in which Alfredo was meeting his daughter's boyfriend, not once did he ask anything about how they were, how they met, or do the fatherly ritual of making sure he was treating Cailey right.

Wasn't that the point of the lunch?

5 The Champion's Charity Gala

Tyler was in the best place in the world.

A cool night breeze whipped through his hair as he continued course at 85mph and rising. The stars in the heavens lit the night sky, while a dim glow came from the skyscrapers below him. He was flying.

Not with his body, of course, people can't fly.

Or so they say.

Any person who got in one of these was, technically, flying. One of Tyler's hands gripped the steering wheel while the other hovered over the control panel, ready to change gears, altitude, or speed if necessary.

For at the moment, Tyler was driving a Dragonfly X, the world's fastest flying car, again. The freedom of flying was so liberating. Up here he could do anything. Be anything. Create anything. Free from the pressure. Free from the people.

The purple glow of the rims reflected off of the buildings as he whizzed around the city skyline.

Tyler hit an arrow on the computer screen. It was time to have some fun.

As smooth as flowing water yet as fast as lighting, the Dragonfly X sped further into the lit up skyline below. Tyler dodged a few more buildings and continued pace, programming the computer when to bank upward.

The traffic down below was getting closer and closer. At first, it looked like a scrabbling bunch of mini lit up ladybugs going one way or another. He saw some interesting architecture ahead that threatened to take off his head.

Yet he wasn't worried.

The Dragonfly X could make sudden movements (such as swinging upward and over traffic before it collided with it) at the press of the touch screen. A smile began to form at the corner of Tyler's mouth. What would the look on Angelica's face be when she discovered one of her cars was stolen by —

"Tyler?"

His vision blurred for a second, as though he was falling asleep. He concentrated harder. That was weird. He couldn't wait to—

"Tyler?"

Oh no…

"Tyler come on, brother."

He opened his eyes to see a figure with slicked back graying hair standing over him, a look of slight amusement in his eyes.

"Late night? With Ms. Lopezzi I presume?" Monty smirked, walking away.

"Yeah…" Tyler said as he tried to simultaneously get the sleep out of his eyes and the disappointment of *not* stealing a flying car out of his system.

"You know, Tyler I realize you have some free time this week. After everything you've been through to get here it is well deserved. However, on that same note, after everything you've been through to get here it'd be a shame to throw out your chances due to foolishness while out roaming the streets."

Ouch. Tyler sat up in bed. He had only missed curfew by a half hour. Was it really that big of a deal?

"Monty, it was only— it won't happen again." He looked around. "Where is Jason?"

Monty's expression darkened slightly, but his face remained, as always, unreadable like that of a champion poker player. What was it with these guys? "Jason is away on other business this morning," Monty said as he unpacked the breakfast he had brought, an egg white bagel sandwich from Liam's down the street.

They were the best.

"But, he assured me that he would be there for the gala tonight."

The Gala! Oh he had completely forgotten that was today, let alone the fact that he was attending. Tyler clearly lacked the poker face Monty had because Monty was able to read him in an instant.

"I see you forgot about this too. Not to worry. It should be a simple event where you and Dei will meet the not as fortunate as you and I, while at least looking as though you are united in the effort to make the world a better place."

Tyler couldn't believe his ears. "Are you kidding me? How are we going to look united with the hate campaign they have been running on me for the past two weeks?" Everywhere he turned, even on major stations now, Dei Jie and his team were boasting he would 'flip him on his head before a minute itself fled'. There's no way the world will believe that garbage?

"Tyler, look—

"No! This is wrong! How can they hide behind a charity event? Someone needs to call them out on their rubbish and I w—

"Tyler that is enough!" Monty yelled.

Given the fact that until just recently you were, no one, what do you think made Jason risk his entire career on you? How could he possibly foresee you making it thus far? Alfredo Lopezzi's words haunted Tyler's yet again, as they echoed throughout his head in the now quiet room. Even the birds seemed to have stopped chirping.

What have you gotten yourself into, Tyler?

"Look...Tyler, I'm sorry but these kids are looking up to you. Some have less than a week on this Earth. Not to mention we have *all* made enormous sacrifices to get here. If you let your anger, no matter how justified, take control of you tonight I can promise you Dei and the media will rip you apart. That would ruin— we can't have that."

He walked over and put his hand on Tyler's shoulder. "I promise you, it will make more sense after Friday. Lets just get through these next four days. *Please.*"

Tyler could feel his heart beating hard against his chest, and even as he promised "okay" he felt a slight feeling of anger starting to bud. They weren't telling him something.

"Now, you'd better get cleaned up fast, or at least brush your teeth! Rosemary will be here any minute, and you know how long it takes her to get you ready!"

Tyler jumped up and ran to the bathroom. Just as he began to brush his teeth, the doorbell to the suite rang three times. Monty sent him off to quickly bathe while he attempted to keep Rosemary at bay, as unlikely as that would be.

For a moment, Tyler enjoyed the hot water as it ran down his body. He took a deep breath. As hard or as crazy as all this turned out, he had to be sure to make the most of his time here. This was after all, a once in a lifetime opportunity.

As he dried off, he stared at his reflection in the mirror. He could handle himself tonight, right? *He's a disgrace to any wrestler ever.* Dei's words made their way into his thoughts. He wasn't sure if he could—

Tap! Tap! Tap! "Tyler Mason! You know better than to keep me waiting! I don't care how famous you are now! You have one minute to get out here NOW!" With that, there was final *bang!* on the door.

As quickly as he could, Tyler slipped on his shorts, finished drying off, took one look at himself in the now foggy mirror, and headed out. Immediately, the smell of strawberries entered Tyler's nose and he had to squint momentarily, until his eyes stopped watering. As they cleared, Tyler was able to see the details of the tall woman in front of him.

There was more to Rosemary Rowling than the strong scent of strawberries, though that was typically the first thing one noticed about her. Standing in nearly six-inch heels, she was quite taller than Tyler. She had a beautiful face, and a smile that could knock any playboy off his feet. The only thing Tyler wasn't sure of was her *natural* hair color. Since he had met her she had always had some absurd hair color.

Right now it was purple, complimenting her dress and hat. In fact, purple was the only color he had seen her wear the past few weeks. When he asked why, she replied it was 'her new thing' claiming to be a trendsetter.

"Fame going to your head now as you keep me waiting?" Rosemary squawked at Tyler, narrowing her bright blue eyes at him. "And what do you think this is, a photo shoot swimsuit edition? Coming out here with no shirt on! Heavens!"

"No!" Tyler shot defensively. "I was just, you know, out last night. I didn't get that much sleep. And I would have had to take my shirt off anyway!"

"Excuses, excuses. Dear Lord boy, it's a wonder how you're going to make it if you win Fri— *when* you win Friday. A Champion's schedule is far more chaotic than yours now, even if you're a bit more popular than most have been."

Tyler had a witty remark lined up, but decided to allow Rosemary peace of mind today. "I'm sorry I overslept Rosemary, it won't happen again, alright?"

"Alright." Rosemary said, looking somewhat surprised. "Well, you did earn some brownie points with me for your outfit yesterday. Considering you came up with it all on your own, and compared to your old repulsive taste when I first came on with you, you've come a long way." Rosemary had her own show on CF, or Champion's Fashion, and she was a very well known designer around the world. Her outfits were known for there 'hidden messages,' whatever that kind of nonsense meant. Tyler did not understand how a shirt could tell a message, unless it was like the elevator who had dating problems.

What was her name again?

Ruckus broke out as Rosemary's two assistants who helped her 'prepare' Tyler for public appearances barged in the room. Chucky Chumpity was a short, round one with puffy cheeks and flaming orange hair (That of which he combed to look like tongues of fire). In accordance to TOC style, his suit jacket was outrageous, his bright blue blazer shot out at you while his orange pants were rivaled in flamboyance only by his orange hair.

Gurdy Gumdrop, the second of the two, wore a 'normal' looking dress compared to her coworkers. What completely set her apart from them, and what was 'trendy' in TOC fashion at the moment, was her makeup. Grant it every woman wears makeup, but its generally not fashioned into things such as cat eyes, eagle eyes, or sometimes even dragon eyes.

She said it was art on her face.

"Bravo, Tyler! I was most impressed when I got the news!" Gurdy raved. "How do you like the art today?" She asked, motioning to her face.

"Oh, it's phenomenal, Gurdy! Tiger prints, right?"

"Yes!" She squeaked, happy someone appreciated her work. Chucky flashed Tyler a thumbs up, as he generally had nothing to say.

"Gurdy, enough! You two bring in his options for tonight!" Rosemary barked, snapping her manicured fingers.

"What exactly are you planning on having him wear?" Monty asked, making his first debut into the conversation since Rosemary's arrival.

"Well Lester Monty, I expect this will be hard for *you* to understand, as you lack taste." Rosemary snapped, eyeing Lester from head to toe. "But tonight, when Tyler arrives at the Champion's Charity Gala for Children, he is on a mission."

Clearly amused and fighting back laughter, Monty played in, "*A mission* you say?"

"Yes Monty, a mission. You see tonight is the night before the big night. Tomorrow Tyler will dress to the nines for the Ball, but tonight, he can't relinquish his jewel, yet he must serve the fans a taste of what is to come."

Monty bit his lip as she went on. Even Tyler couldn't help but chuckle.

"It's a tricky process. Make the outfit too outrageous and you'll drown out the effect of tomorrow. Make it too subtle and people will lose interest."

"Mhmmm." Monty and Tyler exchanged looks before Gurdy and Chucky remerged into the room arguing.

"I told you it would be easier to take the hoverator!" Gurdy groaned.

"Hmph!" Chucky growled.

"Chucky words, dude!" Tyler joked as he and Monty burst into laughter.

"That'll be enough out of all of you!" Rosemary scolded as the two shot dirty looks at one another before directing them toward Tyler and Monty. They guided in what looked to be a mix of a hovering cabinet and a mirror, except there was no mirror. There were two large initials, *R.R.*, engraved on the front.

"Now," Rosemary began. "Let us get you presentable, Mr. Mason." She clapped her hands two times, and the object sprang to life, the crease in between the two R's opening. Rows of clothing on hangers sprang out, along with matching shoes.

"These are your options for tonight. Incase you haven't already noticed, I have not provided you with sunglass options this time. There is a reason for that, which I'm sure you know…"

She looked at Tyler, as if expecting an answer. When she realized she wasn't receiving one she went on. "…It is because this is a charity event. I don't need you blazing in there like some punk rock star with shades on just because you want to stroke your ego."

At this, Monty burst into laughter.

"*Ow!*" Tyler said rubbing his arm with a small smile.

Rosemary turned, glaring at Monty. "Something funny, Lester?"

"Not at all. Go on." He said, biting his lip again.

Tyler walked over and perused the outfits. Clearly, Rosemary was sticking to his signature colors, black and gold. Out of the four outfits, three of them resembled suits, and he had to wear a suit the next two days after this. The fourth however, was a black jacket with golden strings woven into the fabric. Subtle.

"I like…this one I think." He said, showing her.

"You *think* or you *know*? The world of fashion has no room for someone not confident in their looks, Tyler." Rosemary raised a questioning eyebrow.

"Alright! I like this one. I just didn't want to you know, hurt your feelings!"

Rosemary's glare disappeared, and her expression softened as she opened her mouth as if to say something, but then turned and unhooked the outfit. It was rare for Rosemary to surrender an argument like that. *Whoa.*

With that, Tyler exchanged glances with Monty who was of course holding in his laughs. Rosemary made him go to the bathroom and fix his hair before she finally allowed him to put on his clothes for the evening. When he was finished and came out, he felt like a true rock star, although Tyler thought it would have looked better with sunglasses. Despite the fun

Monty and he had with Rosemary, she was very good at her job. The suit jacket conformed to his athletic stature perfectly, and his gold jewelry complimented the hints of gold woven into his jacket.

Immediately Chucky and Gurdy flocked to him like flies to fruit, fixing the slightest wrinkle in his jacket or the tiniest smudge on the already spotless shoes. Then Rosemary came to inspect him, her eyes narrowed in absolute concentration.

"…Shoes…pants…jacket…*hair*"   Rosemary's expression soured as she mused at Tyler's curly locks. She got a comb and some spray and moved it this way and that until she had completely ruined what he did, fashioning what she wanted instead.

"Listen," She said stepping so close to Tyler that the smell of strawberries seemed the only smell in the world. "*Don't* screw this up boy." Rosemary raised a cautioning finger. "Remember, people look up to you. Especially these kids who deserve every ounce of happiness they get. And people look up whom your clothes are made by, and if you behave…*stupidly*…it'll make me look bad. So don't."

Rosemary gave Monty a little nod and trotted out the door, high heels clicking on the floor. "Chucky! Gurdy!" Her voice rang through the hall.

"Good luck tonight!" Gurdy put a hand on Tyler's shoulder, getting a little too close for comfort. "Make the children happy like you always do!" She winked at Tyler and headed over to Rosemary's case.

A round hand sternly gripped Tyler's sleeve and pulled him down until he was eye to eye with the hand's owner, Chucky.

"Don't even *think* about making a move on her." Chucky hissed.

"But Chucky, I have a girl—

Chucky raised a sausage finger to Tyler's face. Turning, he rejoined Gurdy in 'carrying' Rosemary's hovering case out the door, which silently closed behind them.

"What a bunch of turkeys." Monty laughed as he came over to inspect Tyler. "But she does make you look good, and if she wasn't so stuffed I might have a drink with her at some point."

Tyler choked down a laugh, a mixture of cough and giggle came out instead.

"Easy there, slayer. Did I say something funny to you? Mister oh I have a girlfriend nah na nah na nah." Monty asked as his face went red. "Let's forget I ever said that, agreed?"

Tyler smiled. "Whatever you say."

The rest of the morning was spent in traffic trying to get to the radio station for a special interview with all the contenders in each weight class. Tyler's weight class was 165lbs. By the time they arrived to the studio from all the traffic, Dei Jie, Tyler's opponent had already left. Of course, Tyler had no real problem with this.

He had never officially met Dei, but his personal observations had left him with the conclusion that the kid was a self-centered punk, who cared about no one except himself. If the kid's head got any bigger, he wouldn't fit through doorways anymore. The radio interview was brief, as they didn't want to ruin the real interview everyone would watch Thursday evening. Every weight class, starting from 125lbs, would get a shot at the spotlight. Still, after three hours of traffic for ten minutes of airtime, Tyler found himself a bit irritated. As he walked down the hall toward the car, he peered out the window to see Jason. He was in what looked to be a heated conversation with Monty.

Tyler flew down the stairs and out the door. As soon as they saw him, they hushed up and strained smiles onto their faces.

"Tyler! How was the interview? Are you ready for tonight?"

"You bet!" Tyler said, his smile fading as he noticed Jason was not his normal self. "What is it?"

"I have something to— you know what— later. I can't have you looking down when these kids need that smile of the boy with a heart they have come to love." He winked.

"But Jason—

"Tyler later. Please?"

They rode in silence. Whether Jason realized it or not, not telling him was just making it worse. Now Tyler couldn't stop worrying about what it was that was wrong. And they better not tell him everything was just peachy because at this point, Tyler had been with Jason long enough to be able to know one thing, he never saw him like this before. Monty was a different story, Tyler didn't think anyone could crack his code but Jason...he was different.

Was it something he did? Was it something Dei did? Had a new prediction come out that was worse yet? (The current prediction had Tyler getting pinned to his back by Dei in the first of the three period match) Tyler dug deeper into his memory. What was it Jason had said?

"I have a lot to tell you in the next couple days." That statement suddenly meant more to Tyler as he continued to connect puzzle pieces in his head. *"Why would he risk his entire career on you?"* Alfredo Lopezzi's words continued to taunt him. What *did* Jason have to tell him? He thought back to when Jason was recruiting him. He could still feel the icy wind make the hairs on the back of his neck freeze, even under the two sweaters and a coat he wore that day.

"Tyler, I realize how important this is to you. I can see the fire of excitement in your eyes when we talk about this. I see you grab your hands to stop them from shaking. If we both do our part, you know what *can* happen? You can live your dream."

Tyler remembered how he had felt at that moment. He was practically hovering. *You can live your dream.*

That had been the part so vividly engraved in his memory all this time. He closed his eyes, fighting to bring back the second part of the conversation that was so far on the edge of his memory.

"But," Jason went on. "By this point in your life Tyler you must realize nothing is free. There is a reason I have selected you over all others, some of which, no offense are far above your skill level. I have picked you because of this," Jason put his hand over Tyler's heart.

"I'm sorry? I am not sure I am following."

"Let's just say that there are people in this world who are not who they seem to be. As we speak, they are moving to change the future of humanity, and not in a good way. There is nothing I can do to stop them with my skill set. I need you to be a light for humanity, when all other lights go out."

"So basically I am…setting a good example?"

"You could say that. I can't elaborate right now because we are still analyzing the situation, but please exercise caution before you accept my management. What I need from you is very dangerous, and should not be taken lightly. Accepting my offer will almost certainly change your life."

As much as this scared him, he could not live the rest of his life saying no to whatever this was.

"Jason, what if we do it?"

"What if we do what, Tyler?" Jason smiled.

"What if we beat impossible?"

Jason smiled. "If we do that…well, you might just change the world."

Tyler stared across the black seats of the SUV at the man who sat opposite him. He had thought Jason was the best thing that ever happened to him. But now he worried about exactly *how* they would be changing history. He thought he was already doing that, being the youngest contender to be a Champion ever. His life had already been drastically changed.

What more could happen?

"Jason," Tyler began, trying to muster the courage to finish the sentence. "When you told me—

The black door of the SUV opened.

"Sir." A man greeted. Behind him was a red carpet that had a few couples and individuals dotted across it. Hundreds of bright flashes went off every second as photographers snapped photos of every inch of movement. He turned to Jason.

"Later." He mumbled.

Jason nodded. As soon as Tyler was out in the open reporters shouting every question imaginable mobbed him, but he tried to ignore them as best he could as he was escorted to the carpet. He wasn't in a very talkative mood, as he pondered on the thoughts from the car ride.

Was all of it a mistake?

Tyler cursed himself under his breath. He wasn't doing justice to his own nickname when he thought like that. Was that a lie too? Without sunglasses, Tyler had to put on his best fake smile while trying to sound completely normal during the short interviews. They already knew Dei was way above Tyler's skill level, so why did they bother asking him about it?

Getting off the carpet didn't come soon enough, and Tyler couldn't have been happier when he was finally able to do what he had come to do: see the children. He met many, all with different stories and backgrounds. Some had been diagnosed with cancer at the age of six; others had rare diseases that still required treatment unfriendly to any human being, let alone a child, even with the wondrous technology of the world.

"Good to go, sir?" His bodyguard asked.

"Yes, I think we are all set." He was humbled, but his head was still a mess and he was ready to relax. He unbuttoned his collar and—

"Excuse me," a small, very gentle voice said.

Tyler turned around, not sure who he was expecting to see.

She was very small, very skinny, and very pale. Her hair kept falling in her face, and her mom hit a snag in the carpet as she pushed her wheelchair. But it barely shied the beaming smile off of the little girl's face. Here he was, complaining about the fact that he could only live his dream for a little while. What about her dreams? Tyler got on one knee, resisting a tear.

"Hello." He smiled. "What's your name?"

"I'm Alysha! It is so nice to finally meet you, Tyler! You have no idea—

It broke his heart to see her interrupted by her coughing. He helped her get a tissue out of the box she kept tucked on the side of her wheel chair.

"Thank you." She said when she was done. "Nana taught you how to be a gentlemen, didn't she?"

It hit Tyler somewhere he didn't know he had.

"I...well thanks, thank you, Alysha. Yes she, she did."

69

"Oh my pleasure. And I'm sorry you didn't have a mommy. We can share mine if you want?" She smiled. It was so pure a tear slid down his face.

"Well thank you." He laughed as she handed him a tissue.

"Are you going to win on Friday?" She beamed.

"I am certainly going to try my best."

"A lot of people are saying you can't, you know?" She said as she looked down.

"Yeah, that is what I hear."

"But don't worry about them. The doctors told me I can't do it, either. But I said if you can do it, I can do it! Oh my gosh you aren't crying, are you?" She said as she whipped out another tissue for him.

"I'm sorry Alysha, you just make me smile." Tyler said as he looked at her mother. She shook her head with a smile. "Are you coming this Friday?" He asked as he tried to find his center of gravity again.

"Mommy says we can't." The look on her face crushed him. He stood up.

"You don't think you'll be able to make it?" He asked in a hushed tone.

"The bills for her last treatments came in, and I can't pay for the tickets and pay them anymore."

"What do you mean by her last treatments?" He asked.

"She's isn't supposed to make it after this week. These last treatments aren't covered by insurance, but I won't give up. She can do it."

Tyler leaned down to see the amazing little girl in front of him. "Alysha, what if I told you that you were going Friday?"

"How?" She almost launched out of her wheelchair.

"Well, I talked to your mom, and I have a special pair of tickets I want the two of you to have."

"Oh my gosh! Stop. Tyler Mason, you aren't lying to me are you?" She demanded as her little hand grabbed him by the jacket.

"Absolutely not! The tickets are in the first row, center mat, and they are all yours!"

She flung out of her wheelchair and threw her arms around his neck. She was so light.

"Okay, Tyler Mason! Don't you dare tell anyone you made me cry now, okay?" She said as she wiped the tears from her face.

"Only if you don't tell anyone you made me cry." He smiled.

Alysha's bright green eyes sparkled as she handed Tyler a red, heart shaped piece of paper. Scribbled on it as best as possible was:

Yours inspires mine

His heart had never felt so warm.

After tucking it away in his jacket, giving her a kiss, and sending her off with front row tickets to Friday, Tyler headed on to dinner.

He met a few more contenders from different weight classes and chatted a bit. But after his encounter with little Alysha, he found himself unconcerned with politics. Life was so short, why waste it on pretending to feel something you don't? Dinner went well, and as Tyler thought more about the whole Jason situation and Alysha, he began to feel a small feeling of acceptance in it.

Nana always said everything happens for a reason.

Tyler's eyes suddenly locked on a man across the room whose eyes were locked onto Tyler. His gaze didn't even flinch when Tyler looked at him. A not so good feeling molded in the pit of his stomach. There was something about the man that was unnerving. He turned to tell Jason, but when he opened his mouth…

"Ladies and Gentleman," Alfredo Lopezzi began as he stood at the podium in the center of the hall. "Tonight, we have gathered here for a very noble cause: to make dreams come true. Some might say these beautiful children that many of you have met tonight have been dealt an awful hand in life. But, ladies and gentlemen, I stand before you today to announce that because of the efforts of everyone in this room, one day soon we will not only make them smile, but make them healthy! Thank you for joining us this evening, and thank you for your unprecedented generosity! We will see you all soon!"

Applause roared throughout the room.

"Stay here, and stay out of trouble." Jason faced him. "Monty and I have to talk to a few people, and than we'll be on our way."

Tyler nodded, as he glanced across the room, searching for the man. There was no one there.

"Hey? Alright?" Jason insisted.

"Yep! Got it."

"Five minutes."

"How about six?" Tyler joked.

He observed Jason and Monty as stealthily as he could. It started out with only a few people. But within a couple minutes, a crowd of people joined them. Eventually, Tyler got antsy, and couldn't help but try and get within earshot of the group. But each time he would get close enough, Monty would notice, whisper in Jason's ear, and the group would edge away from him.

Soon an hour had passed.

This is ridiculous, Tyler had never been much of the patient type. He decided to get up (yes, he had given up trying to listen in) and go for a walk. Most people were leaving. He looked around, taking in his surrounding for the first time that evening.

The room was massive, complete with a white marble floor, lavish chandeliers, and huge golden TOC eagle in the center. Under the eagle was an elevated stage with the championship-wrestling mat on it. They would move it down the street to the arena early Friday morning. Before any wrestling match, no matter if it was the first match of the day or the championships, he was always nervous. This was no exception, the butterflies in his stomach already flurrying viciously as he imagined himself stepping foot on it.

The roar of the crowd, the cameras, the expectations, none of them got to him as much as the butterflies in his stomach to wrestle the best he possibly could. He always wanted to do better, to be better; he always strived to search for that drive to get him through the grind. That is where most people gave up in this sport. There is no glory in the grind. None. You had to be crazy to be a wrestler.

But it was a good kind of crazy.

To step on that mat Friday, for the most coveted title in the entire world was something he still couldn't believe he was doing.

"Well, well, well," an accented voice interrupted his thoughts. "If it isn't the boy bluffer himself."

Tyler felt his stomach twist.

He turned to face none other than Dei Jie, standing on the stage. Muscles bulging out of his jacket, he stood nearly six feet tall with his hair gelled up in the front, and a Chinese flag lapel pin resting on his heart. But the most unnerving thing about him, to Tyler at least, was his cold, dark, beady black eyes.

"Well, well, well, if it isn't the person I hoped least to see." Tyler said coldly, yet truthfully.

Dei smirked. "Why is that?" He asked. "Because you know I'm going to kick your phony ass." Even with his imperfect English, his vile tone was clear.

"I hope you are aware by now that I'm not going to lay down for you like the rest of your opponents did."

This seemed to have struck a nerve with Dei, whose once cocky expression twisted into an anger. He jumped off the stage, towering over Tyler.

"Hey look!"

That was all it took and within seconds, a crowd was forming.

"Are you implying that I am dishonorable, Mason? That's big talk for someone who made it here off some luck and his manager's connections."

It felt as though someone had punched him the gut. Luck or not, the fact was he beat a state champion who should be here now in his place.

"No Dei, *that* is big talk for someone whose father has enough money to pay off the entire TOC panel to buy you a title."

"How dare you question my honor? Do you want to *test* whether or not I actually need my father to pay anyone off to rip you apart? I think we both know the answer to that. Just wait Mason, come Friday the world will see that you are nothing more than a media produced hype poster. My dad says you're a waste of space."

Tyler felt his fist clench as his eyes darted left and right, he realized much of the room that was empty a few seconds ago was now full of reporters and their cameras. This would be tomorrow's news for sure. *Stay here and stay out of trouble.* He would go back to Jason. This was what Dei wanted.

Tyler turned away from his opponent, taking a few steps away. *You made the right choice, Ty.* In the distance he could see Jason, who was *still* talking.

"Ask your dad to reconsider his waste of space comment, please." Tyler said as he took a deep breath and continued walking away.

"I could tell you the same thing," Dei began. "But then I remembered you don't have a dad to ask. Or a mom. You have nothing. Nothing but that old hag, and where is she? Not even here because she knows you'll lose. Talk about pathetic."

Tyler stopped dead in his tracks and faced Dei. He was fighting hard, but something had snapped inside of him. He could feel sweat begin to glisten on his forehead as his heart beat on his chest faster and faster.

"Something to say?"

"Yeah." Tyler snapped.

He felt the skin on his knuckles peel back as he punched Dei Jie in the face.

6 When it Rains...

It took both Tyler and Dei a moment to realize what just happened.

But after that moment passed, all hell broke loose. Tyler suddenly felt his movement restricted as powerful arms locked around him, squeezing his chest and dragging him back, away from the carnage unfolding in front of him. He struggled to breath as he glimpsed Monty shove the cameras down. Dei's father appeared and grabbed Dei, who was one step away from hitting Tyler. Despite Monty's efforts, the cameras kept flashing. They got *everything*.

The image of Alysha smiling earlier entered his head. As if losing the will to stay up, his head dropped as the image of Alysha's smile faded slowly into tears.

He had let her down.

It was obvious now that the arms locked around him belonged to Jason, and he didn't resist as they dragged him out of the room. Tyler felt a mixture of toxic feelings boiling up inside of him. A raging anger toward Dei, bitter sadness at the example he had just set for his most hopeful fan, and pain that Nana could not be there with him.

He had lost control. Tyler had tried so hard to keep those feelings locked away, and for someone to bring them up in such a vile way...he just couldn't take it!

"Let go, Jason! Let go! I'm fine now!" He struggled but Jason didn't, his grip remained tight as steel as he continued dragging him out through the kitchen. Monty ran behind them and opened a door to an alley, slamming it in the faces of reporters behind them.

"Let g—

With a force as raging as the winds of a hurricane, Jason shoved him into a wall. A sharp pain went through his back, and in that moment he noticed the severity of the looks on both Jason and Monty's faces.

"What? What's wrong?" It was only a bad press day at stake here, nothing more?

"What's wrong?" Jason mocked. "Oh, I'll tell you what's wrong. ARE YOU TRYING TO BLOW THE WHOLE DAMN OPERATION *NOW*, AFTER WE HAVE GOTTEN SO FAR?"

"Jason," Monty said, putting a hand on his shoulder. Tyler had never seen Jason like this, nor did he think he was capable. Jason was right in his face; he could feel his hurried breathes hitting his face. But Tyler had reason to be upset as well. Besides what had just happened, Jason still owed him answers.

It was time to pay up.

"Operation? After *we* have gotten so far? Excuse me, but what the *HELL* ARE YOU TALKING ABOUT? I think it's time *you* gave me some answers! You can't just keep someone in the dark until *you're* ready to tell them what you and your little click are chatting about! This is *my* life we're talking about here!"

"Tyler," Monty said sternly like a parent trying to regain control of their children.

"*Don't* even, Lester! I know your not telling me everything. I knew that about you from day one. But Jason, I expected more of. I didn't think there would be strings attached with him, but Mr. Lopezzi sure did a great job of confirming that for me." The look on Jason's face went from a contorted mix of anger and sadness to utter dismay and confusion.

"Lopezzi? When did you talk to him— look Tyler we're on the *same* team, why don't we go somewhere and we can discuss—

Tyler flicked away Jason's hand.

"I don't give a damn if we're on the same team. I'm not going anywhere until I know exactly what the hell game you two are playing with my life!" Tyler screeched. The mess of toxic emotions inside him had finally hit a boiling point. "What *exactly* are your intentions in having me here? What is your focus? Clearly not to win a championship!"

"Tyler, this isn't the time or place." Monty said sternly, checking the surroundings as though making sure no one was around.

"No Lester, it's time." Jason stated in defeat.

Monty looked as though he had just seen a ghost.

"We can trust him, Lester. We can. We're going to have to. Isn't trust the reason we chose him in the first place?"

"But—" Jason held up a hand to Monty, who reluctantly, stepped back.

"Tyler, the first thing you should know about Lester Monty and I is that we didn't join the TOC Recruiter Program for the career."

Jason paused and rubbed his forehead before taking a seat on one of the garbage capsules. Tyler slid down onto a moldy wooden crate. Monty kept pacing, as though prepping for a sudden attack.

"When Monty and I joined the TOC five years ago, we were doing it as part of a cover."

"A *cover*?"

Jason sighed. "Look, try and keep an open mind. This is going to sound ludicrous when I tell you, and that is what the other side uses."

"The other side?" What was this? An us and them type thing?

"Monty and I work for an organization of," He paused as though considering his words. "Peace keepers if you will."

"Peace keepers?" Tyler repeated questionably.

"It means exactly as it says." Monty snapped irritably. "The people who helped the Americans in the Revolution. The people who stopped the Nazis and the Cuban missile crisis."

Tyler shook his head. This really *was* going to be ludicrous "So let me get this straight, you work for some organization of vigilantes who—

"You wouldn't joke if you could stop being small minded and grasp the gravity of the situation at the moment." Monty snapped. Tyler stood up at this comment, feeling rage still bubbling up inside him.

"Calm down." Jason said irritably.

Stubbornly, Monty went back into pacing mode, slicking back his graying hair with his hand and resuming a pace, once again watching for some unseen foe.

"Tyler, surely by now you must realize that the world is not upfront with everything, very little in fact. A lot of truly important things happen behind the scenes. *We* are the people behind the scenes. We work for the people, not the corrupt. Our work is to ensure there is balance and a set of morals in a world that is becoming increasingly mislead with ideas that money and power are everything."

Tyler felt though he had just been smashed by a bolder. He was trying his best to believe his ears. He had to be dreaming, like the Dragonfly right?

"Well I— I don't know what to say, Jason. Maybe some things seem plausible. Winning World War two was certainly a group effort but—

"Tyler, stop there. Do you really think any country in the world is really capable of making a difference like we can? The leaders are only as good as the world allows them to be. There has to be something, someone, behind the scenes to go the extra mile. To do what is necessary but remain faceless, free from the judgment of the world."

This was too much for Tyler to think about right now with everything else that was already going through his mind. He could see the truth in it to a point but... he still hadn't received the answers he was looking for.

"Alright, nameless and faceless. Two things I am not. So why are you telling me this? Where do I come into this? Is there some rival you guys are at odds with here?"

"The thing is Tyler, I'd be lying if I told you there wasn't."

Tyler looked into Jason's eyes, searching, hoping to see for any trace of a lie in them, but there was none. "Without evil there can't be good, and without good there can't be evil. They call themselves Venom. For thousands of years control has jockeyed from one side to the other. But somehow, we were always able to manage to stay a step ahead. Then something happened, twenty years ago." Jason cringed as he said this.

"The War?" Tyler suggested.

"The War." Jason continued, as some invisible pain of the past seemed to pour out of him. "Venom had nearly defeated us. But somehow we pulled through. At that moment, we believed we finally won. Perhaps peace would finally reign now that humanity had stopped the fighting on it's own, without   our   help."

And it was true. Though neither the United States nor China will ever admit it, at the time of the peace making, both countries were in ruins. Neither was poised to win. "So what happened?" Tyler asked as he tried to wrap his head around the idea of secret organizations that fought for the peace or destruction of the globe.

"*This* happened." Jason said as he gestured toward everything around them.

"What?" Tyler gasped. "No! This was for peace. THAT IS WHY WE ARE HERE!"

"No, Tyler. The man who formed this Tournament is the leader of Venom, and he plans on covering all the world in darkness. Freedom is like a bad joke to them. In their mind, the average person has no need of it."

Tyler shook his head in disbelief. "That's crazy, I won't— I can't believe this. That means...no..." A grim realization popped into Tyler's head. Not for the first time in his life, he was being used. He was no more than a chess piece in not one but *two* people's games if Jason was right.

"Tyler, Jason recruited you because of who you are. You are a good person, and we need a face. And we need that face to be you. Now, it will require training." Monty reentered the conversation.

Spinning.

Tyler's head was spinning. He was struggling to regain control, to figure it out what was going on. "First of all guys, I'm not so sure how good of a person I am anymore. Second, you want me to be what, like a president type thing?"

"No," Jason shook his head. "Much more than that, Tyler. You see, anyone can be a president, but only a few can be a *symbol*."

A symbol. Tyler turned over that phrase in his mind for a few seconds, but he was losing control of himself. He could feel his pulse pounding through his veins like they were going to explode. This was...too much. They...this...

This was insane. *They* were insane. Clearly this was his fault, though. He hadn't taken Jason seriously enough when he said to exercise caution before accepting him as a manager. "But I..I don't understand, why…why now? Why would they run this circus for twenty years?"

"Because they were regaining their strength, Tyler! Don't you see? Look at all the money, the resources, and the connections that this TOC thing has given them. And worst of all, *they* have become a symbol that people are now brainwashed into following. He who controls the people controls the *world,* Tyler. Tell people your doing something bad in the name of good so many times and eventually they'll stop caring. Think about it! Who controls the media? People focus on one thing anymore, the TOC. Every year, they use it as an escape from the problems that are really going on. Meanwhile their freedoms are being stolen under their very nose by paid off lawmakers who are all failing to see the big picture. We are talking about the mass elimination of freedom on a global scale."

It was all crazy, and as much as it made sense, and as much as he wanted to believe Jason, Tyler needed time to think. Second, he wasn't exactly sure what he could do about all of this. He was only one small person in a big world.

"Even if it were all true, what can I possibly do to make a difference?"

"Tyler, you have become more successful than we ever imagined. You now have the audience and the power to influence people in a positive light. You can put out the fire this tournament is trying to cause between the world's two superpowers, and remind people what everything is really about. That's why we were so upset when you punched Dei, because that's only going to make the fire burn even hotter. Everyone knows what kind of person Dei is, but by now they expect more out of you. "

"Jason," Tyler struggled to find words. "I…."

"I am sorry for everything I just dumped on you, and for putting you in this position. I should have told you about this from the beginning. But, Dei is probably enraged about this, and you can bet he will play even dirtier on Friday. We need you to—

"Jason, I'm eighteen years old." Tyler said with the heavy feeling that all his dreams, everything he thought life could be, would be, crumbled right before him. None of it was real.

None of it.

"How in the world do you think I could possibly prevent a world war? How could I make a difference? Even if I could, do you have *any* solid evidence for me that the TOC is corrupt?" He wouldn't allow himself to believe it. He couldn't. Because if the TOC was truly corrupt then that means Cailey's dad…there was no way. She would know wouldn't she? She couldn't. She wouldn't do that to him!

"Tyler, I need you to trust me on this for now. I can tell you more lat—

"Trust you?" A fake, nervous laugh escaped Tyler's throat. "You want me to trust you when you have neglected to tell me about this *little* life changing part of our deal all this time we have been together? Instead, you wait for the most important week of my life?"

"Tyler, this is the most important week of all of our lives! If you would just understand!"

"No Jason! No! Frankly, I don't understand and I don't care! I need some time before I want to see you."

With that, Tyler turned his back to Jason and headed off out of the alley and to the streets. Monty quickly rushed after when he felt a hand grip his shoulder.

"Let him go, Lester. Let him go. He needs time to let things sink in. If you were him right now, how would you feel?" Jason asked. The whole situation had brought up distant memories he had long since tried to bury in the back of his mind.

I would feel like I lost my purpose. He thought.

Tyler continued walking slowly down the empty street. In comparison to the usual circus like atmosphere, it was abnormally silent and dark for the first time Tyler could remember since he had arrived in the ecstatic city. The late night breeze was cool, and gave him goose bumps despite it being late July. Above the shimmering city, the night sky was charcoal black, the stars looked like little glowing night-lights spaced throughout. The yells from the crowd echoed from a few blocks over.

Then there was nothing.

Whatever he did, he had to make sure that he didn't go anywhere near people after the previous situation, which was usually a chore in this city. Considering it had been built just over a year ago and the entire thing was meant to be a resort, it was next to impossible. He would give anything to be in the air right now.

But the idea of being alone *somewhere* in Lanstark City didn't quite seem as impossible if you compared it to what Jason had just revealed to Tyler. Secret organizations? The TOC a complete scandal? Tyler Mason, a *symbol*? It sounded like nothing but nonsense when he first rolled it over in his mind. But...one thing about Jason was he had never lied to him.

Except for all of this...

Tyler thought back to the day he had first met Jason, yet again. After he had gotten over the fear of Jason's alias, Professor Teach, he realized he had found a man he could actually relate to. Not just as a friend, but also like a father he had never had. There was an irresistible charm about this man who was firm, but very much a gentleman. Always polished, hair combed, and relaxed. Tyler normally trusted his gut, and it had told him that this man was all right.

That day he came home, beaming to tell Nana the news that all his dreams were about to become more than just a scene in his imagination. But before he told her, she told him something far more important. She was sick.

Jason visited the hospital with him everyday after her treatment began. It took its toll on her. But she never failed to mention how much she loved Jason. And she was the best judge of character Tyler knew.

A splash echoed throughout the silent silver buildings as he stepped in a murky puddle. As much as Tyler had trouble believing what Jason had told him earlier, he had even more trouble believing that Jason would ever flat out lie to him. Sure, he had covered up some pretty important details, but he had admitted full responsibility for that and apologized.

That would mean all of this was true.

It sounded crazy. Was he being foolish to put so much faith in an individual that, as it turned out, he knew very little about?

He believed everything happened for a reason. What was the reason for this?

His mind wandered back to the night he won states, earning his chance to make it onto Team USA.

He had been sitting alone in his room, hands shaking, and his forehead beaded with sweat. It was easily the biggest night of his life, and at the moment he felt the weight of his entire future on his shoulders. That's why it certainly didn't help when Jason walked in.

Immediately Tyler assumed he knew what Jason had come to say.

"Come to rub it in, have you?" He managed to squeak, feeling a rising sense of embarrassment inside as he fought to hold back his nerves. How is it that he had gotten this far, only to have to face Matt Hooradian-the undefeated, three time State Champion? And Jason was most likely thinking what he was thinking; yet Jason had far more to lose than he did. After all, he had chosen him. He had put his entire career on the line.

"No. No." He said calmly as if expecting that reaction. "I'm here to let you know, no matter what happens tonight, I'm really glad that I had the privilege to meet and work with you, Tyler Mason. You have brightened my dimmed hope in humanity. I want to thank you for that."

As he thought about the memory with what he knew now, maybe Jason really did put it *all* on the line for him that day. Assuming what he had just learned was true. And the more he thought about it, as crazy as all of this was, it certainly wasn't impossible.

A roar of a crowd in the distance was the first sound he had heard in ten minutes.

He stopped walking for a moment and peered up into the heavens, the midnight sky twinkling in its grand design. He was going to make this right. He owed that much to Jason.

"You really do work in mysterious ways, don't you?" He said as he gazed at the sky. At that moment, a shooting star flickered across the sky in its majestic flight, before vanishing in the blink of an eye.

The only thing was, if he did what Jason wanted, and the TOC really was nothing more than a scandal wouldn't that mean his dream, everything he worked so hard for, was a lie? He was finally becoming someone too.

A tear rolled down his cheek. "I was almost there, mom." He said. "I could've made history, and helped others not feel like I do everyday. Without you and dad! Alone, abandoned, helpless...."

He took in a long breath of fresh air, and then exhaled. He would go back to Jason and learn the details of all of this.

He looked up one more time. "I know it wasn't your fault that you left. I just wish...."

He began to head back when he froze in place.

The figure that had been approaching suddenly stopped.

Tyler's heart began to pound harder. Something didn't feel right. He observed the figure in front of him. The man was middle aged, had short sharp facial hair, and was dressed in a normal black tuxedo, not common to the typically outrageous TOC fashion.

But there was something about those eyes.

He had seen this man before! It was the man from the party!

The man began to walk faster toward him now, a treacherous look forming on his face as though he was going to enjoy whatever he was about to do.

Tyler didn't plan on finding out.

He began to run away as fast as his feet would allow. *Why did he leave Jason? How could he have been so stupid?* Lucky for him, he wasn't in terrible shape— and he was banking on this. As he rounded a corner he glanced back, the man was clearly falling behind. Where were all the people? It was no longer feeling like a coincidence. He slipped and felt a stab in his ankle but managed to jump into a dimly doorway.

His heart pounding and sweat beads running off his face, he strained his ears to listen. Pain rippled through his ankle. Had he gotten away? He felt like the man was right behind him. Suddenly, he heard the click of dress shoes pounding on pavement. He peered around the corner and saw the man run by.

A wave of utter relief went through. Time to get back to Ja— a black-coated arm locked itself around his neck.

The last thing he remembered was a sharp poke.

7 Be Careful What You Wish For

A low murmur of voices could be heard, though it was a rather odd thing to hear from outer space.

Looking at the entire planet below, Tyler had never felt so...uplifted. It was so wondrous, big, and free up here. *Free.* For some reason that word seemed to stick in his head. Another murmur of voices, but louder and somewhat clear this time, he could actually make out a word that one of them said: "Friday." He wasn't sure why they were concerned about Friday. If he ever got down from here, he knew what he was doing on Friday: he had a match against "Dei". Well that was strange. Usually when you think to yourself the voice is in your head, not out loud.

"Plan." "Friday." "Silas." The unknown voice was becoming more frequent. *Free.* The word kept repeating in his head, with ever more urgency each time it echoed. *Free.* All right this place was starting to creep him out, he was ready to get down now. *Free.*

Everything went black.

He was falling.

Tyler opened his eyes in panic, suddenly blinded by a bright, white light. The voices stopped as he squeezed his eyes shut, trying to shield his eyes against the unrelenting light. He went to lift his arms but they didn't move. Tyler struggled to open his eyes to see what was restricting his arms. He became aware of the feeling of cold metal on his wrists and his ankles.

Had the voices been in his head? Was he still dreaming? He squeezed his eyes shut. *Wake up! Wake up!*

"Ah, Mr. Mason. So glad you could join us this evening."

Tyler slowly opened his eyes as his heart sank.

This was no dream.

Men of all different shapes and sizes stared at him in cover of the dim light, while he was in the center of the room.

A massive spotlight shined overhead, blasting his presence to all the staring eyes. His vision began to clear. The room was enormous. In the shadows he could make out dozens of glowing eyes staring at him alongside massive computer screens on the walls and desks. They had various images and live feeds of cities around the world. Massive tables had holographic maps of the city that moved with the people in it, and a miniaturized world rotated in sync with its life size counter part. On the wall, instead of the typical TOC logo was instead one Tyler had seen only just the other day, at lunch with Cailey and her father...

"Where am I? Why am I here?" He asked the room, deciding to play the innocent card.

There was a sharp cackle that came from the figure in the shadows. The rest of the men in the room, as though receiving permission, laughed as well. The figure took one more step forward, illuminated by the screen behind him.

"Did you really think we were that foolish, Mr. Mason? Were you truly naïve enough to think that you would fool me?"

"What if I was?" Tyler shot back, throwing away the innocent card.

"Let's not get too confident, Mr. Mason. After all, you are not here by choice, am I right?"

The point put a knife in Tyler's ribs as his hope that he could get out of this situation unscathed continued to fade.

"I will allow you to rejoice in the fact that you came *close*." The voice continued.

Tyler pulled at the metal links that held his arms and legs to the chair, but it only caused the restraints to dig into his skin more.

"That is the story of your life though, isn't it, Mr. Mason? You have always come *so close* to everything you wanted." Tyler felt as though the voice kept twisting the unseen knife, continuing to dig up his most vulnerable feelings. How did it know so much about him?

"I mean you were so close to becoming an All-American. And how about that girl in eighth grade? Oh that girl. You spent so much time on her. You were so close, but not quite *there*. And let's not forget *them*."

"Well, I made it this far, haven't I?" Tyler fought to suppress the painful memories, as they began to bubble to the surface. Who was this man to judge what he was capable of? He had no idea what Tyler had been through. He didn't know the full story. "And who said it was over? You can't exactly get rid of me," Tyler continued. "Two billion viewers around the world will be expecting me on Friday, at 7pm."

The figure was getting closer, and by sheer luck of lighting, Tyler caught a corner of his mouth crease into a smile, as if he was expecting Tyler to say something like this.

"You're quite right about the latter, Mr. Mason. Two billion people will be expecting to see you on Friday, at 7pm." The figure stepped out into the spotlight, and Tyler felt his heart stop. "And you have my word that they *will* be seeing you."

The voice was familiar, because just as Jason had said, it belonged to a very famous figure. Casper Lanstark stepped into the spotlight, a snakelike look set on his face. There was an untouchable air that he carried about him, one that intimidated even Presidents. His dark hair was slicked back to perfection and his suit was tailored to excellence. Perfectly polished shoes clicked on the floor as he stepped closer to Tyler.

"But," He held up a finger. "How they see you Friday is completely up to you."

Tyler really didn't like the sound of that.

"Before I get to that, however, I figured I would tell you a little bit about us anyway? Just for old times sake? After all, don't you want to know about the other side your friend Jason was talking about?"

It was funny, perhaps he had misunderstood, but Casper's tone sounded like it was poised as a question. Casper clapped his hands and the metal clasps restraining him to the chair flung open.

"You are free to go, Mr. Mason. Though I would suggest you stay to hear what I have to say." Although free, Tyler had never felt more trapped in his entire life. He flinched when the metal shackles were released, but his better judgment told him he better stay.

"A wise decision." Casper nodded, clapping his hands again. The various screens and desks in the room went dark, except for the big one he currently stood in front of.

The seal of the snake that he had seen Silas wearing that day at lunch, and that all the men in room were probably wearing, appeared in the middle of the screen. Its glowing green eyes locked onto Tyler, unblinking.

"Casper! Casper!" Choked a raspy voice as a figure emerged from the dark. "Stop this, this instant! This information cannot be shared with *him*! It's too dangerous." Unlike all the men in modern day luxury suits, this man was dressed in robes that seemed to be from the Medieval Era. He wore rings on all of his fingers; his face's old appearance seemed to be from a mixture of old age and disappointment. Tyler instantly recognized Silas Marshall. "You're putting all of us at risk!" He screeched, looking around for others to support his claims.

The room was silent. Casper stood with a look of bewilderment on his face. "I can't quite decide how to respond to your distasteful, disturbing behavior, Silas. It troubles me that you think you can interrupt *me* when *I* am speaking."

Silas looked as though someone had slapped him across the face. "How dare you—"

"Excuse *me*! Should you *ever* be so unwise as to forget whom you are speaking to again, Silas Marshall, so help me God I will BURY you! You're no longer the leader of Venom. I took it from you! We've done things my way for twenty years, and have gotten far more done than you *ever* did." With every one of Casper's words, Silas seemed to grow more and more distraught. "Now, I suggest you sit. Down."

Silas inhaled to say something, but stopped himself, and retreated back into the dark.

"Forgive me, Tyler, and allow me to continue." A smile returned to Casper's face. "You've been told by certain misguided individuals that *we* are the 'bad' guys. This couldn't be farther from the truth. We are here to simply… guide humanity on the proper path."

"Think about it. Are the people of the world actually free? They give up their dreams and hopes to spend their entire lives working to rub a few pennies together under the name of 'freedom!' The countries of the world are nothing more than pawns to the two superpowers of the globe as they try to line up weapons against each other." The U.S. and China began to illuminate on the globe. "*Freedom* is a myth."

"Assuming you're not crazy, how do you plan to stop this, Casper? The work of your organization has caused some of the most devastating events in human history."

"Devastating is only one way of looking at it, Tyler. Remember, life is all about perspective. Please, don't be narrow-minded. Under our guidance, there will be no more false notions of success. People will no longer fill their heads with these lies that if you start at the bottom you can actually go somewhere in this world."

"That is where you are wrong!" Tyler shot. Casper's glow dimmed a bit at this comment as he turned to face his hostage.

"I wouldn't be here today if I had that attitude. Neither would you. You didn't come from money. And how about the countless others who came before the both of us who started with nothing more than a dream?"

Casper's eyes flickered, perhaps with amusement. He began twisting at the large snake ring on his finger. "Tyler," He began, shaking his head. "*We* are the rare people of this Earth. How many people have a dream? Everyone. But how many people actually achieve it? Very few."

Tyler smirked. "So your grand idea is to take away one of the most beautiful aspects of humanity?"

"It would be, relieving them of a pain." Casper proclaimed.

"You're wrong again. People should have the freedom to dream, the freedom to go after their dreams, and the freedom to fail!"

Casper laughed. "Jason was right to put his faith in you, Tyler Mason. You are probably his finest achievement, but you are fighting for the losing side. I am offering you a chance to leave it for the winning side. Join us, and change the world!"

"The winning side? Is that why Jason almost foiled your ludicrous ideas bringing me on board?"

This struck a cord with Casper, as his calm, composed look flipped into a vicious growl, and the true nature of the man in front of him was displayed in brilliant effect.

"*Almost.*" He bellowed as his eyes ripped through Tyler's as though he would shoot him right now if he could. "You know, you silly peasants think you actually stand a chance..." Casper spoke as if thinking aloud.

"You know what's worse? You silly hypocrites who believe you're above everybody...you must have never heard the expression be careful who you step on on your way up, because you'll meet them on the way down."

Casper laughed. "So, I take it you're rejecting my offer?"

"I'm not even considering it." Tyler replied flatly.

"You know, I'm feeling generous today, so I'm going to give it to you anyway. Just for the possibility that you may reconsider your position in a moment." Casper sneered as he paced slowly back and forth. "Whether you cooperate or not, your part in my plan will still be carried out. So just make it easy on yourself and do what any logical person in your position would do, Tyler Mason."

Tyler felt his gut wrench as he prepared for what was next.

"You see Mr. Mason, before you and Jason came to...overcomplicate my show, everything was going smoothly. The U.S. and China have steadily been heading toward a boiling point, and the war that is soon to follow will result in the weakening of the world's armed forces so much so, it will be a cakewalk for us to step in. All of them were falling into my traps perfectly...then out of the randomness of life came *you*. A no one who has attracted *millions* to your cause."

"I'm sorry for being me." Tyler said, a sly smile cracking the edge of his lips and boosting his confidence, even if for a moment.

Casper let out a cackle. "Until very recently, you were potentially the most lethal thorn in my side. As you stated earlier, two billion people are expecting to see their boy with a heart on Friday."

Casper said heart as if the word made him sick to his stomach. Tyler felt his distaste as the very bad knot deep in the pit of his stomach mangled even worse.

"We've been over this." Tyler objected as if trying to save himself from finding out Casper's plan.

"I thought about it for some time, Tyler." Casper continued, ignoring him as his dark grin grew bigger and bigger. "And then it hit me. I don't need to get *rid* of you. I *need* you."

Tyler had only felt all his will power leave him like this one other time in his life. "What... *need* me?"

"Jason had thought he had me beat when he planned on using your reputation against me. But, what if the people of the world saw their brilliant, caring boy with a heart show the utmost misconduct and act like the little punk he is on the world's most televised event? What if you were nothing more than a poster boy, a fraud, a myth?"

Tyler felt every eye in the room on him and his captor. Once again, he was trapped. Not by physical restraints, but by invisible ones that dwarfed the power any physical ones could ever have.

Seeing how Tyler wasn't going to respond, Casper continued on. "So, Mr. Mason what you are going to do on Friday is not only let Dei Jie win, but once he does you are going to hit him. And I don't mean like the pathetic swing you did tonight. Throw him off the podium, hit him where it hurts, what ever you want to do. It really doesn't matter to me. The damage will be down."

He was dreaming. He would wake up any second. He closed his eyes, hoping, praying that any minute now he would wake up safe in his bed.

"You are not dreaming, Tyler." Casper's cold voice echoed in his head, sending a wave of goose bumps all over his body.

He sighed in defeat. "If I refuse?"

"Because I have revealed the concept of my plan to you, you're dead. If you refuse to do this, not only will your death be a lot more painful, but your poor little Nana will suffer a fate worse than yours, right in front of your eyes."

Tyler felt like a sudden ball of fire igniting his insides as he stood up in rage. "NOOOOO! YOU LEAVE HER OUT OF THIS!"

Everyone in the room was clearly shocked, possibly even a little frightened by Tyler's reaction. Memories of the night his parents died finally managed to gurgle to the surface of his mind. *No.* He had blocked them out so well. He would not feel that way ever again.

"Now, please keep in mind, Tyler, this is the scenario where you and I aren't friends. I want us to be friends, Tyler. I really do. We can benefit each other in ways we can't even imagine. So allow me tell you what is in it for you if you do join us."

He collapsed in the chair, his heart pounding and his head feeling like it was going to explode.

"Tyler, I respect you. In fact, I see a lot of myself in you. That is why I am offering this once in a lifetime privilege. Join us. Allow Jason to think you're going to do what he wants of you, but do what I want. In return, I will give you your wildest dreams! Money, fame, a Dragon Fly X, yes…I know of your love for the car. I will even throw in a rematch for the title! Most importantly, we will see to it Nana is taken care of."

How did he know about Nana?

"I know you can't afford the cure, but I can. And I will get it for you." Casper held out his hand. "It's time for you to join the winning side of life, my boy."

It was like shaking hands with the devil. But he couldn't possibly say no. Not with Nana on the line. She needed help, and he refused to continue to feel the helplessness he felt when his parents died again. Jason had lied to him, and led him into this unimaginable trap. This was his only chance to get out of this and find some good out of the situation. Even best of all, he could save Nana.

"Excellent!"

"How do I know you'll keep your word?"

"Tyler," Casper smirked as if he'd heard a joke. "After you do this, there will be no point of going out of my way to kill *you*, I'll be too busy ruling the world."

Free.

Part TWO

8 No Place for a Hero

Jason Teach never liked coffee.

For as long as he remembered, the relationship between him and the beverage had been rocky at best. These days it reminded him too much of his father, bringing with it nothing but pain and anger. Yet as he sat at his desk window gazing out at the city named after a man he hated, he couldn't stop himself from sipping on the despised beverage he had in hand. Oddly enough, it made him feel closer to his father more than ever before.

He took another sip.

Things had been going so well, better than he had ever hoped. Tyler's popularity had rocketed into something he never imagined.

They bet it all on him, Monty, himself, and the team.

It was his fault. He should have told the boy earlier. Tyler had been living his dream. Why would he give it up? If only he could realize what was at stake here! How could he prove it to the boy?

The sound of the door opening and closing startled him, the coffee jolting in his hand. After wiping the hot liquid off of his hand, he slowly took another sip.

"No sign of him. Anywhere. Maybe…maybe he's thinking somewhere?" Monty sighed with a mixture of exhaustion and frustration.

They had been looking for him since the separation in the parking lot. That was almost nine hours ago.

"Lester…the kid is a phenomenon! He can't walk around without being barraged by people! How can there be no sign of him?" Jason screeched, feeling the anger and pain of twenty years rising out of him as he turned to face his oldest friend.

"Jason, I have every man we have on the streets. We *will* find him." Jason felt Monty's firm grip on his shoulder. "I promise you that."

Jason turned his back to Monty to face the window once again.

He hadn't felt this defeated since he was a boy. He could still hear the rain from that day as it hit the ground. *Splat. Splat. Splat.*

Somehow, they had won.

Venom had manipulated the Olympic Games and sparked The War. But as the ferocity of man and his weapons continued to present unimaginable destruction, the people of Earth realized something.

Just how much of a waste all of that destruction was.

But humanity may not have realized this without one individual, known to the people of the world as the President of the United States.

To Jason, he was just dad.

Though he was not his father by birth, Jason was grateful for having him in his life.

Jason spent his early teenage years on the street after running away from twelve brutal years in the foster care system. He quickly learned how to fight and stay sharp as he encountered the staunch realities of living on the streets of Washington DC. He survived with great success in many instances, but at the cost of his heart.

All he cared for was his own well being.

One warm spring morning, he went to a coffee shop to see if he could pick any wallets. He found the perfect target. A man in a two thousand dollar suit would definitely have something worthwhile. But the big-shouldered goons around him were not leaving. He must be a government official, this was DC after all.

"Please, it is okay, Lester. I am only getting a cup of coffee." The man dismissed his detail.

"Alright, sir." Lester hesitated.

This was his chance. Jason moved in. As if knowing what was coming all along, the man quickly sidestepped him.

"Excuse me, young lad. Is there anything I can help you with?"

Jason didn't know what to say. Not only was he shocked he was made, but the man was not angry about it either!

"Well...sir...I uh..."

"Let's you and I have a talk."

The then Senator Michael Cane talked to Jason for the rest of the morning. His Secret Service detail came in only once to tell him he was missing an appointment. He informed them, however, that he would not be attending any of his appointments for the day. They did not bother him again. Jason fought to keep his hard street persona, but the Senator persisted. Before he knew it, all of his walls had come down. Not only did this man manage to bring out his true personality that he believed he had forgotten, he actually listened to Jason when talked. This was something he was not accustomed to growing up in crowded system homes.

Something must have attracted the Senator to this scrappy little teen, because he took Jason home that night. As it turned out, Michael... or as Jason soon began to call him, Dad was lonely too. His wife had passed away in a car accident, leaving him without his love and without children.

Michael sent Jason to school, put him in different extra curricular activities, and tried to help him enjoy the last few years of youth he had left. Soon he even enlisted his head Secret Service Agent and most trusted friend, Lester Monty, to train the young street thug in the art of true self-defense. On the other front, Michael taught Jason how to walk, talk, and act like the perfect gentleman. Michael knew on the inside Jason was truly a good person, but life had forced him to adapt. Almost everyday, Michael stressed to him that the world *was* a good place.

"Jason, I know you still blame the world for what happened to you. I did the same when Mary passed."

"She didn't pass away though, Dad. A drunken idiot killed her! Doesn't that make you angry?"

"You're right, son. She was taken from me. And I did blame the world for a time. I wanted everything and everyone to pay. But what good would that do me? I can promise you revenge does not bring peace. Hate will only tear you up until you are someone you don't know anymore. No matter what, there will always be bad things in this world just as much as there are good."

"I see mostly bad." Jason grunted.

"Change your perspective. Had everything that has happened to you not, we would never of met, and I would have never gotten the incredible son I have today."

Michael was the only person who ever actually cared about him, and the only person he found who could soothe the vast mountains of hate he felt deep inside.

Four of the best years of his life passed, and a lot of things Jason never thought he would live through happened in that time. He attended homecoming and prom, and earned a spot on the wrestling team, cracking the varsity line up as a freshman. He fell in love with the sport, and dreamed of coaching it one day. One night, Michael took Jason aside to tell him about a dream of his own, and asked if Jason would be okay with him pursuing it.

"Of course, dad! That would be incredible!"

Michael smiled. "Thank you, son. I couldn't have done it without your okay. Don't start to worry about the media too much. Lester and I have decided to keep you off the campaign trail, so your life can stay normal."

Jason smiled. He didn't want anything to change.

It seemed like it happened over night when Michael was elected President of the United States. During his time at the center of world power, Jason met a lot of curious individuals. There was something he didn't like about a lot of them.

They all seemed to know something everyone else didn't.

It was also during this time that Jason would meet the other side of the aisle. He wished he were referring to something along the lines of Democrats. But it was far worse. He was referring to the agents of Venom, infiltrating the political realm in secret to supplant any good that was actually done in politics. Yes, it wasn't until later Jason found out Michael was the leader of the organization Jason led today.

Throughout the presidency, Michael continued to keep Jason a secret from the world. And while it grew ever more challenging to keep it a secret at school or on dates, somehow, he managed.

Then came The War.

He had never seen Michael as worn out as he did during this time. All of his cabinet was against him making the speech that would end up saving the world. To be fair, it did seem pretty risky to suspend any and all United States military activity when China was about to launch the biggest invasion in the history of the world. But, out of some wild configuration in the stars, it worked. They had cut Venom off at the knees.

Or so they thought.

There wasn't a day that passed were Jason didn't think about seeing Casper Lanstark for the first time. It was a bright sunny day in New York City, the birds were singing, people were smiling, and there was a new hope in the air. The peace agreements were locked in. They just couldn't come to an agreement over what to do about the Olympics. Everyone agreed that *something* was needed to keep the world busy and to allow people of different cultures to come together to compete in good faith. But with its tattered reputation and so many bad feelings from the Olympics, they needed something new. Unfortunately, no one had any ideas that could be agreed upon. Every proposal had been rejected, except for one, made by a man Jason had seen a few times in the White House hall.

Casper Lanstark.

It was one of the most impressive oral presentations Jason had ever witnessed, televised around the world. Before anyone was able to process what had just transpired, the Tournament of Champions had been made a reality, and peace was finally here?

Somehow, they had missed the fact that Casper was actually an agent of Venom. He had been a grunt, but after this stunt, he *was* Venom. It wasn't until eight long years passed that they were able to figure out Casper wasn't the jewel he had worked so hard to present himself as.

But without Jason, they may have never found out.

If he could, Jason would happily give back the information to the universe, as the cost to get it had been too great. If he had any heart left from his time with Michael, it died on that night long ago.

About a month after the peace treaty Michael was tired. He decided it was time to take a hard earned retreat to his family estate in the wilderness of Virginia. It was meant to be a quiet one-week getaway.

It was all but quiet.

They were the happiest they had ever been when they arrived. The War had been won! There was finally peace and, though there was a lot of rebuilding to be done, the world looked as though it had a bright future ahead.

On the fourth day of the trip, both Jason and Michael were beyond exhausted from the fun that beautiful day had brought. The rays of the sun seemed to kiss his cheek while the light breeze cooled him off. He sipped on a cold soda (he wasn't twenty one yet) without a care in the world. Swimming, biking, riding on four wheelers, and a football game with the Secret Service were just some of the day's activities. Lester even allowed them to hike in the woods *without* a secret service detail.

Jason never thought he would live to see the day.

By the end of the night, they found themselves in the grand hall of the estate. Beautiful white marble beams rose up from the floor, effortlessly holding the weight of a household on their shoulders. The furniture had a classic taste to it with incredible attention to detail, and the paintings that hung on the walls pictured some of the most influential people in history. Not just in American History, but from all corners of the globe. Jason even recognized a few space pilots who did great things beyond Earth, pioneering the Golden Age of space exploration.

Sinking into the soft cushion of one of the chairs, Jason had never felt so hopeful as he gazed at these incredible people who kept watch over the room. The tall, mahogany bookcase with paperback books of their stories was incredible, considering paperback books were nearly extinct. Michael believed in the classic way of doing things just as much as he believed that innovation was key to survival. As he flipped through a book about Miles Young, the famous space pilot who had flown the first ship through the Iron belt, a young Jason Teach felt a feeling of magic and adventure.

Maybe the world wasn't so bad. Maybe anything really was possible.

He gazed at Michael across the room as Lester and the other agents laughed with him. In a room full of legends, he was looking at the biggest one he had ever known. He hoped one day, he could give something back to the world, just as it had given him this family.

Maybe one day soon, his picture would be on a wall next to Miles Young.

Abruptly, the silence of the night was broken with a deafening sound that blew out the windows along the East wing. Jason shook his head, trying to think, as the pounding in his head felt like it was about to split his skull. The ringing in his ears screamed at full volume. He was faintly aware of a sharp stinging in his left arm; he looked to see dozens of little shards of glass had dug their way into skin.

Immediately, the secret service agents surrounded Michael as they shouted into their earpieces.

"Forget about me! Forget about me! The boy is the key!" The President shouted repeatedly as the once joyous scene had erupted into chaos and confusion.

"Sir, we need to get you out of here now!" Lester yelled as he withdrew his gun and clicked his earpiece. "Jack, what the hell is going on out there? Where is the perimeter—

Michael grabbed Monty by the jacket with a look Jason had never seen on the man. "Monty, listen to me, it is over for me. I knew it was only a matter of time before the dark caught up with me. But our light won't go out yet! We have him!" He nodded toward his nineteen-year-old son.

"If they see him it's over, Lester. Get him out now!"

"Sir, I won't leave you!" Monty resisted.

"Go! I'll be fine!"

"Michael, I am not going to leave you! You are my President, my *friend*."

"This is an order, Lester. GO!"

With his eyes streaming, Lester and Michael ran to Jason.

"What is going on? Dad what is happening?" Jason yelled.

"Are you okay, Jay? We have to go now!" Monty said urgently.

Michael put his hands on Jason's shoulders, gripping them firmly. "My son, you are the most caring man I have ever met. Promise me you will be that person for as long as you live."

"Dad, I can't do this without…

"*Promise me.*"

A tear began to slip down his cheek. "I promise."

"I am so happy to have met you, Jason. You're going to bring the world back. We aren't an evil race, us humans. We just get lost sometimes and need someone to help us find our way. My time has come to an end, but yours is just beginning. I love you, Jason." He grabbed him, squeezing tightly. He was never fond of saying goodbye.

Monty had to drag him out of his father's arms and through the halls of the house toward the barn. Bullets ricocheted everywhere while the sounds of gunfire kept goose bumps on the back of his neck. Black clad men seemed to be everywhere as they sprang from the tree lines, their bullets ripping to shreds the house that Michael considered his one place of true peace.

They reached the barn miraculously undetected, and Monty took one hand off of Jason to unlatch the door. That is when the young troublemaker seized his opportunity to run off exactly where the black clad assailants headed to— the house.

"Jason!" Monty yelled as he stumbled and lost his footing. "Jason get back here!"

An explosion erupted from the top left part of the mansion, sending Jason stumbling while his ears screamed their objections to such deafening sounds. Jumping through a shattered window, Jason maneuvered the halls quickly but quietly, determined to see his only family again.

Determined to bring him with.

Shouts of rage filled the hall, so he quickly slid behind a wall as black clad figures marched through. The bodies of the Secret Service agents, many of them his friends, littered the floor.

Resisting the urge to cry out in pain and frustration, Jason continued moving quietly through the house, as the flames engulfed everything in their path. The heat began crawling up and down his skin as he moved toward the center of the crumbling palace.

He knew a secret way to his father; he could beat the intruders and convince him to get out of here. He couldn't lose him. Not now. Much to his surprise, his father had not flinched since he last saw him.

He stood with his back to Jason gazing out of a window ever so calmly.

"Dad!"

Michael turned around. "Jason, wh—how?"

"Dad I am here to save you!"

Jason began to run toward his father when an explosion punched a hole in the wall that took him off his feet, rocketing him into one of the magnificent bookcases that collapsed on impact.

"Jason my son, you're still alive. Thank God."

The darkness was slowly lifting.

A strong pounding throbbed through his head. His body ached and his left arm felt lifeless. He could barely wiggle his legs under the weight of the disheveled bookcase. He squinted his eyes so his vision would stop wobbling. He could see a figure in white…his father…surrounded by darkness…. men. The black clad men.

"Hello, Michael. It's good to see you again." A cold voice said.

The darkness around his father parted to make way for this new dark figure.

"I wish I could say the same." Michael remarked.

The figure laughed. Jason shook his head to clear his vision, but his heavy eyes overtook him. When opened them again, he had no idea how much time had passed.

"—never happen on my watch. EVER!" He recognized his father's voice. His vision finally cleared.

"I am truly sorry to hear your unwillingness to cooperate, Michael." The cold voice replied, his back to Jason and the President.

"I really wanted us to be friends." The voice continued. Almost as if on signal, the guards beat his father down to his knees. "Surely you know what must happen now." Michael glanced back to Jason, lying under the rubble. Their eyes locked.

"You may kill me now, but I will not be dead." Michael said as he kept his sight locked on Jason. "I will live on. And one day, I will be back, stronger than ever. Enjoy your moment while you can, because like me, your time will come."

The man laughed. "You surely have lost your mind in the clouds, Michael!"

"Or perhaps you've spent too much time in the dark!"

The man considered this remark before brushing it off.

"Goodbye, Michael." Illuminated by the ever-growing flames, Casper Lanstark raised his gun on his enemy and did what he deemed necessary. Jason felt his heart crack, and thinking about it still pained every bone in his body.

But his father had been right.

He still lived on today, through Jason, and even more prominently through Tyler. Tyler was just like dad, more so than he could ever be.

He had done some dark things to get where he was today. Tyler still had his soul. He was still pure. They could still beat Lanstark at his own game before the lights went out on the world and they were subject to whatever Lanstark was planning.

He wouldn't leave the boy like he had his father.

"Jason," Monty yelled. "I think I know where he'll be!"

He grabbed the Dragon Fly X keys.

*　　　　　*　　　　　*

Tyler's mind was numb. He felt as though he was coming out of a portal from another dimension. Other than a slight tingling in his veins he tried to itch with no avail, he was not hurt or in pain.

He sat up, briefly trying to figure out where he was exactly. Much to his surprise, he found himself in his bed, in 'his' safe and secure suite. But the walls seemed to be closing in on him as the room began to feel more and more like a prison rather than a home. A cold chill went up his spine as everything slowly came back to him.

Jason. The deal.

Casper. The deceit.

Dei. The match.

Everything. Not as it seemed.

He stood up and, ignoring the tingling in his toes, walked out toward the balcony. The bright sun illuminated his dark apartment as he opened the door. It was a beautiful day in Lanstark City. And everyone was enjoying their time in the sun.

If only they knew the storm that was coming.

Tyler felt different. He wasn't sure what it was. But he had never felt it before. Everything just…looked different. Nothing about his apartment, the cheering of the people, or the city had changed. But they felt completely different.

The lines of good and evil no longer existed to him. His mysterious mentor had more intended for him than he had ever let on. He had also forgot to mention the tiny little detail that coming here could get him killed. It must have just slipped his mind because that detail isn't that important, right? What made him better than Casper? He had used Tyler the same way that Casper wanted, and yet Casper had offered him a way out, a chance at life after all of this. No matter how different that would be that was still a chance, and more than Jason had offered. Not to mention he had offered him a chance to save Nana. Besides, it wasn't like Casper could invade the entire world. Their plan had to have some errors of judgment, no matter how much money they had.

Everything Tyler had believed in, the magic of this tournament, the meaning behind competing here, was a lie. What did he stand for if not that? The boy with a heart found himself no longer believing in everything he was supposed to embody.

Perhaps he was being unfair. After all, was he really the boy with a heart? Had he really come here to make the world a better place? Or had he been in the selfish pursuit of money, fame, and all the entitlements that came with that? What would happen if all his fans around the world found out what they believed in was a lie?

What would happen if they found he had made a deal with Casper Lanstark?

The thought wrenched his stomach.

And, after seeing Lanstark in person and what Jason was up against, perhaps he couldn't blame him for the secrecy. How could someone who had a conscience possibly beat a snake like Lanstark? But his trust in Jason was nearly eroded. Neither of them deserved what they were asking, did they?

The questions pressed on in Tyler's head. He had to get away from it. He had to go to something he knew. Somewhere familiar. And he knew exactly where. Through all of the mystery, there was one thing crystal clear to him.

This was no place for a hero.

9 ...Through Sweat

Be Great.

The phrase shouted in gold on every banner within eyesight in the city. It was a symbol of hope and marketing for the TOC, but to Tyler, it symbolized daggers being twisted into his ribs.

It was a constant reminder of what loomed on Friday. Expected to be the most watched wrestling match of all time, with presidents, billionaires, mistresses, and pop stars all in attendance to see who would be the next Champion.

And it was the day after tomorrow.

Tyler ditched his usual flashy wardrobe in favor of his current wear in order to avoid being spotted by crazed partiers or paparazzi. With his hood up, jacket zipped, and sunglasses on, he made his way up the overcrowded sidewalk toward Jordan's Gym. Everyone and their mothers were out today. Tyler found himself elbowing through crowds of brightly dressed patrons and half drunk hooligans (it was half past nine in the morning) in order to walk the three blocks it took to get to the gym. This was the primetime local for the partiers of the world, the Wednesday before the Championship match.

He could make out the silhouette of Jordan's Gym in the distance; all he had to do was cross the famous Throne Avenue. It was purposely named Throne Avenue. But the thought behind it stirred in Tyler's brain every time he came to the gym. The idea for the name Throne Avenue was chosen because it was said if you trained hard in the gym everyday, you would be able to sit on a throne yourself one day. The one you would presumably earn once you won your championship.

Was that the true definition of success, he pondered?

The light flashed green.

Jordan's Gym, unlike the many silver buildings of the city, was made of large glass panels that curved on the top, preventing the typical look of the buildings in favor of a style that had become a symbol of the sport of wrestling.

Tyler almost broke into a run as he headed up the rows of steps and inside the building, he would be free from the prying eyes of the paparazzi inside. It would also give him some much-needed time to think. He tried to call Cailey one more time as he walked into the main doors but again it went to her voice message box.

Where was she? Dark thoughts entered his head. What if Casper had done something to her? Taken her as some twisted form of leverage should he renege on his part of the deal?

The questions began to hurt his head as he smiled at the receptionist before turning left into the locker-room. He put his palm on his locker, the green light indicating a match to the one coded in its memory as it popped open. He threw his street clothes into the locker in favor of some sweat pants, a tech fit training shirt, and his most favorite wrestling shoes he had ever sported. Comfy, light, and with incredible support, his jet-black Nim Fly Zeros were his babies.

Once he finished tying the Fly Zeros, he grabbed his Nim headgear, and rounded the corner locker rows.

"I see you found me." He murmured.

Jason stepped forward into the light. It was one of the few times Tyler had seen the man without a suit, instead donning a black leather jacket.

"Tyler listen, I know you don't want to talk but—

"No I really don't." Tyler snapped as he fidgeted with his headgear. It was exceedingly difficult to look the man in the eyes when he had made a deal with Lanstark to do the very thing Jason had, secretly, brought him here to prevent.

He had to do it for Nana.

"But if you'll just let me explain, Tyler—

"There is nothing to explain, Jason. The lies are too deep!"

"Technically I didn't lie, I told you I was giving you a chance to *be great*."

Tyler wanted to yell. He wanted to come back swinging at Jason with everything he had. It was his fault he was here in the first place!

"I know you want to be angry, Tyler. I know that feeling all too well. I have felt it for a better part of my life. Trust me, it won't bring you peace. Don't let the hate consume who you are."

As much as it pained him to admit, Jason was right, he couldn't be angry with him. Even though Jason had lied, it was still Tyler who agreed to come. It was Tyler who sought the greatness that was promised. It was on him, and no one else. For the moment, he would have to let it go. These men were the only people in his corner right now.

What was the right thing, to have the guarantee of saving Nana, or no guarantee of saving anyone? His head twisted in pain.

"As much as I want us all to hug it out and eat some chips while watching a fairy documentary," Monty began with a slight grin. "And correct me if I am wrong Tyler, but I believe you came here to train, am I right?"

"I did Lester, yes." Tyler couldn't help but smile.

"Well in that case, I will let you two take care of business, this is your last day of the year to train, after all. Then, we can all talk *later*."

"Sounds like a winner to me." Jason agreed with a smile. He faced Tyler. "You ready to go, champ?"

"Absolutely." Tyler bumped his fist.

"Then for old time's sake, let's get one more hard go in."

The first thing you notice when you walk into a wrestling room is the unbelievable amount of heat that saturates the room and seems to permeate into everything. As soon as he stepped foot in the room, Tyler felt his pores squeeze open. Already small dabs of sweat begin to form on his forehead.

"Dei was already in here today. At this point Tyler, we aren't changing any of your technique, even if we wanted to. He is bigger, taller, faster, and stronger than you. There is only one thing you have that he doesn't."

Jason paused, as if his next word carried considerable weight.

"Heart."

Tyler nodded. Dei Jie was without a doubt the toughest opponent he would ever face on the mat. The scourge of the East, there was no one who dared challenge him for his belt.

"Today is our last day of real training. It is going to be short, but it is going to be hell. Weight lifting, wrestling, aesthetics, balance, we are combining it all into something I like to call…no pain no gain."

"How original." Tyler laughed.

"You won't be laughing when we're done. Kenny here has agreed to be your drilling partner for the day." He gestured toward the large, beefy boy with poky blonde hair who was entering the room.

"Kenny, nice to meet you. No offense, but Jason, Kenny looks to me to be about 180 or maybe more. I wrestle 165?"

"Dei is going to weigh at least that when you guys wrestle because weigh in is tomorrow. He has an entire day *and* night to get fat. You need to be ready for it."

"I am honored, Jason." Tyler smiled.

"For what exactly?"

"You don't think *I* won't get fat."

"Get going!" Jason laughed. Wrestlers were notorious for gaining and losing large amounts of weight in a short amount of time, with a particular talent in the gaining aspect.

No matter how stressed he was, no matter how heavy the weight of life seemed to drag on his shoulders, training always seemed to be able to cut the load. It served as an outlet for him to pour out his anger through sweat, blood, and tears.

That is not to say he enjoyed training.

"Faster! Faster! FASTER!" Jason nodded as Tyler jumped roped alongside Kenny.

Sweat was already furiously soaking through his clothes as they began drilling takedowns. Tyler would practice three shots on Kenny without bringing him to the ground, Kenny would go, and then they would repeat the process.

"Double elbow bine to a high crotch, HIT IT!" Jason watched with almost obsessive precision while Tyler executed each move.

Tyler was strong, and not just kind of strong. *Strong.* But drilling with Kenny at this level of intensity in this heat was already starting to wear him out. Fifteen pounds doesn't seem like a lot until you're lifting it up and throwing it on the ground every fifteen seconds or so. For his part, Kenny was being fair, and not taking any cheap shots on the finalist…*yet.*

"TIME! Let's head over to the pull bar. Don't you dare give me that look you Tyler, we are only fifteen minutes in!"

The weight bar slid through his sweaty fingers as he squatted than threw it above his head.

"That's it! Do you think Dei will stop trying to pummel you into the ground when you make tired faces at him? Do you think life will help you get back up when it knocks you down?"

Tyler felt the burn in his arms while he climbed across the gymnast bars, handle by handle.

"I have news for you sweetheart, it is up to you to get up when you get knocked down. If you don't, you're going to spend the rest of your life there!"

His abs stung as Jason smacked their stomachs while they did his sit-ups. *Keep going Tyler. Keep going. Think about what you're working for. Picture yourself up there…a loser? That's what Lanstark wants. What would Nana say?*

He had to take off his shirt in order to wrestle with Kenny now, as the heat from the hot summer weather and the room together created the ultimate weight cutting room. He was only three pounds over today; by the end of this he had no doubt he was going to be at least six under. He was exhausted. He was thirsty. He wanted to lash out and tell Jason he didn't need to train! He was going to save Nana and that required him to throw the match.

The weight cutting was starting to take over his thoughts!

"This is LIVE wrestling you two. I want to see some action! Move it! WHAT are you training for? WHY are you here? WHY do you keep your body in top shape? WHAT do you want to be remembered for? Do you WANT to be remembered?"

What DO I want to be remembered for?

112

Tyler struggled with this while he battled to stay motivated against Kenny, who was stronger and faster than him. His attempts to grab arms and tie ups were unsuccessful as they were both heaped in sweat. He shot for a double leg, getting as far as wrapping his arms around Kenny's tree trunk legs before getting a forearm to the face as Kenny defended against it. Tyler's hands slid right up Kenny legs as he dropped all of his weight on Tyler's shoulders.

Would Nana really want me to throw what we worked so hard for away for the likes of someone like Casper Lanstark?

"Come on, Tyler you can't sit there when you take a shot and it doesn't work! You have to *move*! Think! *BELIEVE*!"

His arms silently voiced their complaints of holding Kenny at bay as Tyler racked his brain to get out of this.

"This is your opportunity, Tyler! Don't shy away from being great just because you want to give up! That is what is easy to do! The boy with a heart I know wouldn't allow that to happen! SHOW ME you are still that kid!"

Tears of pain blended with the sweat on his face while Tyler contemplated what to do. He could easily just give up and let Kenny score. But neither had scored, and there was only thirty seconds left.

He would be giving up.

"ARRGGGHHHH!" Tyler groaned as he brought his body back under himself, no longer stretched out, which was any wrestlers worse nightmare when trying to score on their opponent through a takedown.

"There it is! I am seeing some life now!"

Tyler diced his thoughts down to focus only on one, to center his energy in his body so he could get to his feet and take Kenny down to win the match. He inhaled...than exhaled...inhaled...exhaled...inhaled...exhaled as he tried to calm his breathing down for just a few seconds.

"FIFTEEN SECONDS!"

Kenny dug in, throwing every ounce of weight and sweat he had on Tyler. His arms felt like they were about to snap as his shoulders writhed in agony. His heart was pounding

113

in his chest, his head hurt from sweating at least ten pounds, and his body pleaded with him to relieve the pressure. Yet...he didn't want to stop. *MOVE.* Slowly, Tyler began to push up and to the right, because if he could just get his feet off the ground he could run through Kenny to finish the takedown. He had a knee up! *PUSH!* Despite his arms objections, they did not give in and he kept his hands locked as he got another foot off the ground and broke into a full out sprint— bringing Kenny crashing into the mat with a giant *BANG!*

"TIME!" Jason called as a relieved look began to settle on his face.

"Thank you for training with me today, Kenny. I know it wasn't fun, but you have a bright future ahead of you. One day, I know you'll be here in the finals too." Tyler said as he stumbled to his feet in a dizzy exhaustion.

Kenny shook his hand firmly. "Thank you, Tyler it means a lot to hear that. Most people tell just to get my head out of the clouds."

"Well you've proving them wrong by being here right now." Tyler thought of what Lanstark had said to him. "Besides, without people's heads in the clouds we would never have made it to mars would we?"

Kenny grinned. "I hope you'll be in my corner. I can tell you I will definitely be in yours this Friday."

"That means more than you know."

Kenny was a good kid. Compared to most of his drilling partners he had practiced with in his extent here, he wished he had been with him before. The partners for the contenders were chosen out of the lineup of people who had come just short of making it into the tournament. The idea was that if they came here, trained with the best, and learned how things worked, there was a big chance they would make it into to the tournament the following year. Most of them however, believed they were better than everyone else and had a chip on their shoulder that they didn't make it. An extreme amount of prejudice was especially thrown at him, as many of them believed they would have made it over him easily. The consequence of this was all the cheap shots thrown at him.

He threw on his clothes, said his goodbyes to Kenny once more, and met Jason in the lobby.

"Ready to go, champ?" Jason said as he nodded goodbye to the receptionist. "You only took *twenty five* minutes in the shower. You know Rosemary doesn't like when you're late!"

"Waiting on you now!" Tyler teased as stepped outside.

The rain clouds had cleared and it a gloriously sunny afternoon was clearing in Lanstark City.

"That was one hell of a workout today." Tyler said as little beads of sweat still formed on his forehead. "I didn't think I was going to make it through it."

"But you did. And that restored hope in me."

"Are you saying you tried to break me?"

"I am saying I tested you, and you still proved me right."

"Right about?"

"You're still the boy with a heart."

10 **The Interview**

Tyler wasn't sure what to think anymore.

He had known this week would be one of the most important weeks of his life the moment after he won his match over Caleb on Sunday. That much was blatantly obvious to anyone who had been following the boy with a heart's story since he came to the world stage almost six months ago. But there was a story behind the spotlight that few knew the *whole* truth about. The boy with a heart had started out with nothing more than a dream, and a really big one at that. Growing up in a small town in Michigan had not set any restrictions on the grand vision he had always pictured for himself.

Tyler owed much of the encouragement for the possibility of his dreams to his Nana, who had raised him after his parents had been killed just after his eighth birthday. He had kept himself locked in his room for a whole week after it happened. When he came out, the death of his parents was something he had masterfully blocked out of his mind.

Nana lived in a small, modest town with immodestly careful people. No one drove a sports car, and no one *wanted* to drive a sports car. No one bothered to make their house look *too* fancy, and no one dressed too fancy either. His neighborhood's design looked as though it had come from a nuclear testing facility handbook. All the houses were exactly the same, lining the street in perfectly straight rows. And the happy, careful residents of Unadventurous Villa seemed content with their middle-of-the-road ways. Nobody stood out in Unadventurous Villa and nobody wanted to stand out, because… well…that would just be crazy. They just existed. No matter what happened in the world around them, they stayed in their shell.

From the start this bothered Tyler who was raised by parents who wanted him to do just the opposite. Tyler saw himself dining with the President, playing golf on rooftops of skyscrapers, driving not just one, two, or three, but *four* sports cars, and, most importantly, changing the world.

His hunger to achieve this vision was only salivated when he would drive six minutes out of Unadventurous Villa and through the city of Grand Staten, where it was as though he drove from Earth to Jupiter. In Grand Staten, it seemed *everyone* was on a mission to stand out from one another. Sports cars left fumes in the air in front of colossal castles while casual walkers in the street were dressed to the nines as if going to a best-dressed contest. Some of the most famous politicians, actors, and innovators from all over the world came to live in Grand Staten. Even though showing off seemed to create tension at times, there seemed to be something that bonded all of the inhabitants together.

Passion.

They had a burning drive to do what wasn't done before. And at this point, many of them had in their own respective fields.

Tyler always found himself envious of their position in the world compared to his. If they had a vision, they had a platform to could execute it on. If he had a vision, it would stay a vision.

Though it was hard at times, he always kept the faith in life that one-day things would work out. Never did he believe he would have the platform he did he today, as he sat waiting for Rosemary to make her entrance into his suite in the Silas Luxury Hotel. *She* was running late this time, even though he had been late himself.

Not only did he have millions of fans around the world that followed his every move, tonight he would have the attention of over a billion people who tuned in for the Contender Interviews. Anyone with access to a TV would be eyeballing him somewhere on the globe.

Of course not everyone was a fan.

The chief editor of *Wrestler Weekly* had already slammed him to the many fans of the sport, calling Tyler's style "pathetic, defensive, outdated, and a disgrace to represent the United States in the biggest wrestling match of a generation."

It was a great note to be going into the finals on, considering how much of the wrestling community read the magazine (all of them, including himself). He worried about the potential effect the piece would have.

He needed all the support he could get for this match.

It was the biggest match of his career, of his life. But the stakes were a lot different than most of his critics or fans thought. The world expected the following would occur should he win: he would go down in history as the youngest Champion ever, and with that he would receive all the glory and everything that could go with it. The people back home in the United States would love him, as the U.S. needed some boost considering the momentum going toward the Chinese right now. Oh, and Jason would probably be a world renowned Recruiter for picking a kid from nowhere and turning him into a Champion.

But there were consequences of this that *Wrestler Weekly* and the rest of the world did not see.

And while it all sounded absolutely insane and could have been straight out of a movie, he had no doubt of the truth in it anymore.

Tyler Mason vs. Dei Jie was part of an intricate plan, a fabrication that Tyler had been a part of without his consent. Casper Lanstark had personally informed him of his options for how the match 'needed' to go, and neither was very promising. The first scenario if he did not cooperate and did what ever he wanted in the match was simple. He would not be killed; instead, the few people he still cared for in this world would be tortured right before his eyes. Then one day, when Casper was feeling generous, they would finally kill him, only after he had gone completely insane. The second option was if he did cooperate with Venom, he would lose the match, and play the poor sport to the audience, tarnishing the United State's reputation and his own. This would be a tremendous blow to the already teetering U.S. and China relations, and Lanstark would do…well, whatever it is he would do in that situation. Tyler's reward for cooperation?

Exactly what he had always wanted. *Four* sports cars, his castles around the world, but most importantly, the cure for Nana that was well beyond his pocketbook as it currently stood.

But what would he be?

The boy who gave up humanity?

Against the warm weather of the afternoon a cold chill gave Tyler goose bumps as he stood up and peered out at the sprawling skyline of Lanstark City, the silver buildings and designs beginning to illuminate as the setting sun gave way to the night sky. In a few hours time, he would be cast into the eyes of the world again in the famous last interviews before the championship matches. It was a TOC tradition, one that was notorious for extremely tough questions.

Questions the world would expect him to answer, despite the fact that he didn't know the answers anymore as he struggled to figure out his place in all of this.

Jason had also made his case.

If he did not stand up for what was right on Friday night at 7pm, who would? Who else had the platform he did right now? It was already Wednesday night and his window to overthink this was closing rapidly. He *had* always wanted to be great. But what does it mean to be great? Was greatness found in fast cars and big houses?

It was curious that Unadventurous Villa and Grand Staten had found their way back into his head today.

What had caused such differences in the towns? Did the people of Unadventurous Villa have a stroke of genius minding their business? They would never end up in the situation he was in now. But, if Venom's plan panned out, then when Lanstark won wouldn't they be subject to his way?

So what made the people of Grand Staten so 'great'?

"Oh, look! There our big hearted boy is!" Gurdy Gumdrop said as she came waltzing in toward him. Today, her makeup design of choice was eagle eyes, and the make up artist had again put in contacts so her eyes looked like that of an eagles. With that she had a matching dress, which was a combination of a light brown and white with subtle feather designs woven in it.

"Hello, Gurdy. How are you today?" Tyler said as he flashed his very convincing fake smile her way.

"Feeling bald." She said with a wink as she kissed both of his cheeks. "Get it, because I am a bald eagle?" She laughed.

"Yes Gurdy I— Ah!" Tyler jolted his leg back as a sharp sting traveled up it. He turned and peered down at Chucky, whose puffy round cheeks were beginning to blend with his fire tongue hair. Tyler was ready knock the little hot headed fireball out. How many times did he have to clarify that he was *not* making a move on Gurdy? Out of nowhere, the scent of strawberries began to permeate his nostrils.

He turned to see Rosemary, whose glaring look still didn't even come close to preparing him for her next action: She slapped him across the face. His once comfortable cheek was now stinging profusely.

"What the hell was that for?" Tyler growled.

"*THAT* is what that is for!" Rosemary shrieked, her gleaming eyes burning holes in Tyler's face. When it was evident he still had no idea what she was implying, she went on. "Don't you remember what I told you yesterday? People look up whom your designer is if they don't already know! And most people know I am your designer! Your little mid life crisis yesterday— it really didn't help either of our images, cupcake! This is a two way relationship, we are a *team,* remember?"

Tyler bit his tongue, as annoyance seeped through his veins. Why should he sit here and take this from Rosemary who, oh by the way had no idea what was actually going on in the world outside of her own fashionable little bubble.

"What am I wearing?" He asked bluntly, wanting to leave the room before he snapped on one of them.

"We have it right here." Gurdy chimed in.

She kicked the large hovering trunk that Chucky guided in, and the huge dresser like case rose from the ground. The brown doors with the letters R.R. engraved on the front swung open and out burst a rack with Tyler's choice outfit tonight. Rosemary had outdone herself.

Black pants with gold trim and perfectly polished shoes were impressive. But Tyler was even more in awe as his eyes traveled upward. Gleaming, glittering, and glowing was a golden suit jacket unlike any Tyler had ever seen.

"The perfect outfit for someone who can change the world." Rosemary said after observing Tyler's face.

Tyler stumbled back, collapsing onto the arm of the chair.

"Rosemary I…I don't know if I can wear this. This is meant for someone …what if I am not who everyone thinks I am?"

"Oh don't be ridiculous dear. Now where are Jason and Monty? The team should be together. We can all talk about this and—"

"They're not here." Tyler said, choking down a swallow. "I …I can't go on, Rosemary. I'm stuck in a corner, I'm stuck in a corner and I can't get out."

Rosemary's face suddenly changed to the warmest expression he had ever seen on the woman. "Tyler…you made a mistake. These things happen."

"I am not who everyone thinks I am, Rosemary. I am not a good person."

"First off, who is they? Tyler, this outfit was inspired by *you*. You inspired it in me because of what you have done on the journey you've been on thus far. I am not the only person who believes this. Just ask anyone of the millions who are also rooting for you."

"Rosemary, what can *I* do? I'm only one tiny spec caught between two vacuums."

She took his hand. "Sometimes, it only takes that one tiny spec to break the vacuum."

"What do I do?"

"You can go out there and do what you do best…be you."

For the first time in all of this, it occurred to Tyler that perhaps Lanstark had made a huge miscalculation in his perfectly calculated plan. Though Lanstark was still in control of the situation, he had unknowingly put control of the most important aspect of his plan- the effect- in Tyler's control. Yes, he was at a *major* disadvantage. But this entire scenario relied on Tyler's actions and Tyler's actions alone. The choices, both easy and hard, were his. Now that didn't mean it would be a cakewalk. Beating Dei would be no waltz in the lily garden.

Perhaps it wasn't the flying cars or the castles that made Grand Staten so great as he had always believed as a child. Perhaps the people of Grand Staten stuck out for a different reason. They worked to change someone's life, including his with their work. Because of them, the world was moving to a better place.

He gazed out at Champion's Avenue, which was aglow all the way up until the plaza. Dressed in colorful costumes and wearing sparkling makeup, every person in the city packed the streets. All of them were trying to catch a glimpse of their favorite wrestler in what would be their last public appearance before the big night. The sidewalks bustled and the traffic seemed to be permanently stuck. Even the flying car routes were backed up today. If their vehicle did not have special markings from the ever-present city security, Tyler felt they would have never reached Champion Plaza.

The thump of his heart on his chest got slightly faster as they continued to get closer to Champion's Plaza. In a couple hours he along with the rest of the world would join the infamous talk show host and public icon, Zeus Clementine. Zeus was known around the globe for his fearlessly controversial questions, his ability to charm his guests to have the ability to ask those questions, and his outrageously flamboyant suits that were questionable even in TOC fashion rules.

Tyler was sure the incident with Dei Jie would come up, and had the uneasy feeling that Lanstark was *very* good 'friends' with Zeus. Therefore, this interview was most likely going to be against him from the start, designed to portray what Casper wanted. Tyler was also upset that both Jason and Monty were not with him right now, though it was at his own request.

He needed time to think.

For as long as he could remember, Tyler had let others dictate the direction in which he was going. He had always had that voice in the back of his head telling him what he wanted to do, but he was never brave enough to take action.

All he did was listen.

The roar of the crowd flooded the SUV as the guards opened the doors. As soon as Tyler was able to see the outside, he was met with an onslaught of flashing camera lights as the thousands of fans outside tried to break the crowd control barriers. Black clad TOC security teams worked to hold them at bay. Without a doubt, Tyler would not soon forget the events of this night.

That seemed to be a trend this week.

As Tyler stepped out of the car, he was dazed by his surroundings. The set was engulfed with people. The sight of the stage in the distance sent butterflies flapping widely in his stomach. That along with the clammy feel of the night really weren't helping him as he tried to stop the small beads of sweat forming on his forehead. The arena looked like a huge dome that was cut in half, then assembled upward with many zigzagging lines that made up its frame. It had always been a childhood dream of his to see it, let alone be in it. Tyler did his best to greet the swarms of people chanting his name and begging for autographs, but his escorts for the evening, ten very unfriendly looking men in black suits, weren't tolerating it. They led him through a long narrow tunnel away from all the press and wild maniacs. He had a hunch they were friends of Lanstark.

At the end of the hall, much to his surprise, Alfredo Lopezzi stood ready to greet him with an arrogant smirk across his face.

Cailey!

He stopped.

She hadn't returned his calls! Where could she be? As always, Alfredo's hair was perfectly combed, and his black tuxedo was fit to perfection. But there was something different about him today. He wore the same broach Tyler had seen on Silas Marshall and on the walls last night... the snake on the broach continued to stare at Tyler; it's diamond green eyes never blinking.

But that would mean...

"Tyler! Good to see you again, my boy. Glad to hear you were willing to help us. If you need anything, please let me know."

Anger filled his heart. Is *this* why he hadn't heard from Cailey? "I didn't realize I was that high on the VIP list to be greeted by such a prominent has-been." Tyler said, some whiplash in his voice.

Alfredo laughed. "So he still has some fight left in him after all? Excellent. You will need it. Besides, you are still a title away from breaking my record. Something that won't be done." Lopezzi replied coldly.

"Since you're here to babysit, would you mind going to get me a snack?" Tyler spat. "Peanuts are fine."

Lopezzi let out a vile scowl and Tyler was tired of being harassed so he disappeared into the comfort of his dressing room. As he was closing the door he caught Alfredo say "Don't try anything, Mason. We'll know."

Tyler took a deep breath and collapsed in the chair, staring into the mirror. Does that mean they are watching him?

Dumb question, Tyler.

He was starting to care less and less. Was he really going to allow himself to be so bitter about his 'greatness' being ruined? All he could focus on was the consequences his choices would have on people who didn't even know what was going on. The silence was killing him, so he switched on the Hologram, which of course was tuned to CC, *Champion's Channel*. He was just in time for the introduction of the show.

"Ladies and Gentlemen, boys and girls from all around the world, allow me to introduce to you the show master of our generation, Zeus Clementine!"

Confident, smiling, well dressed, handsome, it is no wonder Lanstark hired Zeus Clementine to report for the TOC. What better way for him to get his claws into the wallets of the entire planet? Zeus waved and the crowd roared. From his purple suit to his orange shoes and vest, Zeus would be the epitome of the TOC fashion talk tonight.

"Thank you! Thank you! Ladies and Gentlemen, boy and girls welcome and thank you for joining me on this *unbelievable* night!" He proclaimed as he waltzed the stage. "The history of the Tournament of Champions is filled with amazing individuals who have defied the logic of athletics and man to achieve the impossible. This year is no exception. From the east, we have the mighty machine, undefeated Chinese Champion, Dei Jie!"

The audience roared in excitement. Zeus always managed to elegantly weave controversy into his words so effortlessly. Tyler could feel his nerves beginning to get to him, but at the same time, he had an odd but comfortable feeling of... peace...like this was where he was meant to be.

"And from the west, representing the United States of America, a young man who many have said should not even be here because he isn't qualified for this level. Yet he has stolen the record for the youngest TOC finalist contender ever, the boy with a heart, Tyler Mason!"

If any observer had thought the crowd roared loud for Dei, than they may have had a severe misunderstanding of the what 'loud' sounded like. The crowd roared it's thunderous approval of the boy who "should not even be here because he is not qualified." The camera panned the streets showing crowds all around the city dressed in Tyler's signature colors, black and gold.

"The excitement... ladies and gentleman, has never been more REAL!" Zeus bellowed. "But, tonight, on the eve of the greatest wrestling match of the century, I have a little surprise for you all!"

The camera panned the crowd as they hollered in excitement. One thing was already certain about this evening; the surprise would be a surprise for everyone— himself included.

"For the first time in history, that's right, *HISTORY* folks, these two brave young men will come together on this stage one day early, not to wrestle of course, but to talk with me and most importantly with YOU!"

Tyler's nearly choked trying not to spit out the water he had been drinking, the crowd went so insane you would have thought someone was going to get hurt. Zeus started laughing.

"This most wonderful surprise comes as a courtesy from our very own founder, ladies and gentleman let me hear it for Casper Lanstark, and let me hear your enthusiasm for skill versus will, the greatest wrestling event EVER!" The camera panned to Casper, who stood now, waving in his perfectly white tuxedo.

"That son of a—

"Whoa, whoa, language my good lad, language."

Tyler didn't have to think twice as to whom that voice belonged to. He turned and embraced Monty.

"It's great to see you again, Monty!"

"Well you did just see me earlier today, Ty?" Monty laughed.

Jason followed him in, the door sliding shut behind him.

"Just do me one favor tonight champ…"

"What's that?"

"Show them who the *hell* they're messing with."

In that moment, Tyler felt his hope in Jason restored. He had never been happier to have Jason Teach in his corner than he was now. Maybe, just maybe, they could pull this off.

Did that mean his deal with Casper was off?

He laughed as Jason and Monty were fussing about the fact that they had to wear tuxedos that matched Tyler's own jacket. "I hate bowties." Monty complained as he pulled at his neck. Tyler decided not to tell them about the other night and his current internal battle, though he had a strange feeling they already knew.

"Was it originally in the script to have both of us on stage at the same damn time?" Tyler groaned. This was bad for him and him alone, because in the eyes of the world he had thrown the punch. It didn't matter what Dei had said.

"No." Monty said.

"Lanstark himself had it put in a short time after your," Jason paused. "Spectacular headlines came out."

Of course he did.

After about an hour of guest speakers, Tournament and fashion commentators, including Rosemary (who was ever supportive of Tyler), it was time for Dei's individual interview. After over a *minute* long advertisement about mattress cleaner, the commercial break was over.

"Welcome back! Welcome! Welcome! Welcome! In just an hour, we will have for the first time in history, not one but two Championship contenders on the same stage folks! But first, we are keeping to our tradition of the individual interviews where we dive deep into the athletes mind and see what's going on in there. Ladies and Gentlemen please help me give a warm welcome the beast from the east, Mr. Dei Jie!"

The crowd erupted as Dei emerged from the glowing background of the stage. Dressed in a royal red accented tuxedo, he was on the ball with fashion tonight. With his signature evil grin, he waltzed up and grabbed Zeus's hand and then bowed to the crowd. Dei was his usual arrogant self, only something was different tonight…but what?

He was even *more* arrogant.

"I don't know how that kid gets through the door!" Monty joked.

"So, Dei," Zeus said, his voice getting lower and the audience getting quiet with it. "You have been training for this match your entire life. Your father has said on multiple occasions that not only does he expect you to win this, but so does all of China! What do you say to these tremendous expectations?"

Tremendous expectations. Ha!

"All I have to say Zeus is that anyone betting against me is a fool. I've pulverized every real ranked wrestler I've faced in the last few weeks. I expect you saw me whip Marty Jenkins the other day, and he was ranked only one below me. My opponent does not even deserve to be called an opponent."

"Phew…harsh words folks, harsh words." Zeus commented while he shook his hand as though someone had smacked it with a ruler. As much as the arrogance of Dei sent pulses of anger through Tyler, the thought of himself being up there in mere minutes began to sink in. He would have to answer deep, personal questions in front of the entire world. And the next day they would be scrutinized and picked apart.

He shuddered at the thought. At least he still had a few minutes.

"Everyone please give Mr. Jie a round of applause! When we come back, the under dog, the boy who has shattered all expectations, Tyler Mason will be joining us!" The hologram switched to commercials.

So much for his few minutes!

There was a knock at the door; four of Casper's black suited friends were there to escort Tyler the forty-six feet it took to get to the stage.

"You alright?" Jason asked.

"Never better!" Tyler joked as he squirmed in his suit coat, slowly falling into panic.

"Tyler, you'll be fine." Jason said firmly, taking his shoulders before fixing his bow tie. "Just remember what you're out there to do." He said with a wink.

What are you out there to do, Tyler?

He took a deep breath, buttoned his jacket, and followed the men to the stage.

"Ladies and gentlemen, please help me in welcoming a boy some of you might know, a boy who has *stolen* the spotlight this year. He is the youngest TOC finalist EVER, and probably causing some of the most controversy we've ever seen. Please give a warm welcome to the boy with a heart himself, Mr. Tyler Mason!"

As he stepped out into that spotlight, Tyler had never felt a stronger sense of purpose in his life. The fate of everyone here rested on his decisions over these next few days, and he was determined not to misplace the energy he felt inside right now.

He clasped Zeus's hand. Up close, the man's skin was every bit as sparkly as his purple suit. His teeth were so white Tyler felt as though he needed sunglasses to look at them. He looked out to his teammates— the audience.

All he did was smile and give a wave and they went nuts. Tyler wasn't sure what it was about him they loved so much. But tonight he needed them. This was something he could not do alone.

128

"Welcome Mr. Mason, thank you for joining us this evening!"

"The pleasure is all mine, Zeus." Tyler beamed as he glanced at the upper suites in the audience, looking for Lanstark.

"Please have a seat!" Zeus directed him to his seat and they sat down, both simultaneously crossing legs.

"I just wanted to thank you and Casper for having me here this evening, Zeus. It's a real honor." Tyler exclaimed, shooting a look toward the suites again.

"Ha! Hah! I'm sure he appreciates your humbleness." Zeus said.

"Now Tyler, here you are, with me on the eve of the biggest match in wrestling history and your life! After this you get to attend the biggest party on earth in Casper's penthouse! What is going through your head?"

"Well Zeus, as you could imagine it's quite overwhelming if you sit down and think about it. At first when I came here I wasn't sure what to expect, and my purpose was...somewhat misguided, but I have never felt more confident in my reasons for being here as I do now."

The crowd cheered.

"Does this mean you're not nervous? Your opponent had some interesting things to say about you. What about the expectations for you back home? Are the folks up in arms with you, ye=s or no?" Zeus pressed.

"Yes Zeus, they're arms are up in the air, literally, or at least they will be after this match tomorrow."

The crowd thundered.

"Ho, ho, ho, folks! The boy with a heart has some jokes tonight." Zeus wiggled in his coat. "Tyler, you're up against some pretty... steep odds. You're facing an undefeated champion while you yourself barely managed to get here. After yesterday's incident, how do you think your supporters who look up to you around the world are feeling right now?"

Tyler felt like a mouse that a cat had finally caught, and Zeus was digging his claws in hard on this one. He could feel the millions of eyes on him, all wondering what the boy with a heart would say.

"Well Zeus," Tyler began as he tousled his brain for the right words. "That's a great question. The first thing I would like to acknowledge is yes I am considered a nobody who came from nowhere. However, what I don't like about that statement is you implied it like it was a bad thing. Since when does 'where you come from' play a part in sports? This is a place of sportsmanship and goodwill. It doesn't matter who I'm facing and what he has done nor does it matter who I am or what I have done. All that matters is what I'm going to do."

The crowd immediately went wild, and even Zeus Clementine, a master of masking emotions, showed curiosity.

"Do I think all the pressure from the media will get to me? If the pressure hasn't got to me yet then I must not be human because this kind of atmosphere would get to anyone. But life is all about perspective. And the people out there, they keep me going."

"And last night's incident?" Zeus followed, attempting to salvage what was left of his one on one time with Tyler.

"As for last night, I would like to say to everyone all around the world, I'm sorry for what I did. I let the egotistical, heartless champion get to me and I shouldn't have." Tyler cringed as he finished his sentence, because even though the crowd roared in agreement, he had given Lanstark exactly what he wanted.

"Wow folks, as you can see, there is some serious tension going on between these two, and for the first time ever, you're going to see them both on stage together *before* the match!"

Tyler looked up towards the suites, ignoring the crowd as they cut to a commercial break.

There he sat, a smile across his face. This was his doing. Anyone with any common sense would know that to put Tyler and Dei on the same stage together after last night was bad news.

"Ladies and Gentlemen, please welcome back to the stage Dei Jie!" Tyler's head spun around to see his nemesis enter the stage. Zeus's chair moved to the center of the stage, and a new chair rose up from the floor to accommodate their new guest.

Dei looked even *cockier* and angrier, if that was possible. His fans roared, waving red flags and shooting mini rockets off for their hero. He didn't even bother waving to the people; all he did was look straight through Zeus to Tyler.

At first Tyler thought Dei was about to jump him, and all his muscles tensed, but Dei simply grabbed Zeus's hand, and sat down.

"Ladies and Gentlemen for the first time ever we have TWO contenders for the ultimate title of Champion of the TOC here together! Let me hear it!" Zeus screamed as he stood up.

The interview was already difficult enough, and Dei's words foamed back into his mind, despite his resistance. But there was more. Flashbacks of memories, memories he had blocked out of his parents, began to fill his head, a ski trip, an afternoon at a zoo, and the smell of popcorn at the movies…and that night. Tyler closed his eyes, fighting to shut the lid before more spilled out. His sadness began to boil into rage as he fought back tears. Why was this happening now?

"—er? Tyler? Tyler, are you alright?"

He opened his eyes. "Yes. Fine. Shall we continue?"

"Of course." Zeus observed him carefully, before continuing. "Dei, now that Tyler is sitting right across the stage, are you still willing to tell me what you did earlier?"

"Absolutely. I have no problem saying it to his face. Someone has to. Tyler, you don't deserve to be here. You are not a *real* champion. Tomorrow I will shatter the illusion of 'the dream' that you represent."

Dei's words were like daggers.

"Ouch. Insensitive words from an insensitive man. Tyler, what is your response to these statements? You have been widely criticized in the press, especially in the latest edition of *Wrestler's Weekly,* suggesting you don't belong here for your lack of skills as well."

Tyler opened his mouth to respond, but stopped himself, thinking of what he had said last time. *Just remember what you're out there to do.* Jason was right. They were trying to garner a reaction out of him.

131

He turned to face Zeus, who stared at him with unforgiving eyes, constantly trying to suck more out of him, constantly trying to push the limits of his endurance. That's when Tyler noticed it. It was so tiny he couldn't believe he had seen it in the first place. Colored tan to blend in with Zeus's skin, a little earpiece rested in his ear, and Tyler had no doubt that on the other line was none other than Casper Lanstark

"I think that these are very unfair accusations coming from someone who has been wrestling since they were four. I'm sorry that everyone does not have the privileges you do, Dei."

Dei's face twisted while Zeus smiled.

Dammit Tyler.

"Yeah? Shall we put that to the test right now!" Dei roared. "Why do we have to wait until Friday? I'll demolish you right now, you hallucinating little twit!"

"Now Dei," Zeus butted in. "Surely you don't mean that?"

"Oh but I do." Dei growled. "Someone has to show this little fool just where he belongs." Dei locked eyes with Tyler's, and in that moment, Tyler could see the rage that consumed the man across from him. "You are not one of *us,* Tyler. You do not belong here. In fact I am offended I have to face a joke like you in the finals."

Zeus, who always had a comment, said nothing and instead just looked at Tyler. Not for the first time this week, Tyler felt backed into a corner, but that is how is how they wanted him to feel isn't it?

"Tyler?" Tyler felt himself jump even though Zeus had spoken very calmly. "Are you still with us?"

Tyler searched for his words carefully. "I am Zeus, and all I have to say is that I am very excited for this match tomorrow. I'm honored to get the opportunity to face Dei, even if he does not feel the same way about me."

After a few minutes of commercials, the camera cut to Zeus who now stood alone on stage.

"What a night, ladies and gentlemen! As you can see things are extremely heated here. There are many questions on everyone's minds on both sides of the spectrum as to what exactly will take place Friday night at this hour, in the biggest wrestling match of our time. With all of the uncertain, one thing is for certain, the world will be watching."

11 The Biggest Party on Earth

Tyler couldn't see, and anyone who has experienced this inconvenience can relate. However, typically things like fog, rain, snow, or a swarm of bees probably blinded most of those people. It would be more difficult to find a person today who can tell you they were blinded by an unrelenting swarm of confetti like Tyler was as he entered *Veneficus*, the pride of Lanstark City. Towering above the tallest towers, it was bragged about as the most technologically advanced building in the world and the capital building of the TOC.

It was also the host of what has been dubbed the 'biggest party on earth.'

Many were doubtful of course as they watched it on their holograms at home, as it was not unlike something seen in many movies.

That was Tyler's original opinion, until he entered the sprawling palatial like building.

Where there wasn't confetti in the air there was glowing balloons, changing colors as they floated higher into the air. Waiters dressed in slick black suits with a golden TOC seal in the middle of their tie tended to the needs of every guest with a certain madness only seen by a select few. Any status people held Tyler up to was trampled by the titans Casper Lanstark had acquired here to witness his rise to power.

Mistresses in outrageously expensive dresses accompanied sports stars that arrived in sports cars. Inventors chatted with playboys who showed off their fancy toys to millionaires who were trying to befriend billionaires. Famous reporters who tried to get details in specific orders interviewed actors whose cognitive factors were low from not drinking cocktails slow.

It was quite a sight to the average Joe.

Casper was truly a genius at what he did. And he wanted the world here to witness his mastery.

"Tyler, Tyler? Dang it boy this is not a time to lose yourself in your thoughts!" Jason hissed in as low of a tone as possible, despite the deafening sound of voices, music, laughter, and shooting confetti that echoed through the halls. "I need you to be on the guard and be ready to meet some of my...friends."

"Friends? Jason since when do you have friends?"

"There's no time to explain. Lester and I have to be off to do some...mingling." Tyler suddenly became aware that Lester was no longer present. "You're on your own kid, have some fun! And don't forget to watch for my friends!"

As if observing Tyler's dumfounded look, Jason added. "Try and act normal. Maybe go talk to them?" He nodded over to a group of models that were saying they were from Russia.

As Jason left his side, the feeling of loneliness crept over Tyler like a spider making its descent from the ceiling in the middle of night. As he observed the models, his thoughts went to Cailey. She was really the only girl he had truly ever loved.

And she had abandoned him. He hadn't seen her since their date on Monday. He was feeling ever more the fool by the minute.

He had always known it would be too good to be true if a girl like her loved him. Yet he allowed himself to believe that she was sincere on her end all this time. Where was she now that he needed her most? His throat went dry and his heart went cold as he felt a sting only felt by someone in love.

Slowly, he made his way over to the first in a long series of buffet tables. This one had little finger foods, and even though he weighed in earlier today, he still felt guilt for eating them because well... for one thing, it was a pretty big match tomorrow, and for another, he was a wrestler!

But hell, if this was to be his last enjoyable night on Earth, why not?

He grabbed a hand full of fried calamari, trying to avoid as many people as possible. Perhaps in a place full of this many famous faces, he could do it!

In fact, he began to get greedy as he shoved a piece of vanilla cake from a desert tray into his mouth. It was *the* best vanilla cake he had ever tasted. He grabbed another piece. If Casper ended up trying to kill him tomorrow, Tyler was doing it his way: in a kickass suit with some out of Casper's world-class *vanilla* cake.

"You know, for someone who is going to be in the eyes of the world tomorrow rocking glorified underwear," A raspy voice interjected. "I probably would not eat that."

Tyler turned to notice a man leaning on the table a few feet away from him, stabbing a cake with a fork. The man did not face him however; he kept staring into the crowd as though weary of it all.

" Uh...excuse me?" Tyler muffled through the cake in his mouth.

"You heard me." The man stated firmly. Compared to the other guest in the room, this man was not as interested in fashion. His shirt was unbuttoned at the top, and he had long, disheveled dark hair. He was very simple in appearance in everything except the bright silver ring he wore on his right hand, though Tyler couldn't quite make out what it was.

"I'm sorry have we met before?" Tyler asked, a little annoyed that this stranger had the guts to comment on what he should and shouldn't do.

"No, we haven't." The man replied flatly, still gazing into the crowd.

"Well then, please do me a favor and allow me to make my own nutritional decisions." Tyler huffed, unsatisfied with the man's answer.

"So you're going to damage all of our chances for twenty seconds of vanilla pleasure?" The man snarled. "*Brat.*" He hissed.

"You know what mister," Tyler began as he stepped closer to the man. "You have no idea what I am going through in my life so I suggest you stop while you're ahead."

The man startled Tyler as he turned sharply and clenched his fists as if about to say something, but stopped, as he seemed to notice what he was looking for. "Neither do you." The man replied flatly again, and disappeared into the crowd.

Tyler didn't chase after him, too busy trying to take in what had just occurred. Surely he himself would know what was at stake in his life right now, would he not? His own skin and the freedom of all free people in the world, it didn't get any better than that.

"I see you met Lanus." A calm, cool voice said. Tyler turned around to see a tall girl, with smooth tan skin and dark hair smiling back at him.

"Who?" he asked, still confused.

"The tall cranky grouch you just talked too. That was him."

"Right, and who are you?"

"I'm not obliged to answer that at the moment. I just wanted to size you up myself for a few minutes while I could." Abruptly, like an eagle eyeing a prey her attention turned elsewhere. Turning her back to him she went on her way, her walking as seductive as possible.

You could be sure all eyes followed.

At this point Tyler had no idea what to think. Where these people just the weird fans that you never see in public that just decided to show up at random events. Annoyed, tired, and confused, he went to the drink table and took one of the delicate oval shaped glasses off the table and began to drink the delightful green liquid.

"I say!" came a voice that startled him as he nearly dropped the glass.

He turned to see a very plump man staring at him. "Oh please not another one!" Tyler moaned out loud.

"I say dear boy! I promise I am not as rude as Violet, walking away and all. I am more practical and a bit understanding compared to most of our folk."

Tyler decided to just assume Violet was the young lady who he had just encountered. "Who are your *folk*?" Tyler questioned, delighted he may finally get some answers.

"My folk? I say dear boy, they are *yours* as well." The round man fidgeted with his half moon spectacles, almost flinging them off by accident. They looked as though they were about to fly off his rosy red blown up cheeks. His forehead was slightly shiny from the sweat forming and he pulled out the handkerchief that appeared moist already to wipe the sweat again.

"What do you want then?" Tyler snapped, annoyed with these 'folk'.

"Nothing at the moment dear boy, I just had to get your measurements?"

"Excuse me?" Tyler thought he had misheard him, but the man made no indication that he planned on adjusting his statement. "If you think that I am letting you touch me—

"Oh don't worry dear boy, the glasses have already done it." He said, giving them a flick. He glanced down at the undersized watch that rested on his oversized wrist. "I say now, it is time for me to be on my way. Until you we meet again, cheerio!"

The man snickered to himself and waddled away.

Tyler wanted to say this was Jason's doing, but these people seemed a little weird compared to his mentor. Were these his friends?

Now that he had a moment, his thoughts returned to Cailey. Not so much as a phone call had come from his rumored 'fiancé'. Was it something he did? Had she just been with him to have her name in the spotlight? He found a growing resentment toward her. Every memory they had together began to be corrupted in his mind.

He navigated the room toward the massive dance floor where countless people were having the best time of their lives. Through all the glitter and spotlights he began to feel more and more like the eyes of the guards and butlers were tirelessly watching his every step.

Where are you, Casper? You must be close now.

"Great to see you've met the family." Came a voice so calm and comforting it gave Tyler goose bumps as he thought of his mother. Tyler turned to see a very warm pair of eyes looking back at him. They belonged to a woman who wasn't as young as she used to be. Okay, she only had a tiny strand of gray hairs on the right side of her otherwise dark hair.

"The family?" Tyler questioned as he abandoned all hope for this night to make any sense what so ever.

138

"Oh," She chuckled with a sparkle in her eye. "It'll all make sense later." The women had elegance to her, and she commanded respect through her posture but had a sparkle in her voice.

"I suppose you're going to ask me a series of cryptic questions and then instead of telling your name you're going to tell me the name of the large man I just met, before going on your way?"

"Jules? Oh no I promise you I am more straightforward than he. My name is Angelica, but *you* can call me Ang."

"Well thank you…Ang. Not to be… disrespectful, but who the hell are all these people?" Tyler pestered, hoping to get rid of the puppet strings he felts himself being pulled by.

"Don't you see, Tyler? We walk not among you but with you… watching, and protecting, as there is more depth to all of this than you realize. You are to trying to block an experience out of your head, and I am not only referring to the events of this week. Doing this will only make things worse. When you finally tear those walls down, you might find something meaningful." Angelica said as her green eyes scanned him, though he felt she could see right through him.

"Not likely."

"You will soon see this very differently, Tyler. Among the darkness of humanity, there has to be a light to lead them back. Whether you believe it should be you or someone else, fate cares not, destiny will continue moving forward. Accept that most things are out of your control, and do something with the things that *are*." Angelica said.

"It feels like my entire life is out of my control."

"Perhaps you have not yet looked at all your cards." She said calmly, stroking her warm, dark skin. Tyler thought he was seeing things, because he could have sworn her watch just had a stroke of golden light go through it. He blinked to make sure he wasn't seeing things.

Looking up from her watch as if it was a symbol for her departure, Angelica offered one last opinion.

"It wasn't just a marketing strategy, Tyler."

He looked at her, confused.

"Your name, the boy with a heart. Somebody had to see it, no matter how hard you have tried to bury that notion in your mind. You have the privilege to stand for something bigger than you. Stop feeling sorry for yourself and do something with that privilege."

His trance was broken by a burst of laughter by the group next to him.

She was the first person that had not told him that *everything* relied on him. In fact, he felt as though it was suggested that he was not needed at all. This actually made him feel a lot better, and lifted a tremendous weight off of his shoulders. What was truly needed was the idea he had the ability to represent.

It was all slowly coming together now.

And then he saw him. Standing up on the balcony surrounded by some of the biggest names around the world was the man himself, Casper Lanstark.

Tyler had urge to do something somewhat questionable.

Okay, probably really stupid.

He could feel the blood in his veins rush faster and faster as he began his ascent up the stairs. Little beads of sweat formed on his forehead as he fidgeted with his hands in his pockets. But, despite his nervous appearance, he knew what he was going to do. Adrenaline surged through his body as he got closer and closer. Oddly enough, he had never felt freer in his life. The invisible shackles Casper had trapped him in seemed to fall off with each step he took.

The weight of the world was no longer on his shoulders.

Casper, champagne glass in hand wearing his usual malicious poker face had noticed him, and his expression changed in a way Tyler would never expect. He looked as though he was surprised.

"Excuse me, please." Casper said to the group he had been talking to as he faced him. The Venom snake broach on his suit lapel watched all who had the misfortune of meeting the phantom menace. "Ah Mr. Mason, good to see your feeling alright before the big day! Are you ready to make history?"

"I am." Tyler said calmly.

"That's good to hear, because we have found the hospital Nana's in and we will start treatment as soon as the match is over tomorrow."

A sick feeling began to take ahold of him. They found her! Had he known Tyler would get cold feet? Nana would have never wanted him to make a deal with this kind of man, even if it was to save her. He had to be strong for her, for his parents.

"The game ends now."

"Forgive me Tyler, I believe I don't understand."

"Our deal is off. Not only will I *win* tomorrow, I am going to *stop* you."

Casper laughed in his face. "My young foolish friend, the game is only *just* beginning."

"The one between you and me? Absolutely." Tyler said coldly. " But your game with the rest of the world...I hope your pawns are in place, because I am breaking the board."

Casper narrowed his cold, dark eyes. "Do you really think you're going to be able to stop *me*?"

Tyler took a step toward Casper. "Do you really think you can stop *me*, Casper?"

Casper took a step in closer, locking eyes with his young antagonist. "I think you're forgetting who you are *talking* to, Mason."

"I know *exactly* who I am talking to Lanstark, and you know what else? You seem to forget just *who* everything relies on tomorrow. *I* am in control of the outcome."

Casper's nostrils twitched and his eyes looked as though someone slapped him. How many years had passed since the great Casper Lanstark had been challenged?

"I guess the life of your precious Nana means nothing to you. Just so you understand *how* serious I am, if you don't lose that match tomorrow your beloved mentor— excuse me, 'father' as you've been quoted saying, will be dead before he steps foot off this island."

"Ladies and gentlemen may I have your attention, a part of history will be played for you tonight!" All eyes in the room looked down toward the yelling composer in a yellow suit. "A classical history of the world begins now!" The orchestra began to play some classic pieces, and Casper stepped forward to the railing, peering down at the massive hall below.

"It's always the best part, isn't it?" Casper asked him as he gazed into the crowd. Knowing Tyler had no idea what he was talked about, Casper turned back to face him.

"Seeing what all the pawns do at the end of a chess game, just before they lose."

"I agree, though I am not a fan of classic games. They are too plain. My favorite games are when one of the pawns dethrones the king."

"A rarity." Casper snarled.

"A possibility." Tyler fired back.

Casper stepped right in Tyler's face. "Do *not* test me."

"I just did."

Chills went down Tyler's spine as Casper gave him a sharp glare before walking off to his security detail. He had a bad feeling that Casper wasn't thrilled about that little exchange. Tyler's heart was pounding, but he felt a sense of drive unlike any he had ever felt. He made his way off the balcony, away from the glaring guards and high-ranking officials to once again join the crowd that continued to unremittingly party below.

The famous rapper, the Duke, interrupted his otherwise quiet descent to the floor as he paraded around on a gold plated cart drinking champagne from a bottle. Tyler shook his head. Was this what he would have become had he continued to believe greatness came from a sports car?

He shuffled through the group of people while ignoring the paparazzi who came out of nowhere. With a sly grin, he stuck his foot out as the cart carrying the Duke passed by him, causing a rather embarrassing scene for the drunken showman. He pulled out his smartphone to see a message from Jason: *Meet at hotel. DON'T GET LOST.* So they had left him all by himself.

Annoyed, Tyler shoved his way over to the drink table, tempted to snag a good one.

"So this is the boy wonder everyone is rattling about."

Just when the night couldn't get anymore ridiculous.

Tyler flipped around ready to tear into whomever it was that came to harass him. But before he could his jaw dropped, and he lost his words. She had smooth hair, perfectly red lips, and eyes so dangerous it almost frightened him to wonder what was going on inside the woman's mind.

"To whom do I owe the pleasure?" Perhaps one person tonight would be upfront with him?

"You're the first of all the drooling men to formulate a response to me. Impressive." She giggled as she passed him and took a drink from the table. "For that, I applaud you. Oh and don't worry. I won't tell a soul if you choose to drink, assuming that you wont tell a soul what *I've* done."

Tyler paid no consideration to the brown liquid he just spilled as it slowly stained the white tablecloth.

"And what have you done?"

The girl smiled at him from behind her jet-black masquerade mask. "Look at all of them." She gestured toward the party around them. "They really think they are above it all."

"We need justice!" The girl breathed, looking at him if expecting a response.

"So...is that the answer to my question?"

She grabbed his hand, pulling him out to the dance floor and setting his arms around her form fitted sparkling black dress.

"I've only done what I had to do to prepare for the world's ending. You know as well as I do what takes place tomorrow."

Tyler's heart skipped a beat. He got the impression she wasn't one of Jason's friends. Who was she, and how did she know?

"Don't worry, Ty." She said as if reading his thoughts. "I don't work for Casper. Or Jason." She let go of his hand and circled around him. "But enough about me. What about the *great* boy with a heart? What are you going to do at the end of all things?" She leaned in to his ear and whispered. "Tell me you're not a *sellout* darling."

"What exactly—?"

She cupped his face in her hands, kissing him on the lips before she turned and began to walk away.

"Wait!" He called as he wiped the lipstick from his lips. He shoved through some unhappy partiers before catching up to her and grabbing her hand.

"I'll see you in another world, Ty."

Tyler asked. "You really believe it's going to end like that?"

"When the stakes are *this* high? I do."

"Not if I can help it."

"If you can pull that off..." she said with a wink as she leaned in close to his ear and put her hands inside his jacket. Even through his shirt, he could feel the electricity of her touch. "I really will be impressed." Without another word, she vanished into the crowd.

He was about to chase after her when he felt a firm grip contract around his other arm and force him around.

He just couldn't catch a break tonight.

"Tyler, what the HELL was that? Has your ego really grown that big that you believe you can cheat on me?"

As if the night couldn't be anymore of a mess, as he lived and breathed, Cailey stood in front of him with a venomous look in her eyes. Her yelling had attracted the attention of everyone in the area, including the paparazzi. He was not in the mindset to play this game right now. Deep down, he knew the answer to what he was about to ask.

"Was any of it real, Cailey? *Any* of it? "

Cailey looked taken back, as if unsure how to respond to this.

"Tyler...I..." Her tone dimmed and she grabbed his arm, trying to pull him away from the converging crowd of people, paparazzi, and a rather disoriented rapper.

"*Answer me!*" He yelled pulling his arm back. "How could you say the things you said to me—all lies?" He shook his head, as the look on her face seemed to fuel the disappointment in his heart. "You always did have the attitude that you were too good for me."

Cailey looked around as if searching for help. He had never seen such an uncertain expression on her face before. It only confirmed what he already feared: when Jason had recruited him, Alfredo had planted her with him. Had they known Jason wasn't really a recruiter all along?

He opened his mouth to say something more when he felt a strong grip take his shoulder. Within seconds men in black suits were all around them— and they weren't the friendly ones. Tyler felt a sharp poke as the guards began shoving paparazzi out of the way, escorting him out toward the back. Tyler fiercely resisted.

But the more he resisted, the weaker his legs became. They felt as though they were...slowly turning to gelatin. One of the guards slapped a pair of sunglasses on him as the world started to become a blurry enigma. Exhaustion forced itself upon him as he began to slump into their arms. It took all of his remaining strength, but he swung his head back to look behind him. The last image he saw was Casper Lanstark quietly watching him from the balcony.

There was something to be said about that cold, cruel smile that could unnerve even the bravest man.

And then it was dark.

12 **A Billionaire's Change**

"Yes sir, we're taking him there now."

"Good." Alfredo Lopezzi sighed with relief as he unbuttoned his shirt collar. It had been an unnecessarily long night.

Cailey stared out the window as the bright shape of *Veneficus* grew further and further away in the distance. She had disappointed her father; she could see it all over his face. In her defense she hadn't done it on purpose (though she would be lying to say she had never intentionally sabotaged a plan of his). It was supposed to be easy. All she had to do was go in there and make Tyler distraught enough to make a fool of himself. This would of course lead to stories of him being 'unhinged' to circulate, and make his reputation smearing easier for Dad and his people.

Instead of that, she froze up in front of all the paparazzi while Tyler not only remained calm, but made *her* look like the fool.

"Dad…"

"Cailey please. What's done is done."

"It's just…how can you be angry with me?"

"Your job was simple, Cailey! All you had to do was rattle him! Instead you became distraught when he asked you *one* question!"

The right question.

"Don't tell me your conscious is actually starting to come back. Did you *really* develop feelings for him?"

It wasn't like she believed she would freeze up! It was just… seeing his face… the pain in his eyes made her feel…*bad*. She had known the entire time she was doing something wrong. She wasn't heartless. Just a little messed up.

"Dad, it was almost like he *knew* what I was going to say before I said it!"

A tear escaped from her eye and splashed on the screen of the tablet that sat in her lap.

"Are you really telling me you've done this for almost a year now, and you had to feel bad about it *today*?" Alfredo snarled, clearly not picking up on the problem his daughter was suggesting caused this disaster. There was no way Tyler was going to stop them. He was confident in that. *However*, as much it twisted a knife in his ribs to admit it, the boy was right about one thing. The influence he wielded over people. It was a weapon he could use to destroy them if the circumstance were right. It was a minor chance of this happening yes, but still a chance.

And it was not a risk Venom planned on taking.

"I am sorry I am just not as used to stabbing people in the back as *you are*."

Alfredo Lopezzi looked at his daughter, a disturbed expression forming across his face.

"Really? Is that how you feel, Cailey? Because it certainly doesn't seem that way every time you swipe my credit card! What do you think pays for the party? May I remind you that *you've* been stabbing him in the back everyday for the past year as it stands!"

"You always thought you were better than me."

Tears streamed down Cailey's face as Tyler's words replayed in her head. When her father had first approached her about dating the shy kid who wasn't exactly a rock star in high school, she was hesitant. But he insisted it was necessary.

He promised to compensate her thoroughly, buying her everything she could want and more. There were only two unbinding conditions. The first was that she had to plant bugs in all of Tyler's electronics. This made her uneasy more times than she could count, but she did it. The second was also very straightforward: don't fall in love incase he turned out to be an enemy.

Easy enough, right?

Soon it even became beneficial to her own fame, as Tyler became an overnight celebrity with popularity around the globe that hadn't been seen in ages. No matter how big Tyler got however, he always treated her just like he did when they first met. And this was a quality she had never found before.

147

This led her to begin to consider being with him after all this was over. Consideration began to turn into want and before she knew it, she fell for him. He had still not been deemed a threat, so she assumed her father was wrong. This was the first man she might actually see herself with long term, and the feeling of happiness it gave her caused her to smile brighter than she had before. For the first time since mom left, she was happy.

That's when it happened. She tapped into his electronics for her father's tech wizzes for what was going to be the last time. Using that as a springboard, they hacked into his manager, Jason's phones and computers. They soon discovered something in Jason's messages that led to a wave of chaos.

Her worst fear had come to pass.

Tyler was now deemed an imminent threat.

Her father didn't tell her until after their lunch with him at the *Common Club*, and almost overnight, she was instructed to cut off all contact with him. While it was tremendously hard, she hoped by cooperating there would be a chance for Tyler to be cleared and things could go back to how they were. To accomplish this, she helped her father's people craft an offer for him. She knew Nana was sick, and he couldn't afford the treatment to get her better.

Relief flooded through her veins when she got the news that he took the deal Casper set forward for him. She even planned on talking to him about it tonight. But on her way to the party, her father called her to inform her Tyler had rejected the deal mere minutes before her arrival.

How could she have not seen this coming, she knew Tyler.

He had realized just who it was he was making a deal with. Cailey was aware her father and his cronies weren't the greatest people out there.

She was probably no different than him now...

Her nerves rattled as she racked her brain, trying tediously to figure out what tomorrow would bring.

Cailey longed to go back in time to when they bumped into each other in the hallway that day. She longed to tell Tyler not to enter the tournament before inviting him to her house, free from the vicious fangs of Venom. What could she do now?

It was far too late for that.

Part
THREE

13 **The Pawn's Decision**

He was suddenly aware of a staunch throbbing in his head.

Tyler tried to lift up.

It collapsed back onto the pillow, feeling as though it weighed two tons. His neck felt like steel, all flexibility seemed to have vanished. His entire body was aching and weak. The sunlight that penetrated the room blinded him, and it took at least five minutes to get his eyes to adjust to the light. Slowly, Tyler managed to sit himself up. How did he get back here? The party… Jason's 'friends'… the girl… Cailey… the last face of the night…*Casper*.

His fingers went to the stinging dot on his neck. What did they do to him this time?

He stumbled off the bed, barely making it to the bathroom. The first thing he noticed were the large bags that rested under his eyes. Speaking of his eyes…they looked like they were straining to stay open, the veins in them bulging. His shirt from last night was saturated with sweat stains.

"Do not test me."

Lanstark's words haunted his mind like the growl of a wolf sends chills through the wool of a sheep. He struggled to twist the handles of the sink as his hands continued to shake.

"Argh!" Finally, he spun the handle. He splashed water on his face, its coldness providing direction to his disheveled head.

He managed to throw off his suit jacket onto the bathroom floor and stumbled into the living room to find something to throw on and get out of here. He had to find Jason. A cold chill seemed to take ahold of him. He had to make sure Jason wasn't…dead. He wobbled over to his dresser, trying to grab some clothes off the hooks. Instead he ended up taking everything out, and dropping it out onto the floor.

Angrily, he smacked the door.

Swiveling on his heel, he nearly slipped as he stopped dead in his tracks.

"Going somewhere?" The cold, unmistakable voice asked. Casper Lanstark sat dressed in a white suit, no other color on him except him his black tie, and the serpent pin that sat in the middle of it. Had he been here the entire time watching him? The thought of Casper Lanstark watching him all night sent fear into the deepest crevices of his heart.

"Well now Tyler you are welcome to sit down, this is *your* room after all! Won't you join me for some tea?" He nodded over at the chair and teacup across from him. Tyler didn't move. Was this the end? Was Casper cutting the game short?

"You were very forward last night, when all you're friends were around. Are you telling me now when there is no camera around that Tyler Mason has lost his stomach?" Casper mocked, licking his lips as he took a drink out of the white teacup in his hand.

"What do you want, Casper? You've already taken everything."

Casper laughed slightly, amused. "Oh my dear boy, do you really think I have taken *everything?* Now please stop wasting time! Sit! And drink up. It's a big day and you'll need what is in this glass to recover from the serium administered in your system last night."

Tyler wearily observed the teacup in front of him as he slumped into the chair across from Casper.

They sat in silence.

"Oh for heaven sake just drink it! I can't kill you, not yet anyway. I need you for the show tonight. *Everyone* will be watching. I have made sure of it."

Tyler managed to pick up the glass, which felt as though a thirty-pound dumbbell had been somehow inserted in its tiny glass frame. Cautiously, he drank the warm caramel colored liquid. It tasted…*good,* and within seconds of sipping it, he was already feeling better.

"Why are you doing this? What purpose will it serve you to take down the world? You already have everything."

Casper winced again, as though Tyler insulted whatever morals he *did* have in his heart. "Everything? *Everything?*

Tyler, do you really believe in your small-minded head that *everything* can be defined as something as common as money? Houses? Cars? Women? Islands? I thought you were better than that."

Indeed, there was a time, a long time in his life, where Tyler believed that having those things really meant having everything. He wasn't so sure anymore.

Casper leaned forward in his chair. "Tyler, let me tell you exactly what *everything* is. Everything is influence. Real power is not found in material things, it is found in controlling the most resourceful thing on the planet, people. Think about it. If I can control, even a generation of people, in how they think, act, and what they believe, than I can bend their will exactly the way I want it. War? It will be nonexistent because people won't disagree. They won't know how! Money? No one will care for such a thing, as they will be told they don't need it! *Imagine* what we could accomplish as a society of one were no one stands out."

"Where no one stands out except for you?" Tyler grumbled, beginning to feel like himself again as he sipped the caramel liquid more.

Casper sat back in his chair nodding. "You truly had potential, Tyler Mason." He stood up and buttoned his suit. "You would have made a great apprentice. No matter, you will still be the instrument to my biggest success yet." He smirked and began walking to the door before turning. "How ironic. Oh, and one more thing, if you think I don't know about your co conspirators who, 'have me snow balled,' know that the men outside your door won't be letting you leave until I deem it time." The door slid shut.

Silence.

He slurped down the rest of the caramel liquid, and shot to the door, peering out the peep whole. Sure enough, two black clad guards sat in watch outside. Worse, he had no idea where Jason was. Had he been captured? His chest rose and fell faster and faster as he tried to figure out what would happen now. He ran to the table and grabbed his smartphone.

No service stared back at him. There had to be a way out of this!

His brain soon began to tire as time slowed down to turtle speed, each passing minute felt like an hour. It really was a big day for him today. After all, he was dying!

He walked out onto the balcony, ignoring the rain as he tried to imagine what the day had in store for him. He really had no idea what to expect...something rattled his nerves and shook the very foundations of his being.

"So tell me Tyler Mason,"

Nearly falling out of his chair, Tyler stumbled to his feet.

"What do you want to be remembered for?" The voice continued.

At first Tyler had no idea who the hell stood on the balcony next to his own.

"Who..."

The man calmly observed him, his long hair billowing in the wind. "What's the matter? Don't recognize me?" The man's clothes looked as though they belonged in...medieval France!

"*Silas?*"

"Let me tell you something my young little friend, the day you die is something worth living for!"

*   *   *

Dei Jie impatiently paced his room awaiting his father who was on a 'very important' business call. It really pissed him off every time his father came over to see him and than talked on his mobile instead. His heart was racing. He would admit to no one that he was nervous for tonight. It embarrassed him to admit it to himself. The fool didn't even deserve to be here like he did.

This was *his* title.

Tyler hadn't been through what he had, as he thought back to the first time he had won his a national wrestling title back in China. His father had nearly broken him that season. The training, the mental preparation, and how could he forget the dreaded weight cutting.

But he didn't break. Against the odds, he triumphed. That was the last season he had spent being the underdog. After that, he had traveled the world beating any who stood in his path with ferocity no one had ever seen before. Any who dared to say they knew the art of the sport of wrestling better than he had would be obliterated. He was the most feared, respected, and popular name in the sport.

The TOC title was without a doubt his this year.

He would bring the title of Champion to the East, the first to do so. The West had for too long stood so arrogantly against them.

So why was he nervous?

"Shi shi." His father hung up his mobile.

"Who was that?" Dei asked emotionlessly, just as his training had taught.

"The president." His father gushed, the sweet sense of victory evident behind the square glasses that rested on his nose.

"What did he want?"

"He said he looked forward to being there to see your victory over the American tonight. He expects that the West should finally end its streak of foolishness and come to terms after this public blow. Failure is *not* an option."

Dei found no emotion in the news of the VIP who would be watching him tonight. Not even a stir. "Was there ever any doubt in your mind father? The fact that any of you think that this fool deserves to be on the same mat as me is insulting!" Dei hissed.

"Dei!" His father screeched. "What did I teach you in all that training? I told you no matter who it is your facing, this is one of the few sports, if the only where *anything* can happen at any moment. An attitude will not help you in this! Don't you dare forget all the time and money I have put into this! You will not dissolve my honor!"

155

"Your honor?" Dei found himself ready to snap at all of them. But before he could the annoying musical tone of his father's mobile interrupted.

His own father squabbling about *his* honor? How dare he? His father hadn't done this in years. Not until just recently when some nobody from America began to miraculously climb the American Wrestling Organization brackets, beating the best in the country to gain a spot to go to the TOC.

Did his father really believe Mason stood a chance? Rage seemed to reach a boiling point in Dei's heart.

At the time, Dei was even impressed, scowling at how terrible competition in the United States must have been for this to happen. But the kid continued winning his matches, beating 99-1 odds to make it to the TOC, climbing the ladder all the way to the finals to challenge him. What made him ever more upset...Mason stole the spotlight from him! It made his father skittish and annoying, as he was starting to return to his old methods of trying to train him.

Despite this being *his* life, what should have been his decisions were decided by his father while his feelings were swept under the rug. Soon it was about the state and what they wanted him to do. And his ball-less father obliged every command because of his obsession with the country. Many thought his father did it for money, but that was simply untrue, they already had money. He realized a long time ago his father was doing this for *power*. However, he never realized the extent his father was willing to go until the buffoon made a deal with a new entity other than the state. Dei had figured out it was somebody related to the TOC board, but he couldn't figure out who. It didn't matter anyway, at this point it seemed his father would sellout his son to anyone if power was promised to him. The Chinese government, his father, and this mysterious stranger had guided his public image and actions since.

If it were up to him, he would have approached Tyler as he had every other opponent he had faced before he got here and the politics got involved in the sports. It disgusted him, how much the press hyped this kid up and fueled his hype like he would *actually* beat Dei? How dare they? Just because a kid beats a few kids and breaks a record he is the new beginning for the sport? He would show all of them by smashing his challenger pitifully. Not only would he prove to all of the fools that he was the best that ever was and ever will be, he would wrangle control of his life from his father.

He almost wanted to be free from all of this as bad as he wanted the title. It confused him when he thought like that, and he would never admit it because he was always taught never to show weakness. But that is what he wanted.

To be free. Free from being a pawn on other people's boards.

"Dei!" His father snapped as he slid the mobile into his pocket.

"What is it now father? Do you want me to go out and meet the President?"

To Dei's surprise, his father nodded.

"Even better." His father beamed. "You're going to meet the man who is going to give us *real* power son."

There was a knock at the door. His father quickly opened it. Dei's heart skipped a beat. He had only ever seen the person who walked in on TV, and had to admit even he was intimidated.

"Hello Dei. Ready for your big day?" Casper Lanstark smiled.

*   *   *

Not for the first time this week, Tyler was doing something most would consider off the wall. He sat in the back of a car with none other than Silas Marshall, the guy dressed in medieval robes.

Tyler remembered him from lunch with Cailey's father and also as one of the few who stuck up to Lanstark when he was kidnapped. To say he was a character wouldn't be entirely fair to the man. Bizarre seemed a lot more… reasonable.

"So let me get this straight," Tyler said, still trying to figure out why he had trusted this man enough to get in car

157

with him. "You want to help me even though I am the primary target of your organization?"

"Yes." Silas joked as he coughed into a silk cloth.

"May I ask why exactly?"

"Let's just say that for the lifetime I have spent committing sins, I had a change of heart." Silas croaked as he coughed again. Tyler noticed that Silas did not have his broach on anymore. Had he really defected from Venom? Or was something else going on here?

"Forgive me Silas, but it is hard for me to believe that considering you were once head of the world's most lethal terrorist organization."

" You got into the car didn't you?" Silas coughed as if offended. " And terrorist you say? Terrorists nay, we once had a purpose, one other than world domination."

"Are you trying to tell me the bad guys weren't always bad?"

"No son. We only did what was necessary. Doesn't excuse the sinful nature of playing God but…we only sought to control or if necessary eliminate those who were sinners of the earth. Overtime however, our methods slowly fell more and more into the red. Finally, when it was clear we had lost our way and no longer served our true purpose, we faced a great schism. When my family took over Venom, we tried to bring it back to the old methods of doing things but we failed miserably. Greed and power had corrupted everyone."

"Why cause the War if you wanted to return the organization to the old ways of doing things?"

"That was a suggestion that came from a place other than the council. There was nothing I could do, as they had already set things in motion. I was ousted from leadership after the disaster of The War. Our organization was about to disband, and perhaps that would have been for the best."

"So what saved it? There is no way Casper could have stopped all of this?"

Silas looked at him with a painful expression in his eyes. "But he did. And if anyone believes for a moment that man is using all of this for the betterment of man kind, they are insane."

Tyler felt a pain rising in his heart. Sports were meant to be something sacred, a place for people to come together, not apart.

"Lanstark's plans have been hitting snags. There were some internal sabotages."

Immediately Tyler thought of Jason. "Jason?" He gasped.

Silas nodded.

"You knew but said nothing?"

"As I said, I don't agree with the new rule. Our mission was never to take away freedom from all of mankind. Only those who deserve it."

"Which is still not justified! Who gave humanity the right to play God?" Tyler shot.

"Everything has a way of catching up to all of us in the end anyway." Silas said. Tyler noticed how he put his hand on his heart as if remembering something. "Lanstark was on the verge of launching a plan destined to fail until he found you."

There it was again. Why did they all believe everything hinged on him?

"I don't understand what I have to do with any of this! I am *not* a saint! I never was!" Tyler screamed angrily.

Silas coughed into his cloth a few more times before tucking it into his robe. He began to toy with his rings as though this was not the first time he had encountered a conversation such as this.

"Tyler, no human being on the planet is all good, or all bad. We all act in the name of both based on what we believe in. Who you are in your soul, is what defines you as a person. And you have a good soul Tyler. Right or wrong is something in the brain we only figure out later when it's too late. That is how life is. But you're looking at this entire situation all wrong. Is it really a curse knowing what a few human beings are going to try and do to the many? Imagine being one of the billions who know nothing. Imagine how they are going to feel if Casper succeeds. They have no choice but to deal with what happens to them. You have a chance to change what is happening."

A week ago he was just a teenager who didn't care about anything but buying a mansion and driving sports cars. That was how he believed he would make history before living a long and happy life. Now...

"You see Tyler, anyone who has their soul intact is pretty obvious to those of us whose souls are *not*." Silas said softly as he gazed out the window. "This was evident especially to Lanstark when he first saw you. He was so pleased when you took his deal. I am glad you rejected it. You need to show that same rebellious nature to the world tonight. It's time you accept the cause the universe has given you."

The raindrops that smacked the window seemed to smack a little harder as Tyler let all of this sink in. Whether he liked it or not, he was in this. And it was real.

The car made a sudden stop that sent him smack-dab into the window. The tires squealed to a halt on the wet street. He squinted through the rain to see two figures in black emerge out of a building coming toward the car. He turned to Silas who was still looking out the window.

"Silas?" Tyler began unbuckling his seat belt as panic began to spread through his body. The figures were getting closer.

"SILAS?"

His door swung open and Tyler threw up his fists ready to fight.

"What the hell does he think he is going to do with those?" Came a female voice.

A surge of joy went through his veins as he recognized the girl from the party, and with her Monty!

"Where you expecting some one else wise guy?" Monty grinned.

Tyler grinned and began to get out of the SUV but stopped. "Thank you, Silas. You're not so bad for someone who walks around in medieval robes."

Silas smiled, Tyler felt maybe the first real smile in years.

"You're not so bad yourself...for a short little punk."

Tyler shut the door grinning.

"Are you ready to go? We have a lot of things to figure out and no time to do so." Monty said as he and Violet grabbed his arms, escorting him into the building.

"That's okay." Tyler said. "I'm ready."

Or at least he hoped he was.

*   *   *

"What is it that you wanted to meet me about?" Dei said with no hint of respect in his voice. While he was originally surprised to see Casper Lanstark at his door, unlike his father, he did not kiss feet just to get what he wanted.

"Well Dei, it's a rather small request I have of you. One, which should be rather enjoyable for you." Lanstark stated patiently, not affected by Dei's tone of voice.

"If I do this for you, I am done Lanstark. I want nothing more to do with any of this. Whatever nonsense my father is involved in, this will be my only contribution." Dei said flatly, ignoring the glares from his father.

"Absolutely." Casper agreed. This unnerved Dei, as he doubted a man like Lanstark ever went along with anything unless it had benefit to him.

"Go on." He grumbled.

"You have been conducting yourself toward Tyler in a very disrespectful manner, and you have been doing it rather successfully especially of late. It is not good enough."

"I'm sorry?" His father questioned.

Dei wasted no breaths with useless words. "What are you saying?"

"It's simple. Tonight, I want you to humiliate Tyler with extreme prejudice." Casper said, sitting crossing legged in front of Dei.

"I already planned on it." Dei said. He was known to get rough with opponents— especially the ones he pretended were his father.

"I'm happy to hear that Dei a—

"So can I be on my way then? Incase you forgot I do have to prepare for the big night."

Dei rose to his feet and went to the door.

"Excuse me Dei, I was not finished talking."

Dei wanted to throw Lanstark through the wall, and he would…if it didn't mean certain disqualification.

"I expect you to execute this manner of behavior whether you win or lose."

Dei stood in disbelief. His fist was clenched, and he was fully prepared to punch Casper Lanstark square in the jaw, no longer worried about disqualification.

Casper stared back with an arrogant smile awaiting Dei's reply.

"You better hope *you* don't step foot on that mat tonight" Dei hissed, storming out of the room, sliding the door with a *SLAM*! Casper felt a vibration in his suit jacket and read a text from security: *The boy is gone. Still figuring out how.* He smiled. Everything was going as plan.

As Dei paced through the halls, shoving staff out of his way as he walked, he felt hate. Hatred towards the boy who was trying to steal his year, his title, his honor! The TOC had not given him the respect and the status he *deserved.* He had trained *too* hard. He had been through *too* much. *What* was so special about this boy?

What he *did* know was that tonight, Tyler Mason would bare the brutality of his hatred. Tonight was a night no one would ever forget.

14 What You've Been Waiting For

"Good evening ladies and gentlemen, boys and girls! Welcome to Lanstark City! My name is Zeus Clementine and TONIGHT is *the* night that you've been waiting for!" Zeus yelled with expert precision of words and emotion going into each of them as the camera panned him to reveal his shimmering navy and gold suit. He stood on a glittering stage inside a magnificent arena, filled beyond capacity with *thousands* of people.

"That's right, folks. Tonight, in less than two hours you get to witness one of the biggest rivalries ever seen in the history of the sport of wrestling come to a finale. Yes, I know it is slightly disappointing. But I think the question on all of our minds is who will win? Am. I. Right?" The cameras panned to show the thousands of screaming fans waving, their costumes almost as flamboyant as the world's richest talk show host. Seas of red, white and blue blended in with the seas of red and gold as everyone tried to catch a glimpse of Zeus.

"Some say that every year on this night there is not an inch to spare next to any TV or hologram anywhere around the world. Seeing the hundreds of thousands before me and the many more filling up Caesar stadium at this very moment, I can honestly say that I believe this statement. Despite the incalculable amount of questions floating in all of our minds right now, there is one we know the answer to!" He yelled, as though more excited than the thousands around him.

"Tonight history will be made!" He bellowed. The roar of the crowd amplified as Zeus's bright white teeth emerged as his mouth drew into a smile. He pointed at the audience who screamed even louder. Girls with tears smearing their makeup could now be seen on the big screens behind him.

The camera then panned to the thousands of people who looked like tiny dots amongst the enormous silver and black building that illuminated the Lanstark City skyline. The world's biggest phenomenon was drawing to a close for the year, and everyone wanted a front row seat.

"Just because you're walking behind me does not give you exclusive permission to stare at my rear end." Violet snapped, glancing back at Tyler.

"Well how about I walk next to you then?" Tyler smiled, speeding up to walk alongside of her. "I do believe we need to develop our relationship anyway!"

"Our *relationship* huh?" She chuckled.

"Yeah!" Tyler began, a big smile on his face. "You know my name and probably everything about me but all I know is your... name?"

She rolled her eyes. "My name is Violet."

"Violet." Tyler repeated. "Beautiful."

"Thank you, Tyler. But before you get your hopes up, I don't date younger men."

"For now." Tyler threw her a wink. "So Violet, can you tell me what the top secret plan is for tonight? You guys left me in the dark for the party last night and I don't think it turned out well."

She laughed. "Well, I will let you in on a secret, we are going to your room right now if you really must know. It's a big night for us! We have to get you all dressed up in your glorified spandex! On a serious note, I know how stressful a wrestling match on its own can be, so I could only imagine your nerves right now!"

In that moment, Tyler gained a massive amount of respect for her. She was the first person to actually acknowledge that! A wrestling match alone was a major play on one's nerves. Tack on the fact that it was for the championship that was being broadcast to one billion people, and oh by the way there are these two ancient orders using you and you have yourself a nerve casserole.

"It is actually. Thank you." He said in appreciation. As they walked through the long chrome walled corridors, he passed pictures of former TOC champions. They than reached the picture that represented the final match tonight, its large frame empty. He stopped for a second when they came to

Alfredo Lopezzi's picture. He thought about how his life might have turned out if it had not been cut so short. Would he have ended up like Alfredo?

"But I am slightly confused."

"About?"

"You said it was a big night for *us*."

"Here we are." Violet said pointing to his dressing room. He stared at her until she shot him a glare so scary he decided to let it go. He turned to look at the door. Sure enough on the door *Tyler Mason* was inscribed on a gold plaque.

He pressed his thumb against the keypad, and the door slid open revealing his quarters before the match. A hologram of TV controls floated above the table, the walls were tinted a light metallic gold color, and the furniture was all black. He turned to Tavy.

"Thanks?"

"Absolutely." She said. "Jason and Monty should be around soon. Good luck."

"Yeah." He was tired of people wishing him for tonight.

"Oh and one more thing," She said, glancing back at him. "Don't lose your head."

More riddles. Tyler thought. He was never going to get an answer out of any of them was he? Maybe this was part of some cruel test they were putting him through to see if he was worthy to be a part of...well, whatever it is they were a part of. Hadn't he proven he was trustworthy already?

He threw his jacket on the couch and looked at the person who was staring back at him from the mirror on the wall. He thought back to the person he was a mere four days ago.

How trivial that something as common as money was able to make it onto the top of his list of priorities. So perhaps he owed Casper Lanstark a thank you. Casper had saved him from becoming just like him. Tonight he was going to show him that the people of the world were not pawns to play with on a chessboard.

He walked into the washroom, and on the table was his gear for tonight. His signature jet-black Nims lay on the table with gold lacing and *TM* sewed onto the back of them. His singlet matched his shoes, jet black with gold stitching traveling up and down it. But on the front was something new…a huge gold eagle.

Not an eagle that looked vicious and powerful like the TOC's. This one looked…happier if that made sense. He was perched as if about to blast off the ground and take flight. He felt a spark inside of him as he took the image in. He nodded his head, smiling. He couldn't possibly stop the power of Venom tonight. And he was at peace with that. Tyler lifted up the singlet and a small piece of paper tumbled out.

He picked it up and unfolded it to find a variety of different handwritings drawn on it.

Good Luck Tyler. If you don't screw this up, everything should be fine.

- *Percival*

Sorry about him mate. See you soon.
-Alvis

Sorry about Percival Ty. Don't lose yourself out there.

- *Alekto*

Tyler, stay contempt out there. Any tactical errors will cost us. You need to do this.

-Deimos

You already know us. Can't wait to see what you do now that it is your turn!

- Orvar and Girisha

A surge of happiness filled his heart. While it was true that he really didn't know who most of these people were, this note gave him hope. It made him feel like he wasn't alone in this. And according to note, he would see them *soon*, whatever that meant? Maybe they would be there watching tonight.

Tyler slowly got dressed, feeling as though he was a gladiator assembling his armor as he prepared to enter the arena and fight for his life. His nerves rattled as the sounds of the crowd began to get louder and louder. He was wrestling for the *championship*.

Tyler laughed at this thought. "I am wrestling for the *championship* baby!"

With everything that had gone on during the week, he hadn't stopped even once to consider that amazing thought. *Appreciate the small things Tyler.* Nana had always said that. If only she could be here today. He hoped to see her again.

He was tempted to turn on the Hologram, but decided against it. He really preferred not to have to listen to hundreds of different reporters predict his defeat. Dei was after all, the fear of the East. Undefeated, calculating, and brutal. Some of his past opponents had come out of matches looking like they had been in a boxing match rather than a wrestling one, especially if they upset him in some way.

With what had conspired between the two of them in recent events, he thought it was safe to assume Dei probably hated him. So much of his attention had been spent on all the absurdity this week that he had done no research on Dei at all.

Let it go Tyler. There is nothing you can do about it now.

He finished tying his shoes and stood up and walked to the mirror. For one of the many countless time in his life, he observed himself. He studied the outlines of his face, his dark curly hair, and his arms. It was funny how humans judged each other by observing as he was now. Really they should be concerned with what was underneath.

The boy with a heart.

Did he really deserve that title? Whether he did or not, he would earn it tonight. He thought about a life after this. Was there going to be one? He had so much living to do yet. What if he snuck out the back? Would anyone notice his disappearance once he blended in with the chaos on the streets? Who would care? Slowly, an image of a heart began to form in his head, but it was not the kind you would see in a science book. Rather one that had been crafted out of love. Little Alysha had given it to him. She had been faced with the idea of dying a lot longer than he had. But you would never know it when you met her.

All the odds were against her, just like him. And yet despite her fragile body, the tough treatment she had endured, and the number the doctors gave her until her time would be up she was one of the most hopeful people he had ever met.

And she would be there tonight, cheering for him. Did he really want to turn his back on her?

He heard a scanning noise coming from the hall and suddenly the door slid open and yet again Tyler found himself poised to defend himself if necessary.

"But those down before you hurt yourself! It is just us old men here!" Jason Teach laughed as he glided into the room. Despite everything, he seemed calmer than Tyler had imagined. The only thing that was weird to Tyler was that his black tuxedo seemed to be slightly more… bulky tonight.

Did Jason put on fifteen pounds in a night?

"How are you feeling champ?" Monty asked with a strange conviction about him. "Are you ready to bring this one home?"

"I'm as ready as I will ever be!" Tyler stated. He was ready to go. It really didn't matter if he lost this match, all he wanted to do show he still had heart. No one had ever stood up to Dei and been happy about it. This was his time.

"Good to hear champ. It is time someone gave Dei a licking. I have no doubt that this will be the biggest wrestling match in history." Monty said as he gave a smile. "Jason, I have to run and check in with our guests."

"Let me know if anything comes up." Jason replied.

Monty nodded. "Tyler, do me one favor."

"Anything Monty."

"Just kick his ass."

"Absolutely!" Tyler smiled.

With that, Monty disappeared into the hall.

Jason touched his ear. "Alright, I'll let him know. They are on their way bud. It's time."

"*They?*"

"Security. Apparently they are worried about some 'rambunctious fans' trying to break in and get to you."

"Do you really believe that?"

"Of course not! But who cares. Tyler, they are going to come at you with everything they can tonight."

"Jason—

"Make sure you are grasping what I am saying when I say *everything* Tyler. You can bet that Lanstark has had conversations with Mr. Jie to play on his emotions like he did with you."

"How…"

"Tyler please!" Jason burst. "Please, can we focus on what is important?" He pleaded. His voice was calm again. "Whatever you do, don't let it rattle you. That is all they want, for you to be rattled and lose the match. Anything you say about them after that will just look like slander because you lost."

"Jason, I can't just let them walk all over me! It isn't right and it isn't fair!"

"Promise me that no matter what happens out there, you will be the boy I know you are."

Tyler closed his eyes and took a deep breath. "I promise."

"Having some last minute pep talks are we?" Alfredo Lopezzi stood in the door, flanked by black clad guards carrying… assault rifles? Why were these necessary to control rambunctious fans?

"I guess I missed the memo saying that employees could storm into private VIP rooms didn't I, Alfredo?" Jason mocked Lopezzi, his eyes still locked with Tyler's.

" If I recall *I* am the one who got the promotion Jason." Alfredo hissed as he welcomed himself into the room.

Jason smiled almost mischievously. "It was never about the promotion, Alfredo."

"The loser always makes excuses to the winner, Jason."

"And the winner always assumes the loser has lost, Alfredo."

"You never have gotten over the fact that I have always been ahead of the game, Jason. And now you've prepped this poor young sheep for slaughter, no offense, Tyler."

"None taken, Mr. Lopezzi. After all, the loser always makes excuses to the winner, and considering I have trampled your records, I see why you are so sour, *sir*."

Jason's face lit up while Alfredo's truly did sour. "How dare you. I—" Alfredo stopped as if choosing his words more carefully. "Bask in your glory while you can, tonight you have to face your true test of greatness." He turned to Jason. "As for you, count your blessings." With that he led Tyler out the door to the guards.

"Will do." Jason snapped as he jumped to his feet. "Blessing number one: you're leaving."

Alfredo stopped, his fists clenched. However, he did not say anything and continued out of the room. Tyler turned to catch one last glance at Jason.

"I'll see you out there, champ!"

15 **Six Minutes**

The crowd roared with such fury that vents rattled as Tyler and his escorts made their way down the chrome halls. It sounded like a thousand mini marbles bouncing up and down, echoing through the endless metal tunnels until the sound escaped with the cold air from the air conditioning and met his ears. He could feel the anticipation in the air.

The night everyone had been waiting for had finally arrived.

He still couldn't believe the amount of people chanting his name. When he thought about where he started, an underdog from nowhere to be here now in this moment was unreal. It was every young wrestler's dream to compete in the TOC.

Since it started, the Tournament of Champions had transformed itself into the ultimate advertising, entertainment, and athletic arena, leading to its domination of pop culture. It always seemed like a far off thought in his head when he used to lie in bed, imagining what it would be like to wrestle on the world's biggest stage.

So when a man, whose crooked smile approached him on a chilly fall day, Tyler knew opportunity had come knocking. The man with a crooked smile was none other than Jason Teach. After that meeting, everything seemed to flow perfectly. It was as if all the forces of the universe agreed this was his path to take, some may call it fate.

Alfredo Lopezzi held his finger to his ear. "Got it." He turned to Tyler, a satisfied expression on his face. "It's time, Mr. Mason. Are you ready to change the course of mankind?"

"As ready as I'll ever be." Tyler spoke calmly.

"These gentlemen will escort you to your hoverpad." He began to walk away. "Oh, and one more thing, Ty," He stopped. "When did you plan on telling Cailey goodbye?"

Tyler felt like he had just been punched in the gut. If more confirmation on the fakeness of their relationship was needed, that was it. He felt one of the guards nudge him with their rifle. "Alright!"

Up until today, he had considered all of the events of the week exquisite misfortune. Today however, he viewed it as a blessing. 99% of the world had no idea what was happening behind the scenes. Not only did he know, he had the ability to change the course of the events. While he was frightened of what would happen when he resisted Casper and Venom, (he could see himself getting shot on the spot) adrenaline coursed through his veins at the thought of it all.

They reached the hoverpad. Or what was supposed to be a hoverpad? There was a rectangular cut out in the floor with a shaft going above ground. Where was the pad? He turned to the guards, who did nothing but stare back silently.

"Step forward." One of them commanded from behind his black mask, finally breaking the silence.

His voice is really light for a guard.

Suddenly Tyler had a terrible idea formulate in his head. *I am about to die?* Was this it? All that hard work for nothing! "Whoa we can solve this another way guys I—

"Step forward NOW!" The other one commanded, his voice deeper and far more intimidating. He raised his gun so it was level with Tyler's chest. The other one followed.

"You can't do this. They're expecting me!" Tyler struggled for a way to get out of this.

"Oh yes we can. Now step forward and stop making this any harder than it has to be."

Tyler took a deep breath. All of this for it to end like this? No, Jason would have seen this coming and stopped him from going, right? Tyler closed his eyes and stepped forward, trying to brace himself for a blistering cold piece of metal to end his life.

"Finally." The deeper voice guard said. "All of this commotion just to get on a damn hoverpad."

What? Tyler peeked at the floor through closed eyelids. It looked like nothing more than the outline of a hovering rectangle. Suddenly, the outline began to glow a bright white and Tyler stumbled as the thing began to rise. Of course! It was

172

similar to the one from *The Common Club*. A wave of relief went over him as he began floating upward. The closer he got to the surface, the louder the roars of the crowd became. Echoes of Zeus Clementine's voice could be heard throughout the stadium, along with the other announcers he was with.

He had no idea what to expect. He thought it wouldn't be that bad because he had seen it on TV, but being here proved to him just how wrong he was.

The hoverpad reached the end of the tunnel and he was suddenly above ground. As soon as the crowd saw him they began to scream thunderously.

"There he is ladies and gentlemen! Tyler Mason of the United States of America!" Zeus Clementine's voice boomed, echoing in every direction around the goliath-sized stadium.

It was unlike anything Tyler had ever imagined. His hoverpad rose up to be level with the fourth row of seats, but there were hundreds of rows rising up toward the night sky. The stadium formed a huge circle where his hoverpad had risen up from the ground before meshing into what looked like a hallway that lead to the center of the arena and the wrestling mat that hovered in the middle. Colossal screens that had live feed of him right now stood on the top of the stadium. Below the screens were thousands of fans forming a screaming sea decked out in black and gold. In the distance beyond the wrestling mat, he could see the arena took on a similar shape similar to what it did here. Was that where Dei would emerge?

He felt a jerk and stumbled to catch his balance as his hoverpad slowly began to move forward. He had to force himself to remember to wave to the crowd, still in awe of the sheer magnitude of how many people were here. He nodded and smiled at some people down in the first row, they yelled back, all dressed up in costumes with face paint outlining their eyes.

But today there was something new. Each fan had what looked like a poster board, except it wasn't paper. They looked like giant smart tablets. The crowd would start a chant until it caught on, and than all of them would hold up their tablets next to the other in unison. Together it formed a giant image. Glowing on the tablets right now was a video of Tyler himself, dressed in his uniform staring at the real Tyler. A bald eagle flew and perched itself on his shoulder on the screens as fireworks erupted. It was one of the most amazing things he had ever seen. The energy of the crowd was surging through his veins.

All these people had no idea what was really happening here. They deserved a chance, a chance to live their life the way they wanted, and give all he had to ensure they get it.

Now was his time.

"Weighing in yesterday at 162 pounds, Mason is the slimmest we have seen him all season. Does this mean he is faster or has he just been skipping some gym sessions?"

"Well, Zeus I can tell you right now that despite what the critics say, I think that Mason will put up more of a fight to Dei than we imagine."

"It's great that you have so much faith in the boy, Daniel."

Despite the enormity of the speakers in the arena, Tyler did not hear a single word they were saying. He was too transfixed with the swarms of people. Girls hooped and hollered to him, while boys ripped their shirts. But he was looking for one very special audience member...one brave little girl.

He scanned the crowd as fast as his eyes would allow. Though it was not the girl, they did catch something, however. A suite above all the other seats, with a large golden eagle fiercely looking down on everyone below. There was no doubt of who was in that box.

His hoverpad stopped in the center of the arena near the wrestling mat. He was surrounded on all sides by screaming fans who held up there giant tablets with even more moving pictures of him...at least up until the sea of U.S. fans ended. Chinese fans shouted in victory as Dei approached from the other end, making no effort to wave to the crowd. His headgear already on, Dei had a vicious look in his eyes as he glared at one person: Tyler.

The Chinese fans were dressed in red and gold, Dei's colors, as they held up their tablets displaying Dei with dragons floating behind him. Tyler looked to his left, Zeus and the other announcers sat behind a desk, a large golden eagle on the front of their hoverpad.

Zeus's voice became more apparent to Tyler as his focus on looking for little Alysha slowly dwindled.

"Look at him! And weighing in at 165 pounds on the dot there is no doubt Dei Jie is really pushing just how muscular he can be. Another ounce heavier and he would not have been aloud to wrestle, as he would have been over weight!" Zeus shouted.

"I'll tell you, Zeus he looks more serious and determined right now than he has the entire tournament. I would hate to be that person on the mat with him."

"Oh I agree, Daniel. And to add to that point *Wrestler's Weekly* released a poll this week where people were asked to pick who would win this super match."

"What came out of it Zeus?"

"I can tell you that it is not looking good for Mr. Mason. The polls showed a whopping 80% of people believe Jie will win."

All the bug spray in the world could not control the butterflies in Tyler's stomach right now. As he stepped onto the center of the mat, he felt as though he was at the center of the world. Everyone was watching. He spotted Jason and Monty on a hoverpad to his left. They nodded reassuringly. *Don't worry guys, I got this...*

Dei and Tyler walked to the center of the mat. The referee began examining both of them, making sure there were no ointments on their skin and nothing in their headgear. During this entire period of time, Dei and Tyler did not break eye contact.

The referee was called to the corner of the mat by the other official, leaving the two of them virtually alone except for the hovering camera that circled them, projecting their images onto the big screens in the stadium and millions of TV's around the world.

"Ready to be embarrassed Mason? You don't belong here!" Dei snarled.

"What makes you think you're so entitled Jie?"

175

"We were born different. It's in our blood."

"You're right. You were born with a silver spoon in your mouth and I've had to work for everything I have."

Dei clenched his fist. "How dare you question my honor!"

"I have no problem doing it again, either."

With that they turned their back to each other and paced, waiting for the referee to begin the biggest wrestling match ever. Tyler could think of doing nothing more than ripping Dei's face right off, until he noticed one last hoverpad floating toward the mat. There was a woman on it.

One Tyler knew *very* well.

Angry and confused he watched as Cailey walked toward Dei Jie. She gave a pat on the shoulder and said something to him. Rage bubbled inside of him, like lava in a volcano. He felt himself slowly slipping into a rage only felt in a man's heart when it involves a woman. If he had looked up at Casper Lanstark, he would have seen the wicked smile etched on the man's face.

Cailey began walking toward Tyler. The expression on her face was a riddle, even to the boy who had been dating her for a year. Her dress was a deep black with what looked like glistening white feathers sticking out all over. Her nails and makeup were jet black with hints of white: a very deceptive angel.

"Cailey what are you doing here and what the *hell* was that?" Tyler stammered with anger.

As if she didn't even hear what he said, she gave him a hug and whispered in his ear, "Good luck, Tyler." Her tone grew even quieter and he strained to hear what she said over the sound of the crowd. "Don't forget the cameras are *on*." She squeezed him tightly, and gave him a kiss before returning to a hoverpad that carried her away.

"What a nice exchange between young love there, Zeus."

"Yes indeed, Daniel. I'm sure that exchange just calmed Tyler's nerves in the presence of all of this."

Tyler felt as though he wanted to scream in rage and throw up in confusion at the same time. What? When? How? *Who?* He was desperately confused now. He was desperate for answers and desperate to be out of the spotlight and back to the safety of a normal life and out of this madness.

"You can't tell me that wasn't on purpose! He hasn't seen her in days, Jason! And she suddenly shows up out of random *and* gives talks to Dei?" Monty hissed.

"There is nothing we can do now, Lester. It is on him." Jason said calmly.

They were all in here.

Tyler felt himself starting to hyperventilate. He had to calm down. He felt like the reality of the situation had finally come crashing down on his shoulders and on top of that his heart felt as though it had been stung. *Composure, Tyler, keep your composure!* The words were useless as his mental state continued to deteriorate. The referee walked to the center of the mat, signaling Dei and Tyler to join him and shake hands. Tyler stumbled to the center while Dei pounced like a wolf ready for attack.

"What is going on with Mason, Zeus?"

"I'm not sure, Daniel. It'd be a shame if he is having second thoughts about this now when the world is watching."

"Shake hands." The referee commanded. Tyler shook Dei's hand, and as soon as the whistle blew he felt as though he was forced onto a roller coaster, doing nothing but going through loops with no way off.

Immediately Dei's forearm came crashing down on the back of Tyler's neck, rattling his brain to the core. Instinctively Tyler threw his arms up in defense, opening his legs to Dei's attack. The next thing he knew he was on the ground and already down 2-0. The Chinese fans went wild, holding up their tablets to show a montage of Dei's most famous takedowns. The U.S. fans booed in disappointment.

"Well, as of now, Las Vegas odds are standing true." Zeus commented as he looked on.

Tyler felt lost. His heart was racing, his head was pounding, and all he wanted was to be somewhere else in the world. Anywhere else.

Tyler was able to resist Dei's barrage of attacks to turn him to his back and pin him, which would have won him the match. Struggling, he worked his hips up, and got to his feet to go toe to toe with Dei, yet again. The score was now 2-1 for the escape. Tyler resisted more attacks and took a shot of his own, but was way off the mark. Dei just laughed and attacked Tyler's head again, slashing his forearm across Tyler's face. Blood spewed from his mouth before he caught a punch to the stomach as Dei ran his forehead into Tyler's gut and smashed him to the ground.

"Well I have to tell you, Zeus, Tyler doesn't even look like he's with us."

"He looks as though he doesn't want to be here, Daniel."

Tyler was staring into the crowd, but he wasn't looking at them. He was seeing stars as he tried to figure out how they all ended up in this game that they were playing. Dei cracked his elbow into the back of Tyler's skull, but even that didn't wake him up from his daze. Everything Dei was doing was illegal, and yet the referee said nothing. Did nothing. They all were against him. He was fighting a losing battle.

Why try?

The buzzer rang and Dei pushed his weight on Tyler as he got up. "You don't belong here, fool! Ahaha!" Dei snarled as he strut to his end of the mat. Tyler stumbled to his feet, before retreating to his own side. The audience was screaming many different things at him. But he didn't hear a word; despite all the noise he had never experienced such silence in his entire life.

"Tyler! Tyler, are you okay? What's the matter? Come on kid you got this! The score is only 4-1." Monty yelled as he slapped Tyler's shoulder. Jason did not get up however. He sat on his chair on the hoverpad without uttering a word. It was as if he was waiting…hoping for something. Did he have a plan? Tyler really hoped so. Jason stared at him before looking up at something behind him. Tyler knew exactly what he was staring at: the box where Casper Lanstark was perched.

The referee whistled before flipping the coin to decide who would got to choose the starting position for the next period, a custom in the sport of wrestling. Surprisingly, Tyler won the coin toss. Perhaps, despite everything today being rigged against him, something was on his side, even if it was a piece of metal.

Tyler differed, meaning Dei received choice for this period, and Tyler would get choice in the final period of the match. Dei chose neutral, where each wrestle would start on their feet.

They went back to the center of the mat, where the sound of the whistle left Tyler's right ear writhing as the noise bounced off his eardrum. Dei immediately moved in for the attack.

"Daniel, your boy seems to be defending better this period, but I can't help but notice he has come out flat, yet again."

"It's easy to kick a man when he is down, Zeus. The score is only 4-1, and with Tyler's history you never know what could happen."

Dei faked a shot and brought the top of his head into Tyler's face. Tyler screeched in pain as a shot of blood erupted from his face, but the referee did not stop the match. Dei dove into Tyler's gut and drove him straight into the mat.

"You better make that 6-1 now, Daniel." Zeus commented, a satisfied look on his face.

"The referee should have stopped the match, that was a *clear* violation of the rules. They are not being fair!" Zeus shot Daniel a dark look.

"Well Daniel, mistakes are made everyday. The only difference is some have consequences."

On the mat, Tyler was completely unfocused. The crowd shouted their frustration but it seemed to have no effect. Tyler continued to glance blankly into the crowd while Dei continued his abuse on top. Tyler tried struggling to his feet, but he seemed to have lost his will, falling bluntly back to the mat.

The buzzer rang, and a triumphant Dei Jie got off of him and raised his arms in victory shouting, "I told you all! He doesn't belong here! He will never be on my level!" He proclaimed while pointing a finger at Tyler as he turned and spat on him.

Tyler didn't seem to notice. He worked his way up to his knees and looked blankly into the crowd, yet again.

His heart skipped a beat.

There she was.

She looked so innocent, staring at him with puffy red eyes from the front row. On her shirt was a heart stitched to the front, with her little hands clasped together. Of all the unrelenting dark that surrounded Tyler in the arena today, she was his light. It felt as though someone had slapped him, and he suddenly realized everything that had happen to him over the last two periods.

He winked at little Alysha and rose to his feet.

Monty sat looking on in horror over the last two periods. And with the way Dei had been treating Tyler, Monty could just see the look of embarrassment overtaking the U.S. President's face. Surely, there would be consequences. "It's all over, Jason." Monty squeaked. The color had drained from his face, he felt as though he was about to throw up.

"There it is!" Jason exclaimed hitting his shoulder. "THERE IT IS, LESTER!"

"What?" Monty asked in confusion. It was very rare for Lester Monty to miss anything tactical, so the fact that Jason has seen something before him was a surprise.

"IT." Jason beamed.

"What is *that*?" Daniel questioned as he observed Tyler.

"What is what?" Zeus asked.

"Don't you see it?"

"See what?"

"The change in his posture!"

"Daniel, what in Lanstark's name are you talking about?"

Tyler stood up straight and firm, wiping the spit off of him. He directed his gaze directly at Dei. When Dei turned around from waving to the crowd his expression changed, not expecting to face the determined set of eyes that were locked with his own. The referee asked Tyler what position he wanted to start the final period of the match in.

"Neutral." Tyler raised a confident brow.

There were gasps in the crowd.

He knew exactly what he was about to do. He was going to show the world he was not weak, and that he did belong here. They would rue the day they were ignorant enough to think they could step on the 'little' people of the world.

The whistle blew and Tyler faked a shot in on Dei and brought his elbow slicing across Dei's face, making a devastating impact with his nose. Dei let out a cry of surprise.

The referee quickly blew the whistle and began yelling at Tyler, but none of the words registered to Tyler's auditory receptors in his brain. He was still focused on Dei, who was getting his bloody nose cared for by the medical staff. The referee issued a warning on Tyler.

"What is that? They definitely did not issue any warnings on Dei for any of the punches he threw earlier! I'm seeing favoritism here!"

"Daniel, please that is a very serious accusation! Perhaps the referee didn't see it before."

"Yes well he must be blind."

It turned out the referee had awarded Dei a penalty point, making the score 7-1.

"Say what you will Daniel, but with one minute and fifty eight seconds left, it is clear to anyone that Dei Jie will be the next Champion of the TOC. Look! You can already see the Chinese fans projecting it on their tablets."

It could not be said that the same joy was being felt on the mat. Abandoning his waving and celebration, Dei stomped to the center of the mat with a glare that would have frightened Tyler on any other day, but not today.

A 7-1 victory would not satisfy Dei. He wanted to humiliate Tyler. He wanted to destroy him. And now Tyler had drawn blood.

This was war.

The whistle blew and Dei charged at Tyler with the force of a freight train, but Tyler dodged it —narrowly, avoiding the loss of breath that would have cost him the rest of the match.

Dei turned and ran at him again going for a take down that Tyler sidestepped.... but only by the skin of teeth. Frustrated, Dei reshot let out a cry of rage as he shot again and tripped on his shoe, jumping back up as if his life depended on it.

Tyler brought the match back to the center of the mat, trying to set up a shot to prevent Dei from staying on the edge of the mat. Dei seemed to be moving more cautiously than he had just moments ago. Seeing this, Tyler felt even more energized and moved, it was now he who brought his hands smashing on the back of Dei's neck.

"Wow Zeus, it looks like Tyler's confidence continues to grow while Dei's continues to retreat."

Zeus gritted his teeth, and in a rarely seen moment, the TV personality found that things were not going his way.

Tyler took a half shot at Dei's ankle, but Dei saw it coming and with lighting effectiveness he quickly dodged his foot out of the way. However he did not attack while Tyler continued to press his assault.

"Despite any possible shift in momentum, there are only thirty seconds left on the clock, Daniel. If Tyler is going to have a chance of doing anything, he needs to do it now." Zeus commented.

"I wouldn't be so down Zeus, you know what they say."

"No I don't ."

"Nothing is over until it's over."

"Twenty seconds." An automated voice boomed, filling the arena. The crowd was absolutely ridiculous, on their feet taunting the other side.

The look on Dei's face was one rarely seen on the champion of the East. Confidence was replaced with what looked like a mixture of distress and fear. Out of nowhere Dei swung his elbow around and nailed Tyler square in the face.

182

Inside Tyler's stomach the sparks of anger transformed into a forest fire fueling the pain in his head. Dei brought both of his arms up as if he saw the flame of anger take over Tyler's being.

In that moment Tyler saw an opportunity to hit one of the most basic wrestling shots there was— all he had to do was pop Dei's arms and he could hit a double leg takedown, a football tackle with slightly more finesse. Without thinking, Tyler blasted Dei's arm skyward and threw himself at his legs.

Dei let out a gasp so loud it could be heard over the crowd. Dei slammed onto the mat gasping for air on his back.

Flat on his back!

Tyler locked up, holding him there with all his might! This was it! If he could pin him, the match would be his no matter the score! Dei pushed up and swung his hands at Tyler's face trying to get up. Tyler's sweaty grip was starting to slip as he struggled to fight.

"Five seconds." The automated voice boomed.

Tyler closed his eyes. They weren't going to give it to him. Lanstark had rigged this so well that even though Dei should have been pinned here, the referee would not call it. Hope sank from his heart as his grim fate matched that of the worlds.

The whistle blew, signifying the end of the match.

Tyler collapsed off of Dei in defeat.

I blew it.

He opened his eyes to see the referee slam his hand on the mat… signifying a pin. A pin!

He had *won*!

16 Aftermath

What just happened?

Everything was a blur as adrenaline surged through his veins like a dangerously overcharged battery. He looked to the crowd for help. The U.S. side was going absolutely nuts while the Chinese side began to falter. The adrenaline finally became too much and Tyler found his feet carrying him around the mat like lightning in triumph. He raised his arms in the air and yelled with the crowd!

Now it was *his* turn to humiliate his rival. It was *his* turn to brag about his glory. And he couldn't wait. He stopped running but continued to hold his hands up in triumph, and that is when their eyes met.

Lanstark sat in his box smiling. Tyler's pent-up anger began to fade as he watched the smile that crossed the man's face. It was a look of utter satisfaction.

Keep going, Tyler. You are almost done. Lanstark's voice haunted him. Slowly, his arms fell to his sides.

Tyler turned to see the pathetic image that lay across the mat. Dei Jie had rolled over onto his stomach and lay with his head buried in his hands. The United States fans, seeing they finally had a leg up over China's wrestling team, continued to taunt the Chinese fans who sent insulting signals back there way. The rowdiness in the stadium could be felt by anybody.

Tyler took one step toward Dei and the crowd went berserk.

"Show him who is boss, Tyler!"

"It's about time we teach them a lesson!"

"We will always be better!"

"Well Zeus, what do you have to say for yourself now? Your eggs were in the wrong basket." Daniel Louis mocked Zeus. What he didn't see was that Zeus had a similar smirk on his face as his boss did.

"Perhaps Daniel, perhaps. But sometimes things work out better when they don't go as plan."

184

Tyler tapped on the sweaty shoulder of his rival. As if knowing his turn had come, Dei slowly rolled over. The look on his face sent chills through Tyler's spine. The confident and hungry young man he had seen minutes before seemed to have disappeared completely, replaced with a distraught, frightened expression. His shoulders seemed to sag even more from the weight of shame that had been placed on them.

"Go ahead. Do it." Dei croaked, trying to keep his tough persona.

All the things Dei did to Tyler played through his head like a movie: the insult about his parents at the party, the taunts, and the fight. The temptation of hitting Dei in the face grew hotter and hotter. He clenched his fist, ready to take ten months of anger out on this spoiled oaf.

He felt his muscles begin to tighten as he wound his arm up. He was so ready for this. Dei deserved as much, just like he, Tyler deserved to do it, right?

Somehow, through every image in his mind right now, the image of Casper Lanstark smiling managed to squeeze into his head. That cold, evil smile stuck. He stood, frozen. The weight of the repercussions for what he was about to do seemed to formulate like a massive weight on his arm. He looked down at Dei, curled up in a defensive position.

Slowly Dei began to peer out to see what fate had in store for him.

"What are you doing?" came Dei's surprised reply as he stared at Tyler's outstretched hand.

"I'm putting our past behind us." Tyler had to force the words out of his mouth, but they still came out.

"What are you doing? You're throwing away everything." Dei questioned.

"No, he doesn't care about either of us. We are just pawns to get what he wants done. But if we do this, if we stick together... maybe we end this."

Dei stared long and hard at Tyler's hand as if beginning to realize Tyler was right. Slowly, he began to raise his hand.

Tyler tightened his grip as he felt Dei's sweaty palm take his. He felt the urge to do what he believed the punk deserved, but what if he was no more than a misguided puppet himself? To the surprise of everyone in the arena he pulled Dei up to his feet. There was absolute silence in the arena for the first time in TOC history. Tyler quickly turned to see the smile washed off Casper's face, replaced with a scowl that looked more furious then Tyler had ever hoped to see.

Well, you've done it Tyler. You've managed to piss off the world's most evil man. But hey, if a difference was made it was worth it. You've finally done something worth doing.

Tyler's eyes searched for Alysha in the crowd. Everyone was standing still, as if they didn't know what to do. Just like a bright little flower, she stood beaming at him. She gave him two thumbs up and shouted as loud as her little voice could manage, but thanks to the silence everyone heard it. "You did the right thing, Tyler. We love you!"

She clapped with great joy, her tiny hands echoing their call throughout the arena. Hesitantly, her mom began to join her.

People were reluctant at first, but emotions and biases were slowly replaced with rationality and soul as people realized it was the right thing to do. A ripple effect seemed to set in, and soon the entire stadium was clapping. Tyler gazed around in awe at the extraordinary event as the entire stadium cheered in unison. But the bad feeling in the pit of his stomach kept growing more and more, like a fleet of black clouds encroaching on a rainy day.

He turned to Dei and even he was clapping! Except he wasn't looking at Tyler— he was looking up to box...toward Lanstark. Now, more than ever Tyler was terrified of him. As they met eyes, Lanstark's scowl deepened. He shook his head very slowly at Tyler.

Casper rose to his feet, buttoned his suit jacket, and nodded.

Tyler spun around as if urgently trying to find a sudden attacker or men with guns coming after him.

But there was nothing.

Relief flooded him, and he began to smile as fans shouted and cheered to him in joy.

"Hey man that was a really brave thing you did out there!" A guy with spiked hair and sunglasses shouted.

"We are all one, the sooner we realize that, the better!" Howled another.

"Hey champ, my daughter was watching from home tonight, thank you for setting a good example for her!" A mother yelled.

Gently, a tear began to slip from his eye. He proved he was the boy with a heart. Not just to them, but to himself. The scene gave him an ideal of hope. Mankind could still come together, no matter the differences.

The silence of the announcers began to bother Tyler. Where were they?

Had Lanstark been bluffing the entire time? He looked in his corner. Where were Jason and Monty?

He was ready get to kick the dust on this city and head back home, away from these egotistical, power hungry billionaires. None of the money or fame would have ever brought him sense of purpose Alysha did today. He would take her home with Jason and Monty, getting her all the help she needed.

Tyler signaled over a hoverpad. He was ready to end this chapter of his life. He had thought he wanted all of this, but he was wrong. He faced Dei, ready to say his goodbyes. He didn't really care to stay for the victory ceremony.

What was that?

A piercing howl ripped through the usual sounds of the evening, a wave of panic going up his skin and through the crowd as everyone tried to figure out what was going on.

Tyler was the first to know.

A splash of red liquid splashed from Dei's chest with ferocity like water when smashed into rock. Tyler eyes locked with Dei's. Within seconds, Dei's life had come to an end. Darkness overtook the stadium as the lights went out, nothing but tiny emergency lights flickered on. The cameras collapsed powerless in their places. Tyler took a step toward Dei until he heard another piercing sound while the crowd went up in screams. As if fueled by instinct, his feet began to move as he started running. He could see rows of black clad figures begin to poor into the crowd.

A rush of air sliced right by the back of his neck. He imagined the person taking aim at him in their scope; he quickly rotated routes back and forth. There was only one way out of this...he quickened his sprint for the hoverpad that had stopped fifteen feet away from the platform the wrestling mat was on.

If he could just get to that...

A gaping hole in the mat was blasted right in front of him, he stumbled, almost losing his balance. He could swear his chin came within inches of the ground but somehow he managed to stay on his feet only to realize he wasn't going to make the jump.

He had to try.

As soon as he was in the air he heard a tremendous *BOOM*! He felt the brush of extreme heat smack against his exposed skin as it the explosion catapulted him over the hoverpad.

Scream after scream meshed together as an orange glow lit the arena. The ground grew closer, but Tyler was accepting of whatever happened now. He had done his part, for better or worse. Casper was making his move.... it was the end.

As if snapping out of a trance he realized he was nearly forty feet from either hitting cold hard concrete or a soft padded platform. "Argh!" he grunted as his eyes watered from the unforgivable air whipping into them. Shifting his body weight, he hoped to alter his angle so he would survive the fall. A sharp sting dug across his back and he let out a cry and lost focus, as he looked left to see metal shards from another exploding hoverpad flying everywhere.

This was really it. Tyler squeezed his eyes shut, bracing for impact. He felt a soft cushion as he collided with hoverpad, and slid to a halt as he hit the ground.

His back burned, as though someone had scrubbed it with sandpaper. He couldn't move, trapped in his own body. As much as a he resisted, a tear squeezed itself out of his eye.

For a second he almost forgot what was going on as he closed his eyes.

The darkness was very comforting…

The pounding in his head was unbearable. He had never had a concussion before, but he guessed this what they felt like.

Wake up! This is all a dream! None of this real!

Slowly he opened his eyes, hoping to see he was back in Unadventurous Vila. Nana would be down in the kitchen making breakfast for him before school. But it was not a dream.

He was still in Lanstark City.

Parts of the arena had caught on fire from the hoverpad explosions. Most of the people were gone. How long had he been out for? An occasional popping sound here and there could be heard in the night.

He was gasping for air. The wake of a missile glided over him and a deafening sound erupted were Dei had come into the arena from, followed by a massive wave of heat. Twisted pieces of metal flew everywhere, and Tyler saw one that looked like it was coming dangerously close to him. Closer. Closer.

ROLL!

There was a loud smash and the ground shook as Tyler traded places with the chunk of metal.

It was time to go.

Tyler scrambled to his feet and ran for the door along the outer wall of the front row seats. A shower of more metal pieces rained down on the entire portion of the arena he had just been in. A gouge of gnarled metal sat between him and the door to getting out of the arena. He tried to lift, but his body rebelled in more ways than one.

Hope began to fade, as no more exits where in sight. The black clad soldiers were beginning to escort the remaining people out of the arena. Tyler hid behind the metal chunk as a group of soldiers on hoverpads came into the sight from the direction he entered the arena from.

"As soon as possible." The voice from the soldier was very intense, as if everything depended on it. Tyler strained to listen, but explosions in the distance muffled the sound.

"No sign of him, sir." The soldier who looked to be in charge said, his hand up to his ear.

He took his finger off his ear shaking his head.

More explosions rocked the ground, and Tyler pounded the debris in frustration. All the soldiers sped off, leaving the captain. He hovered a bit higher and pulled out a grenade.

Oh no.

Dropping the grenade, he too sped off.

As soon as the grenade hit the ground a wave of fire began engulfing the entire lower part of the arena, coming straight for Tyler. Adrenaline coursed through his veins as Tyler moved with a speed he didn't know he was capable of as he fought to remove the metal out of his way.

The flames were getting closer. Tyler could feel the searing heat on his skin already!

Come on! Come on!

The metal chunk finally began to give as the flames closed the last thirty feet between them. With the strength of all his heart and body, Tyler strained as hard as he could to move the barrier. The flames were less than ten feet away. With the last ounce of strength he had he pushed as hard as he could. Miraculously the metal piece flipped over just in time for him to get inside.

Tyler screamed in agony as he slammed the door shut.

It felt like thousands of little bugs of fire were crawling on his back. The fire had just singed him as he slammed the door shut. Outright exhausted, he collapsed to the floor.

The darkness invited him again.

Gradually, the world started coming back. Panicking, he jumped to his feet, only to be engulfed by the feeling that someone just clunked him upside the head. He fell to his knees gripping his forehead. What on Earth could he do now?

Baby steps Tyler, baby steps.

He observed his surroundings. It looked he was in some kind of suite. From the furniture, to the refreshments, this could have been a five star hotel room.

Gradually, he made it to his feet. His singlet was tattered. He had to find more clothes. His burns couldn't be visible, otherwise they would most likely be exploited. Tyler swung open a closet door, frantically looking for anything to cover his wounds.

Inside were some dress shirts and suits. They would have to do. Tyler shuddered in pain as he surgically removed the tattered materials of his singlet from his body. It took him twenty minutes of grimacing, lip biting, and swearing to get it off. His wounds seared as he brought the dress shirt around and put it on his back.

The cloth stuck to his back as though it was wet.

His hands fumbled and shook as he buttoned the shirt. The ringing in his ear and pounding in his head seemed to get worse every second. He flinched as he heard some screams. A similar process followed to get his jacket on.

At least the pants were easy.

He quickly gulped some water down from the sink before glancing into the mirror. Blood was beginning to stain through the shirt as the fabric stuck to his wounds.

Tyler cautiously made his way out of the room and into the hall, ignoring the water that streamed from bullet holes in the wall.

As he moved further through the complex, he came to a fork ahead. A pool of red liquid slowly slid from the left side. He wanted to tell himself he was wrong about what it was, but as he got closer he saw someone's arm. *What had happened here?*

A sickly feeling took ahold of Tyler as he rounded the corner. At least a dozen bodies were there. *Was this his fault?* This is exactly what he had wanted to avoid when he chose to stand up to Lanstark, and now...

Anger overtook his sorrow. He had to find Jason and get out of here. He stepped forward to—

"Tyler?"

Tyler spun around ready for anything but with a combination of shock, awe, and panic he slipped and fell over, narrowly missing one of the pools of blood. He stumbled to his feet.

"What the *hell* is..." He grunted.

"Tyler please! We don't have time for this!"

"Cailey, I can't even look at you right now!"

"Tyler please...

"No, stay back Cailey! Don't you dare come any closer to me!" Tyler screeched as he stood up. A piece of the shirt snagged off his burn on the back and sent a searing ripple through his wounds. He groaned as he collapsed to the floor.

He needed to relax.

"Tyler..." Cailey threw off her heels and kneeled down. "How did this happen?" Tears streamed from her eyes.

"You... your dad... that's what happened!" Tyler growled weakly. He had just wrestled an entire wrestling match, ran for his life, and narrowly escaped being burned alive.

He was exhausted.

"Tyler please, *listen* to me. It wasn't real." Cailey cried. "Not at first. I admit that. But I fell for *you* Tyler. For this!" She put her hand on his heart.

Tyler didn't know what to think.

"What about what you did in there?" He muffled as the tears slid down his face. "In there when I needed you!" He pointed toward the way he had come, the once majestic arena now in tatters.

"Tyler," Cailey shook her head. "I had no choice. But I am my own person! I am not involved with dad or his company." She pleaded as her makeup followed the path of her tears. "

Tyler looked away. *No you can't. You can't trust her!* The soft familiar touch of Cailey's fingers gently slid down his cheek and turned his head toward hers.

"Tyler, I'm *not* one of them. Not anymore. I'm here now with you, here at the end of it all. We're going to get through this. We just have a little bit further to go." Cailey assured. "But we have to hurry, Tyler! My dad is looking for you!"

Slowly, Tyler let his guard down. Cailey leaned and gave him a warm kiss. It made him feel as though everything would be all right.

Cailey held out her hand. The feeling of loneliness disappeared as she helped him up. Cailey through his arm around her back and they began to walk.

The world was a blur. He closed his eyes, hoping the spinning would stop and he could actually focus again.

It felt like they had been walking forever. Parts of the trip were black...had he passed out? That would have meant Cailey had dragged him all by herself.

"How much... longer?" He murmured, his eyes heavy.

"Not much farther." Cailey said. Perhaps she was running low on breath. He struggled to resist but it was no use.

Tyler fell into darkness again.

He was flying high up into the night sky, the stars lighting his way. He felt his lips curl into a smile. *He was flying! He was actually flying!* Throwing his weight forward, he flew even faster. The glowing city below looked a lot like Lanstark City. He wasn't going back. As fast as he could, he sped toward the water, away from this wretched place. Suddenly, he heard a scream. Tyler wanted more than anything to leave. But the scream seemed to tug him back. He resisted and broke the invisible force. It came back again and this time it took longer for him to fight it off. The third time he panicked as he began falling from the sky...the force was too strong.

"NO! TYLER! DAD DON'T YOU DARE TOUCH HIM!"

A sharp pain banged on the back of his head and back as if he fell. It felt like he had been thrown against something. Had it been the hard concrete of the city streets? Feeling in his hand slowly came back...it didn't feel like concrete. It was cold tile.

An ominous feeling that he was being watched began to take ahold of him. Slowly, he opened his eyes.

He was surrounded on all sides by black clad figures, the TOC logo emblazed in gold on their chests.

17 **Loose Ends**

"What's the matter, champ? Did someone wake you from your slumber?"

There came a derogatory remark from one of the armored figures that stepped forward. Tyler refused to answer, instead opting to glare at the guard. He flinched, but reacted too late and a steal toe boot came smashing into his stomach. His throat stung as he coughed up blood.

"Now, now." Came a familiar voice. "Let's be nice, boys, there will be more of that later. For now let's just have a talk with Mr. Mason." The guards cleared a path in their circle. As they did, Tyler noticed that he was in a huge round room with large glass windows; he was most likely in one of the towers of the arena. Despite everything going on, all the treachery, it amazed him how the night sky looked the same. Nature and the rest of the universe went on, no matter how foolish humanity acted.

"WHERE IS CAILEY?" Tyler demanded.

"She is just fine. A little disappointing though. She thought she could get you out!" Tyler recognized Alfredo Lopezzi as he stepped forward out of the shadows, still sporting his suit and acting as though this was everyday business.

"And you, my sly little friend…you just couldn't stick to the plan could you?" Alfredo continued, letting out a slightly relieved, slightly upset cackle.

"You really have made us work much harder than necessary, Tyler. Do you know that?" Alfredo continued, a hint of madness in his voice.

"Cailey? Where are you?" Tyler squeaked as his strength continued to leave him, while every breath he took was hampered with pain from the blow to his stomach.

"All you had to do was go out there, get your ass kicked, get shot and be done! Everybody wins! But no!" Alfredo screamed manically.

Tyler struggled to breathe; his lungs were stinging as

194

they gasped for air.

"Do I look like I care about your issues?" Tyler hissed. Alfredo flinched. He quickly shot looks at all the guards who were looking at him and then proceeded to stab his shoe in Tyler's stomach. Tyler violently coughed again. He refused to be weak in front of them.

"You...you – Tyler was cut off by his own wheezing, as his lungs begged for air.

"What's the problem, Tyler? Never been in the big leagues before? That was your idea wasn't it? To play on the same chessboard we do?" Alfredo's voice was now consumed by the maddening slaphappy speech that was escaping his throat. "You can't handle it!"

The words tore at his confidence, and it was because they both knew he was right.

"That may be true," Tyler wheezed. "But that's not what I was referring too, Lopezzi."

"Then please explain, Mason. We might as well give you some time since this is the last conversation you'll ever have." He shrugged as he thought for a moment. "Maybe your last sane one anyway."

All the pain he was in became obsolete at the thought of what he may face. Death was too good a gift for him now. They would never give it to him. He got a grip of himself as best as he could, sucking in his tears and looking Alfredo directly in the eyes.

"Your own daughter?"

Alfredo looked puzzled. "Come again?"

"CAILEY!" Tyler screeched, followed by coughing.

Alfredo still looked confused. He opened his mouth for a reply, but Tyler interrupted.

"You made your own daughter get involved with your lunacy?" Tyler yelled with all his strength.

"Do you know how we found out about Jason's plan, Tyler?" Lopezzi smiled. "Cailey would bug your phone for us, and we used it to hack into Jason's phone." The resistance in him seemed to falter.

"So," Alfredo chuckled. "The reason you are in this mess is because of *her*."

The last glimmer of hope began to fade from Tyler's heart. "So you see Tyler, had you never met her, you would not find yourself in the sad position you are now." He snorted.

"You know what Alfredo," Tyler struggled. "You can torment me all you want, but I broke your record. You are no longer the greatest of all time...*I am.*"

Alfredo's face twisted as he took a pistol from one of the black clad soldiers.

"You know what Ty—

BANG! BANG! BANG!

A large white light blinded him, while explosions and shattering glass sent his ears screaming for dear life. Chaos ensued throughout the room and the piercing, sound of gunshots, now all too familiar to him, echoed throughout the tower.

Strong hands grabbed his arms. He fought back, but blinded, bleeding, tired, and breathless there was little he could do. They set him down against a wall, the sound of the shots quieter than before. He felt a prick in his arm. Gradually he regained his sight, and rays of hope sparked in him once again.

Jason and Monty stood in front of him.

"Tell me this is real!" Tyler cried out in happiness.

"Realer than real, Ty." Jason laughed.

They were in the hallway of one of the exit doors, and he jumped as he saw black armored men next to him.

"Jason, Jason these are not our friends!" He panicked.

"No! It's okay, Ty!" Monty yelled placing his hand on Tyler's shoulder.

"These are *our* guys."

"*Our* guys?" Tyler repeated.

Monty aimed out the door and took some shots. "Jason, our window is approaching!"

"Copy that!" Jason yelled.

"Jason! I have so many questions! How did you know where I would be? Did you know I would survive? When did—

Jason's hand muffled Tyler's mouth. "Tyler, look I know you have a lot of questions but now is not the time. We have to get you out of here." Jason pulled Tyler to his feet.

"Let's get you out of here, champ!"

Tyler shook his head in despair. "I failed Jason. I failed. Look what is happening."

"Tyler..." Jason shook his head. "If anyone should be sorry it should be me. You have done beautifully, more than we could have ever hoped. You've given people an ideal of hope once again! Now—

An explosion blasted a hole the size of a person in the wall a few feet from where they stood. Tyler's ears rang furiously yet again, as if voicing their distaste to the terrible sounds.

"Jason, we have to get the *hell* out of here!" Monty yelled as he took point at the window while the other soldiers began to cover his position.

"Tyler, we'll have time to talk later!" Jason yelled as another mammoth hole was blown through the wall. "Right now, it is time to get the hell out of this nut house!" He signaled the other soldiers to cover them as they passed the door.

"DO YOU REALLY THINK YOU'RE GETTING OUT OF THIS, TEACH?" A cracked, howling voice screeched as loud as it could go. Tyler peered through a bullet hole in the wall to see a piece of metal being thrown over on the floor. He noticed a once perfectly polished shoe emerge from underneath it, now completely tarnished. Alfredo Lopezzi emerged from a pile of debris. His perfectly tan face now had a new compliment, an agonizing gash that extended from the top left corner of his face down to the bottom right corner of his mouth. He wobbled to his feet with difficulty.

"YOU ARE GOING TO LOSE, JASON! MARK MY WORDS! I WILL KILL YOU!" Alfredo Lopezzi screamed. A wounded soldier was being carried out, his gun dragging behind him. Alfredo snatched the weapon and kicked the soldier, taking aim in their direction.

"NOW!" Jason yelled. He and Tyler took off running, the wiz of bullets could be felt on the back of his neck. He glanced behind them. The two soldiers helping them flew backwards, a red stain forming in their armor. They had died trying to save him.

He turned around just in time to see Monty and another soldier smash two windows out. They took a gun off their back, with what looked like a harpoon sticking out of the barrel.

The sound of relieved tension followed as the harpoon like point shot out from the barrel, a rope followed.

"Come on, baby, come on." The soldier next to Monty prayed. Hope turned to disappointment as Monty's shot missed. Tyler wasn't sure if it was out of anger or necessity that Monty threw the gun out the window as the cable fell down to the street below, clicking and clacking off the sides of the building. But the soldier's shot hit its mark, a *CRACK* sound ripping through the night.

Tyler had never wanted to go zip lining. But he did it when he was eight. That is also when he fell off and broke his arm.

"Something wrong Ty?" Jason asked.

"It's just that...I uh— He stopped to wince as a soldier behind him latched straps across his chest while another snapped the metal latch of his belt. "I've actually had poor experiences zip lining in the past!"

"Tyler, you've almost been blown to bits, shot, and incinerated. Are you really telling me you don't want to zip line to freedom?" Jason smiled, uncharacteristically calm.

Monty, who was uncharacteristically ruffled, stormed through the squad to them.

"What is the issue here, Tyler? We are on the clock! Lets go!" Monty hollered as he hooked Tyler's latch to the cable.

"Whoa! Monty, I am not ready for this I—

"Tyler, these men and women are here risking everything, fighting against unbeatable odds, and not complaining at all about what they are afraid of when this whole trip would be grounds to quit. You are the lightest out of all of us. You can do this!"

"Monty," Jason began.

"No." Tyler interrupted. "He's right. He's right." Tyler hopped onto the windowsill, ignoring the pain in his ribs and the burning on his back. He turned to see the soldiers at the end of the hall buying him precious seconds, sacrificing everything for *him*. Blood spattered from the man at the door as he collapsed on the ground.

With a heavy conscious, Tyler pushed off the building and immediately panicked as the rope started lashing downward as it grasped his weight.

But it didn't fall.

He thought he saw his stomach splash as it hit the street below. He peered across Lanstark City's skyline. Smoke blossomed from the arena on his left. But the rest of the city looked untouched. He swore he could here the sound of jets, somewhere in the distance. To the right, the clouds were aglow from sporadic bursts of orange light. Were they the jets? The way they illuminated the night sky and reflected off the ocean made them look like they were something of beauty. Something you wanted to continue happening.

How deceiving.

Ahead, he saw the lower level roof of the building he would be landing on.

A sudden jolt on the rope made Tyler panic. He glanced behind him to see another soldier sliding down the rope. It was Jason, who antagonized him with a small wave. Tyler turned around just in time to see the end of the wall ten feet in front of him.

"Sh— He flipped the latch off the line.

Cold pebbles dug into his bare skin, and provided an uncomfortable landing as he crashed into them, rolling through all the momentum. A stab of pain shot through his ribs. But he had no time to rest anymore. Using the wall for support, he forced himself up.

"Tyler, are you alright?" The sound of impact behind him suggested Jason had just landed, and the hands under his arm for support confirmed it.

"Yep." He gasped. In truth he was out of breath, sore, tired, thirsty, and probably had some broken ribs to go with his burns now. But he was alive. That was more than some people could say today, something that was haunting him more and more with every passing second.

"I thought you guys left me." Tyler managed.

"We didn't think Lanstark would shoot Dei, and by the time we figured out what was going on, you were no longer in the arena."

"How did you find me?" He asked.

"Cailey...believe it or not."

At that moment, Monty came crashing down.

"We have to move now! We are being overrun, not everyone is going to make it out." He yelled grimly. Two more soldiers landed within seconds of each other —too many were using the rope at the same time. Tyler looked to see the bolt jerk in the wall.

"Move!" He was shoved forward and he quickly followed Jason who took point ahead of them.

He thought about Cailey for a moment...maybe she really hadn't betrayed him.

"There is a shortcut we're taking rather than the alternate route!" Jason yelled as they reached the other side of the roof. There was a section of the roof that looked incomplete, as the wall was missing. It was almost as if it were an opening of some kind...then he saw them.

One by one, hoverpads emerged from their building, and traveled all the way across to the city's private airfield a few clicks ahead. The pods were used to pickup the baggage of wealthy clients, and transport it back here.

"Alright, everyone on the pads." Jason commanded. "The ride itself is about ten minutes, be on your guard for anything that doesn't look good. As long as we're on these things, we're sitting ducks."

"What about everyone else?"

"They'll be okay!" Monty said. "We've wired it into their HUDs, they know where we are going."

"But they are outnumbered!" Tyler interjected.

"This is what they were trained to handle. Now please, get on a hoverpad, Tyler or all will be for nothing." With a heavy heart Tyler stepped onto the next one as it emerged from the building, while Jason and Monty hopped on after him. As they began their descent, he could see the rope in the distance, the last few soldier sliding down.

Perhaps they had made it unscathed after all.

"They volunteered to come, Tyler. They knew what they were getting into." Jason offered, putting his hand gently on Tyler's unburned half.

Within a few minutes, the rest of the soldiers all had made it onto hoverpads. Now all that was left was to make it to the other side.

The sudden silence of the night made the hairs on the back of Tyler's neck standup. He looked to the East toward the ocean, the 'fireworks' had stopped. It was nothing but darkness, now.

"It's so...quiet." Tyler whispered, afraid someone would hear him. He glanced behind them at the other soldiers of the squad. There were three of them on each hoverpad, with five hoverpads total not counting their own. Eighteen of them against Casper Lanstark on his own turf, how on would they manage this one?

"Hopefully, that means peace and quiet." Jason commented. "Monty, did you check the area?"

"The bulk of the force chasing us is waiting on the lower levels of that building." He pointed to the right. "We would have never made it out had we stuck to the original plan."

"So we are good?" Tyler asked, hope rising in his stomach.

"Not exactly," Jason began as his eyes darted around in his eyeglass. "The radar is picking up nothing."

"How is that a bad thing?" Tyler moaned in confusion. Didn't that mean there were no enemies? When had a thing like that become bad news?

"Because, Tyler! Think! We are in the heart of enemy territory! We should be surrounded by red dots of some shape or another whether they are coming after us or not!" Jason seemed be panicking now, while Monty loaded his gun. Tyler looked down at the cold piece of metal they shoved into his hand. He had never fired a gun in his life, nor had he imagined the day would ever come when he would have to. Would he be able to do it if it came down to it? Would he be able to fire this pistol and take someone's life? The image of the soldier with the blood bursting out of him stuck in his head. He thought of Dei collapsing backward without warning, without a chance, without knowing he had just lived the last moments of his life.

Was that because of him, or had they already planned on doing it? Had he made the right decision doing what he did?

How was he still alive?

With three blocks left to go and tension that could be cut with a knife, the eerie silence continued to haunt him. But it was peaceful, in that no one was trying to kill him for a moment.

Perhaps the night would finally quiet down.

18 Revelations

As soon as the guns had started, Daniel Louis knew that the plan had clearly not gone according to plan. They had grossly underestimated just how far Lanstark would go to achieve a total victory, and it appeared that he had forwarded the timetable for all of his plans to tonight.

Venom was going all in.

Originally, he was to meet with Zeus for a celebratory dinner, and maintain his cover. But the only thing Daniel Louis wanted to do right now was get out of this vile city. He flipped open his compass, and a map of the city projected up from. Jason and company currently hovered on a ridiculously exposed line of hoverpads. This was a change in the plan! They must have been headed to the airport. There wasn't a sign of enemy movement. He felt his excitement peak. Could this be anymore perfect?

Daniel grabbed his wig and flung it off. Forget the cover. He was getting out to fight another day. He opened his drawer, pressed his thumb on the handle to open the secret compartment under his desk, and withdrew his silenced pistol from it. He cocked the pistol and moved for the door, expecting the coast to be clear. His anxiousness and fear seemed to over power his caution…until at the last minute he turned on his heel.

The same reason he was so excited was becoming the same reason he should be fearful. There was no enemy movement. But that made so sense because they were in the beating heart of the Venom. Hope began to fade as he thought about this further. Was there any movement?

He pulled out his compass and the map of the city flickered to life once again. There was no movement but his own and Jason's team. This couldn't be right.

Trap. This is a trap. Trap. Calm down, Daniel. Technology, more specifically the intelligence aspect of it, was in fact his other job besides being a fake talk show anchor. In the training they had learned a strategy to conceal everything from the radar but the enemy themselves, and they often used it to escape or ambush their much stronger foes.

Ghosts.

The strategy had been called Ghost protocol. It had been quite sometime since they employed the strategy once the enemy caught on. In fact they really didn't even have a protocol to safe guard themselves against it…

But it couldn't be a problem the program had been developed in house. It was years ahead of anything they were working on over at Venom. Daniel ran his fingers through his hair and wiped the festering sweat off of his brow.

He himself had over saw the team. *Think Daniel. Think.*

That was it! He dialed three buttons on the compass, hitting the red one twice. It was the strategy the enemy had developed to stop ghosts, and now he was using it against them. He breathed a sigh of relief as nothing happened. Perhaps they really were this lucky. The boy not dying in the arena was lucky enough but this was incredible.

He sighed in relief and he began to dial a few buttons to let Jason know his plan. His map suddenly flickered, and nearly shut off before shifting and revealing what was *really* around them. Red dots surrounded his entire position and were moving toward him meanwhile a mass of red moved toward the airport to intercept Jason's team.

He began to shake as panic overtook him. He shook himself out of it and threw the compass to the ground. It satisfyingly shattered.

The door slid open and he turned to see Zeus Clementine surrounded by black clad TOC guards.

"Zeus, to what do I owe the pleasure?" Daniel asked. "Dinner is not for another hour." He quickly stuffed the gun in the back of his pants.

"I recognize a threat when I see one, Daniel. I know what you were trying to do earlier, making me look bad in front of the world because I picked the loser."

"So what are you saying exactly?" Daniel asked, trying to contain his urgency.

"You are gunning for my spot. You are gunning for *my* status." Zeus snarled.

"Zeus brother, you're looking at this all wrong."

Zeus whipped a gun out of his jacket. "A lot of people are dying today, no one will notice when you join them. I am sorry, Daniel. I really did enjoy working with you."

"Zeus, give a friend a chance and hear me out..." Daniel pleaded.

Zeus stared hard at him as he contemplated what had just been said. Daniel closed his eyes.

*   *   *

"Daniel, do you copy? Daniel? He's offline." Jason said with a hint of worry in his voice. Monty shook his head.

"What does it mean?" Tyler asked. He could feel a rising sense of panic in the air. And with the way this night had been going, he wasn't sure he could handle anymore.

They both stood silent.

"Jason? Monty? Frankly I think I have a right to know considering we could die at any minute tonight. Enough with the secrets. You brought me into this, so forgive me if I bring my own rules to the table." Tyler felt a searing in the burns on his back, but gritted his teeth as to not show it to the other two. Not right now.

"It means our last connection inside Venom is gone." Monty stated grimly. Tyler immediately regretted what he said, but he was learned a hard lesson this week, this place was no place for a nice person. There were times teeth needed to be showed.

He turned and gazed toward the airport. It was right along the beach. One of the top things he had wanted to do in his time here was visit the beach. The sands were some of the finest sands in the world, shipped from the nicest beach resorts and put together here. The night was cold, the warmness and excitement from the celebration seemed to be phased out by the ever-growing darkness of the night. They were only a block and a half away until they would be able to get off of this doom device and get on a plane to freedom.

He turned to Jason and Monty, who looked alert and nowhere near calm, but thank heavens not worried. All had been quiet, and still nothing had appeared on radar. The only activity that had taken place was the disappearance of Daniel's signal. But if Daniel had known about this plan, why would his signal go offline when he knew that now of all times was when they needed him most? Red flags flashed in Tyler's mind, as there was only one answer he could see.

"You said Daniel is undercover, right?" Tyler asked.

"Right." Jason confirmed.

"So how do we know he got caught?"

"Because we lost his signal." Monty interjected.

"How exactly is a signal lost?"

"The bearer of the compass would have to destroy it, because even if you are killed the compass will still be active and transmit KIA."

"So what do you think happened?

"We aren't sure. We have never had a glitch in the system before. Our guy is one of the best. He is working on it as we speak and insists he can find nothing wrong." Jason said.

"What if *that* is the problem? What if no signal is Daniel's way of telling us something else?"

Jason and Monty exchanged glances.

He began to open his mouth and argue his point when he became distracted by it, something ever so slightly cutting through the silence of the night

It was a faint at first. Whatever it was it sounded... strained. One solid mundane hum, and he was beginning to think the only reason it was getting louder was because it was...getting closer.

He looked around the buildings, there was nothing? He squinted into the night sky, nothing. But it was getting louder and louder, some kind of awful screeching noise, like nails being slowly raked across a chalkboard.

He turned to Jason and Monty for help, hoping they had an answer. They didn't.

In fact they looked no different than when Tyler had last peered at them.

"What is it?" Tyler asked. Surely they knew since they weren't panicking, but he didn't have that blessing.

"What is what?" Monty asked as he checked the clip in his gun.

"That noise..." Tyler found his tone rise slightly in frustration.

It was becoming louder and louder to the point were Tyler's hands flinched to cover his ears.

"What is wrong, Tyler?" Jason asked as a look of concern graced his face. The noise went from its monotone sound to a high frequency pitch that caused him to scream and drop to his knees as it seemed to explode in his ears before suddenly stopping.

Silence.

He quickly got to his feet and peered in the sky as if expecting to see something. Instead, it was only the dark grey misty clouds of the night.

"It might be gone..." Tyler exclaimed.

Jason and Monty appeared confused while the noise returned, but this time Tyler dropped to the floor, pulling Jason and Monty with him as what looked like an oversized metal bird swooped down at them with a screech.

"Holy hell!" One of the soldiers on the other hoverpads screamed as more of the tin birds swarmed them. Gunfire brightened the night sky as the soldiers fired on their attackers.

"Why the *hell* didn't these pop up on radar?" Jason shrieked as he took some shots to the sky, an explosions following a few seconds later.

"I couldn't tell you, Jay! Perhaps the kid is right!" Monty said as he ducked. The first wave was short.

The second wave came back with a vengeance. This time they had weapons pop out from under their wingspan. Within seconds of their decent two of the hoverpads carrying part of their team exploded in balls of flames.

"Jason!" Tyler yelled.

"What?"

"Give me some ammo!"

"You have no experience! You could hurt someone or yourself!"

Tyler banged the hoverpad with his fist in frustration, quickly forgetting the pain it caused when he looked up and got a good look at their attackers. They truly did look like metallic birds, with their bodies pieces of armor welded together. They had mini cannons and guns under their wingspan, as well as razor sharp claws that could grab you and drop you to your death without breaking a sweat out of their metallic silver paint job. But perhaps the most disturbing part of their design was their glowing, red eyes. They looked as though they belonged in a nightmare.

Three of them flew right over their heads, barely missing them with their claws. Unfortunately the soldiers on the hoverpad behind them were not as lucky. Two of the birds swooped down and grabbed them by their necks, severing their connection to the body before dropping them to the street below while the third launched a missile that sent the rest of the platform into pieces. Tyler spun around.

"Jason! Did you see that? GIVE ME A CLIP!"

As if *finally* realizing three guns was better than two in this situation, Jason yelled for Monty to cover him before lowering his gun and grabbing a pistol clip. He threw it to Tyler.

"I am sure you know how to pull the trigger!" Jason yelled as he handed some of the clips.

Tyler gazed at the gun. He had never fired one before, and it scared him…the power that it gave was too much for one individual. The ability to take away something so precious and do damage so permanent… at least he was firing at metals birds….for now.

"Tyler, one more thing, the recoil is a pain!"

He had heard of people firing a gun for the first time and breaking their nose from the recoil. Frankly, he had gone through enough for one day, and was not looking for an egg in the face…or a punch. He took aim at a bird and followed it as it moved closer to him; summoning his courage he readied himself to pull the trigger when the bird suddenly exploded into fire.

He turned to see a sly grin on Jason's face.

"*Jerk!*" Tyler couldn't help but smile. Even in the darkest of circumstances, the fact that Jason was still able to put a smile on his face showed something of the amazing spirit inside of him. He looked up to this man, and despite the twisted dark fantasy that they called present day; he couldn't wait to see what he could do with his guidance.

It gave him hope.

The birds were few and far between now, the rest being picked off by sharpshooters, Jason's best. The last few explosions faded, and the night sky returned to it's dark grey.

He observed ahead, they were less than forty yards away from the other building, and the end of what had been a terrible ride.

"Here," Jason exclaimed as he stepped toward Tyler and took the pistol. "This is the safety." *Click.*

"Switch it off again when you need it. I have a sneaky suspicion this night is just beginning."

A chill went up Tyler's spine, and the shiver that followed reminded him of the current burns and cuts that riddled his body. The temporary period of relief immediately ended the moment his conscious revisited this train of thought. He winced in pain, but did not feel sorry for himself. People had *died*. A little bit of pain wouldn't kill him.

"...great, that will be our strategy going forward. Make sure the rest of the squad knows that they are not to kill *any* civilians. That is not our way."

"Copy that," Monty said in agreement. "Copy that." Before there was even a moment wasted, Monty was off on the other end of the hoverpad issuing code words and orders to what remained of their squad.

The pod suddenly shuttered, and came to an abrupt stop. They were inside of a peculiarly square shaped hangar. He looked down below and saw nothing but more pods moving toward the ground through a square shaped tunnel.

"Quick, off!" Monty commanded as he grabbed both of them and jumped onto the platform. They waited until the others arrived, and then moved into the building. It was a maintenance building, so it was rather empty compared to anything that was related to the thousands of fans on the island.

The rest of the team jumped onto the platform with a slight sense of urgency as their pods began the descent downward after twenty or thirty seconds.

"What's next, Jason?" One of the soldiers demanded. Tyler could swear he had seen him before…but where? Then it hit him, the ball! The night his whole life went to hell! What a way to remember someone, present the night your life went to hell. He could swear he knew that girl behind him too, if only she would take off her helmet, then he would know.

"Move!" Monty's voice snapped him out of his daze. The squad moved as silent as a kid tip toeing through the hall to sneak a few cookies at midnight.

"Alright kids," Jason began. "There comes a time in your life when you are faced with some deep dodo. In that moment, you have to make a choice! You have to decide whether you want to back down and falter, taking the easy way out because you don't think you can do it. Or, you can choose to be the best version of yourself! You can choose to challenge yourself, and be great!"

They continued toward a large row of windows overlooking the airfield.

"Boys and girls, for all of us, TODAY IS THAT DAY! I choose to BE GREAT! What do you choose?"

A huge smile creased Tyler's face as he took these words in and whispered to himself.

"I choose to be great."

19 The Only Easy Day...

"We are getting reports that wide spread panic is overtaking many countries around the world. Some of the world's militaries are scrambling without leadership, trying to figure out if they should act or not. In some cases people are beginning to riot for information about the situation. The biggest question on everyone's mind is exactly what is happening in Lanstark City? Just seconds after Tyler Mason secured the biggest upset in history all screens went dark, and no one can establish communication from anyone on the island. This is especially concerning considering that many of the world's leaders are still present..."

The holoTV went dark.

Walking out of the room, Casper Lanstark emerged onto the balcony of his full floor apartment, gazing at his city. Despite the scattered fiery glows in the distance, there was nothing to disturb the peace of the night...other then the occasional distant gunshot.

His right hand cradled a drink, from which he sipped occasionally. After all, a celebration was in order. Not only had he kidnapped an army of the most powerful people in the world, but he had also orchestrated stock market crashes around the world. The sole benefactor: him. Why? He had shorted every single stock he owned, and among other arrangements, had been behind events that would cost trillions of dollars. The best part of all was that no one knew a thing about the impending events. With the world stripped of its money, he would buy back everything at a much cheaper price.

Casper had waited years for this moment, and having just been informed that all the world leaders in attendance were in an adjacent conference room awaiting him –not by free will of course – his heart skipped a beat in excitement.

Finally, his plan to bring Venom to where it needed to be was in full motion. And this was just the first step in his life's work. Being here now caused him to think back to his childhood. He had had nothing. Not a penny to rub together.

No father to look after him. And a mother who wasn't sober enough to tuck him in at night.

He was on his own.

Trying to survive the unforgiving streets of Detroit was no easy task. By age eleven, he had begun taking karate lessons to beat up the bullies who tormented him at school. By sixteen, he was in incredible physical condition, and the bullies had become the bullied. After high school he went to college, no thanks to his family.

He stole – or as he preferred to say, "borrowed" – identities and bank accounts from rich kids he befriended at parties he attended in order to pay the monthly bills, all the while absorbing knowledge like a sponge. Outside of college, local street fights and betting provided extra income but more importantly, brutal fighting experience for an already deadly weapon in the making. It wasn't long until gun and knife fights were his second nature. By the time he had finished grad school, his mother had began to feel sorry for herself, realizing she had done nothing for the last twenty years.

She became a nuisance, telling him to quit his current line of employment as a highly skilled assassin. But he ignored her, holding out hope that something in this world would go right for him. He picked up the bills, and made sure they were always fed. He moved them to a nicer place and tried to rebuild the family that he was now the leader of.

Six months went by and all seemed to be going well. He was even considering letting go of his current profession and getting a real job. But fate intervened.

He came home one day to find that, after years of neglecting his family, his loving father had showed up. To make matters worse, he apparently had gotten there at a time when his mother wasn't there and convinced his little brother and sister to come with him for a better life away from their drunken mother. His father turned to him; gun in hand, pointed at his mother who lay on the floor crying.

"Come on son." The fool slurred. "Leave her here and we can finally be together as a happy family." The needle marks on his arms and his mother's bleeding face suggested the man had greatly underestimated his oldest son. He had a bald head, with prickly remnants of hair sticking out of it, bloodshot eyes, a face that looked twenty years too old, and tattered clothes to match the stench of a man who hadn't showered in days.

"Listen, Stan, if it's money you want I can give you that, but no one is leaving here today."

"What did you call me?" His father asked in shock, as if he couldn't see that his son was not five anymore. Casper refused to ever acknowledge this man as his father. He had left them. Clearly, he was nothing but a drug junkie in need of money to overdose. He would be more than that. So would his siblings.

He took a step toward the man that was responsible for his conception. "Put the gun down now, and I'll get you your money and you can be on your way."

His father had now turned the gun on him, but his hand began to shake and he was beginning to perspire. He was going through withdrawal.

"I just have to get across the room to the safe and you'll get what you need." He spoke calmly.

"Don't try anything or you'll die!" The man screamed. Casper gave a reassuring look to his sister. She was not even this man's daughter and he was too messed up to figure out he only had two kids with his mother. The look on her face changed Casper Lanstark forever. It was in this moment he realized what a cold, nasty place the world was. It was the red blood seeping into the white carpet from the wound on his mother's bleeding face that caused any sympathy that Casper Lanstark had left in his bones to be iced over.

He walked over to the safe, trying to not make any sudden movements as he opened it and removed the thick bag of money. Slowly, stared at his father, who stood in their living room with a gun pointed at him.

"Okay Stan, I am going to walk toward you and give you the money, ok?"

Stan nodded, the gun beginning to slowly lower to face the ground. He was just three steps shy from his father.

He didn't even know what happened. He just heard his sister scream.

"Mommy!"

A loud pop rang throughout the house. There was a thump. His mom lay on the floor, a bullet hole in her skull. His sister buried her head in a pillow crying while the Stan didn't even flinch.

"What. Happened." Casper fought to control his anger.

"She moved." He shrugged.

"What. Do. You. Mean. She. Moved." He stammered on, he could feel his blood boiling, his body shaking slightly and his impulses bubbling up inside of him.

"I told that filth not to move! Now give me my damn money!"

"That filth?" Lanstark was in awe of just how much some people thought of themselves. "Okay, Stan. I will give you your money and than some."

He unzipped the bag and revealed the stacks of 100-dollar bills. He saw the gnarled, eroding black teeth of Stan as he smiled. Humanity disgusted him. Nothing but filthy, greedy, pleasure addicted ego inflators.

Stan pocketed his gun as he took a stack of money. Casper through the bag in his face, disorienting him before placing a few well placed punches and swift kicks, immobilizing Stan's legs and his left arm.

He than snatched his throat so hard his face began to turn purple. Stan tried to reach for the gun but Casper was too fast, shooting his left hand with it.

"Casper.....Li-s-t-e-n" But he didn't. His father's veins perturbed from his neck as his grip got tighter. The crunching sound confirmed that his father would no longer bother them. He let the body hit the floor with a *thud.*

Grabbing his sister and brother, he helped them gather their things, and sent them to the car. He gazed at his mother's lifeless body.

She was finally at peace.

It had been a turning point in his life. He had figured out his path, and a new vision for the world and his life emerged, but at a great cost. How would he accomplish his newfound ideals? Time alone would be the sole judge of that.

At 25, he felt empty, and resentful of a world that could care less about his existence. He had always known he had been destined for greatness. Why did they refuse to see it?

For three years he did nothing but his usual work acquiring the money he had always wanted, but not the power. By the start of the fourth year he had begun to lose hope, until he got a job from a mysterious cloaked figure he had not been familiar with, which was odd considering he knew everyone in the business.

The man wouldn't reveal anything beyond his perfectly polished shoes, the rest of his body stayed in the shadows. It wasn't the job that had struck a cord with Casper, but rather the payment. It wasn't money. It was access and membership to a legend the local street gangs had only joked about while touting their egos. 'Venom' they had called it. He was automatically hooked, and he could honestly say up until that moment he never had worked so hard in his life.

However, when he finally made his appearance before Venom, everyone in the room dismissed him, including a man wearing what looked to be medieval robes. He was the worst of them all, and argued against his acceptance. The person who hired him for the job never stepped forward.

In the end, however, they held the deal.

Casper felt as though he was the bearer of bad fortune as time went on. Their rival had not only gained control of an American President, but also had secured large funds from private Chinese investors. This put the war Venom had worked on for decades, constructing the tension, forcing arms races, and inciting nationalism out of commission. The two superpowers were emerging more united than ever.

The rest was history. He, Casper Lanstark had done what was probably, no not probably, *was* the biggest power grab in history. And the future looked like it couldn't get any brighter. By the end of the year, he planned to control the world's major military installations and space centers. Who knows, with the amount of money and power soon to be at his disposal, perhaps Venom would explore its grip into space, and the world's unknown.

At this point in his story, he was sure that all of the people who knew of everything he was doing believed him to be a power hungry monster that cared about nothing except for said things, with some major issues in the head.

But this simply was not true.

Long ago, someone said that people who are crazy enough to believe they can change the world do. He was one of those people, and history would remember him for what he was currently in the process of doing. Establishing the most peaceful time ever, allowing people to finally be free of the illusion that they must be great, and allowing all of humanity to prosper.

From its very beginning, humanity had needed limits. Otherwise it would be destroyed, or destroy itself. Casper represented those limits. He, and he alone, had a bright vision for the future of humanity.

There was just one thing that could pose a potential threat to the bright future they were on the verge of achieving, a person who he saw a lot of himself in.

And that frightened him.

Once he was broken, there would be nothing left to obstruct his vision for the future of humanity.

Casper Lanstark clicked a button on his wrist.

"Yes sir? "A soldier's voice echoed in his ear.

"Is it done?"

"We have their location locked at the airport sir. It is only a matter of time before we get the boy."

"Be sure to let me know when we have him."

He was no longer interested in killing the boy. No. He would either corrupt him, and if that couldn't be done...

He would break him.

20 Legends Never Die

They were half a football field away from freedom.

Tyler gazed out the window from the 2nd floor, wondering how on Earth they would ever get there. It wasn't the distance that was the problem.

It was all that stood in their way.

Tyler couldn't believe he had held out for this long, carried on by pure adrenaline and nothing more. Burned, bleeding, dehydrated, and beyond sore were just half of his problems. If not for the simple reassurance provided by Jason's presence, Tyler couldn't imagine the mental breakdown he would be in right now...or worse. He was holding him, all of them, together.

"What do we got?" Jason asked.

"It appears they knew we were coming. They rolled out all the bells and whistles to stop us." Monty said as he checked his HUD.

"They have at least a six squads posted up on the rooftops as well as hidden throughout the track." A soldier with a hologram projecting from his wrist added. "It is also very likely they are going to have more mechanized units like those that attacked us earlier on the pads?"

"So basically it is going to take every last bullet and grenade we have to get through this?" Jason smiled.

And Tyler thought the odds were against him when he faced Dei.

"Roger that. We seem to be okay here, but once we hit that pavement, the fireworks begin." Monty said.

"How far away is our ride?" Jason asked.

"ETA: fifteen minutes out." The soldier chimed in as he closed the hologram.

"Can't we just wait it out right here?" Tyler chimed in.

"If only life were that kind." Monty kidded.

"We have to make it to the end of the track in order for the craft to have the cover of the buildings, otherwise their anti air fire will cripple the shields and we will be shot down. Or worse."

Tyler didn't like the or worse part of that sentence.

"Alright fellas, looks like we are Oscar Mike. Let's keep our head on a swivel, guns up, and trigger fingers ready," Jason directed. "Just don't shoot me in the ass." A few laughs could be heard as they began their descent to the pavement.

Jason's effect on people was constantly apparent, a true legend among the men.

The runway of Lanstark City International Airstation wasn't long, but when traveling by foot, it wasn't short either. It was right on the ocean, and Tyler wondered how the pilots didn't fret about crashing into the ocean while making their descent...he knew he would. Private jets from all the wealth that was here to see the big match littered the runway... and he was proud to say that he didn't disappoint, even if the whole thing was rigged and micromanaged against him from the start. In the distance he could see Air Force One on the landscape, as well as planes from China, the UK, and many others. He wondered where those leaders were and if they were hurt. No matter, they had plans in place to leave in case of an emergency, right? Lanstark wouldn't dare kidnap world leaders.

Right?

As his feet hit the pavement, Tyler saw black clad movement from behind the various fuel and luggage boxes that were scattered among the planes of the runway. There must not have been any takeoffs scheduled for today, if there were the plane would be going through a maze. He still had the pistol Jason had given to him in his hand, and his grip was so tight he felt he was bending the handle. His hand was soaked with sweat, and his body seemed to be getting weaker every step.

"Tangos on the right!" Someone yelled. Harsh popping sounds ripped through the silence of the night and two black clad bodies fell from the top of a building across to the right.

They kept in single file formation spaced out and moving from cover to cover, gunning down the defenders when they had to.

"Two more over on the left Jason, behind the barrels!" Monty shouted.

"Roger!" Jason confirmed, hitting a setting on his gun, releasing a blinking red projectile that brought the barrels up in flames.

It seemed to be a losing battle for the black clad TOC thugs. It is not that they were not good, but these were the best of the best men Jason could throw at Venom. Not people to be trifled with.

They were reaching the half waypoint of the track and Tyler's outlook on the situation completely changed. Not only did he believe they would all make it home safely, but his outlook on the mission and everything they had to do began to turn from sour to doable.

"Incoming!" Monty yelled. "Take cover!" Jason grabbed Tyler and threw him behind a stack of huge metal boxes and took cover himself, peering at the sky. Tyler didn't have to look to know what was coming, he could tell from the awful shrieking sound that he had heard earlier this same night.

"Hurry! Get an EMP blast up there now or we are all dead!" Jason yelled as a soldier scrambled with the metallic weapon on his back. Tyler peered around the edge and saw the swarm coming at them and his heart dropped. The night sky was alit with hundreds of pairs of glowing red eyes.

Little pieces of pavement and metal shavings began to explode like confetti, as the birds opened fire on their position. At that same moment he saw more black clad troops approaching, but these weren't like the ones he was used to seeing, and he couldn't quite tell why…wait, they were bigger soldiers, bulkier in size than their predecessors. He watched as bullets bounced right off of them. They didn't carry guns, because they looked like they could tear you apart with their bare hands!

He took a few shots at them, but missed.

"Jason, we have incoming!" He yelled.

Jason momentarily turned away from the birds to peer at the new threat…

"Monty, we have troopers incoming!" He yelled whilst shooting a bird that erupted in a ball of fire.

The troopers were getting closer and closer. Tyler could feel his blood boiling. If the birds didn't kill them, than the troopers would. The birds began swooping in, ripping soldiers in half with their claws. What were they going to do?

"Do you got it, kid?" Jason shouted. "Time is of the essence!"

"Yes, sir!" The soldier shouted. His name was Mat, Tyler had found out.

The troopers and were closing in, and the birds getting ready for a second run in. Tyler gritted his teeth and closed his fists, ready for anything.

A sound of force building up began to fill his ears as though it was sucking in all hell, then, just before Tyler thought his ears were going to explode off of his head, a loud sonic boom echoed throughout, as a blast of purple light jetted into the sky. The hundreds of glowing red eyes suddenly went out and the shrieking stopped. Gravity began to play its part. Everyone threw their hands over their heads as it rained metal shrapnel. Balls of orange heat exploded all around as the birds dissolved in orange flashes. Tyler lurched forward to help some soldiers a bird was falling toward but it was already too late.

They disappeared seconds later.

The blood on his hands grew darker. He peered around to see the troopers bearing down on them. They numbers were dwindling fast; getting caught in the deadly rain themselves.

Tyler ducked and pressed his back against the metal that shielded him, he had to be smart. With his mangled and broken body, he would be out in seconds if he went to face them head on. He would wait until he could jump on the back of one. However, even the thought of killing, let alone injuring someone haunted him. Someone else's child, someone else's father...

Suddenly a huge trooper jumped over the boxes, where he was seeking temporary refuge, throwing Tyler's protectors out of the way. He charged down the track to the back of their line and grabbed a soldier, beating the pulp out of him. It was truly a horrific sight to see, one that would never leave his memory. More jumped over around them and began fighting with the other soldiers that were in position around him.

Another came from out of thin air and grabbed Mat from behind, throwing him to the ground. Tyler couldn't stand to see it. Mat did the best he could to defend himself, but he was outmuscled and out armored.

What to do? What to do? What to do?

Tyler felt himself begin to physically shake. Jason was nowhere to be seen and everyone else was engaged in combat.

You're not going to let this kid die, not if there is anything you can do about it!

Tyler rose to his feet and ran toward the back of the trooper and jumped on his back, clasping one arm around his throat and smashing the butt of the gun on the trooper's head repeatedly, trying to crack his armor.

The trooper stopped attacking Mat and threw Tyler off of him into a pile of crates that shattered on impact. Tyler felt a searing pain run through all of his burns, and his left arm was numb from using all his strength to keep that strangle hold for as long as he had. He scrambled to find his pistol, and then he saw it —over at the foot of a recovering and slightly bloodied Mat.

He tried to stand, but his feet slipped beneath him. He observed his armor clad attacker. He wondered if there was any soul behind that dark mask, if the person behind it had any heart at all? He braced for what came next. The trooper grabbed him by his bullet proof vest and lifted him off the ground until they were eye to eye, though Tyler could see nothing of his attacker's face. The trooper brought back his fist, and Tyler could already feel his brain bouncing back and forth in his skull.

He closed his eyes.

The next thing he knew he hit the ground, sending more pain into his wounds. He opened his eyes, dazed and confused. Jason stood before him with the troopers neck grasped in his hand. With a swift and sudden movement, Jason's hand was no longer there. The soldier collapsed in a heap of armor on the ground.

Two more came out of the battle zone and Tyler saw a side of Jason he had never seen before. Jason had incredible speed, fluidity, and precision in hand-to-hand combat. Even though it was two against one, he would have felt outmatched being one of the two as Jason masterfully played them against each other's every move. He blocked one punch and twisted the man's arm and set him stumbling into the other. Jason made a few more lightning fast movements and the soldiers collapsed, motionless.

"Tyler?" Jason came over to help him but Tyler ran to check on Mat. His bloodied mask worried him, but he opened to see a smiling face.

"You crazy fool, you!" Mat exclaimed. "Who attacks a trooper with absolutely no armor on?"

Tyler smiled and helped Mat to his feet.

"Good to see everything is under control here." Jason smiled.

"Well, well, well." A familiar voice echoed throughout the airport. The assaulting enemy troops and drones simultaneously halted, as if it were an order.

They peered to the top of the platform in front of them. Alfredo Lopezzi walked out to greet them. With him of course, was an entire squadron of troopers.

"My friends," he continued, a very arrogant tone in his voice. "The battle is over. We all know who the true winner will be. So, I have called off everything, from the fleet of drones, to the squadron of troopers here with me, to the swarm of hell birds you don't yet see…"

They all peered into the sky to look for signs of the ferocious creatures, as their EMP weapons were out of commission for the time being.

"And I have generously given you this time to think logically. If you surrender now, you will be treated fairly. Don't surrender, and we will kill everyone you love before we are finished with you." Lopezzi looked satisfied with his deal.

"Jason, you see that?" Monty asked.

"What?" Jason asked as he ducked behind cover, his thinking face on.

"On his wrist."

Tyler squinted around the corner of the box to try and see Alfredo Lopezzi's wrists. He didn't see anything out of the ordinary....he squinted harder, straining his eyes. There it was, he caught a glimpse of a little red bleeping light he could see when Lopezzi lifted his arm. Was that what they were talking about?

"Monty I don't know how you have such great eye sight as an old man but thank the heavens!" Jason exclaimed giving Monty a quick knudge.

"What is it?" Tyler asked.

"That my friend is a command link!" Jason said.

"It controls the entire drone fleet under his command." Monty chimed in.

"Which presumably is every bird in this area?" Tyler guessed.

"Now you're catching on!" Jason said.

"So what are we going to do?" Tyler asked.

"It's quite simple really," Jason exclaimed. "We are are going to shoot every bit of explosive and flash bang we have up there. All those explosions are rigged with EMP elements now, so they will zap anything electronic the grenade doesn't take care of. "

"Combined, they should have enough of an effect to disconnect that bracelet's signal, even if it is only temporary." Monty went on.

"Why not just use the EMP gun?" Tyler asked. They pointed to the right, and he turned to see a disheveled Mat holding the broken EMP gun in his hand.

"Are we thinking we are doing this?"

"Well the odds are about 48% that this will work." Monty countered.

"But we are going to try it, yes?" Jason said.

Yeah, what could possibly go wrong? All we would do is piss off the lion in his own den if this didn't work. Alfredo Lopezzi will be furious. Tyler got the suspicion he had been taking it easy in hopes of capturing them. He was expecting this to be an easy win. Trying to blow him up would for sure land them on his bad list.

As Jason and Monty signaled the plan to the rest of the squad, Tyler observed way off in the distance toward the end of the runway a very brief blink of a green light. One second it was there, the next it was gone. He had to double check himself and make sure he hadn't imagined it. Perhaps it was their ride out of here.

Perhaps.

If it was, he really hoped it would be here soon. He had already seen enough death, destruction, and abuse for one day. He couldn't get the images of the soldiers who passed out of his head.

What made it worse was that all of it was for him.

*   *   *

Alfredo Lopezzi stood poised and confident. He looked at his prey like rats in a barrel. All he had to do now was spin his revolver and choose which one to shoot first for sport. Had these been any other rats, he would have killed them already. He had the might of an entire battalion under his command.

But these were no ordinary rats. He had given everything to crush this rat, even his own wretched daughter who cared about nothing other than attention. And yet this rat had escaped him. This puny, little object of no importance to his world dared to believe that he mattered. It was insulting to a man of his stature. This could set a dangerous trend if this ant wasn't stepped on immediately. Every man, woman, and child would begin to think that they were equal.

The very thought sickened him.

He had learned from his mother, rest her soul, of the filth of those kinds of people. They pollute the world with their ideas, believing they can rise up and take everything he worked so hard for. He hit a holographic button on his wristband, setting the hawks on alert. Once they surrendered he would kill all of them but the three he needed. They would be an example of what was to come in the new world order.

He could smell the sweet scent of victory. He could smell the fear and defeat that the rats reeked of. Oh yes, he couldn't wait until they bowed before them. Humanity now answered to him and him alo—

He strained his ears, listening.

If he wasn't crazy, he had just heard a tap.

"What was that?" He demanded.

"I don't know sir."

Tap. Tap. Tap. Tap. Tap. It was like it was starting to rain without the rain. He looked in the direction of the rats. Nothing.

Than what was it?

Accompanying the taps was now a beeping sound. Almost like a... grenade. But that was impossible. He looked at the rats again; they had launchers pointed right at him! How dare they.... this wasn't how it was supposed to go! This wasn't how it was foreseen! Death was not worthy of him yet!

The night sky began to glow a bright orange.

*   *   *

Tyler remained fixated on the scene in front of him as sweat stung the burns on his back.

The entire platform seemed to crumble and collapse right in front of them with debris flying in all directions. Nothing happened, and the glowing red eyes of the metal devil machines above him seemed to focus in even more. The fact that they had no feeling at all scared him beyond belief. They didn't hate him, or love him. They were indifferent to him whether they killed him or not.

He braced to fight them off, when their eyes started to flicker. They began to wind up and down in the air as if they were fighting gravity. Even the TOC soldiers looked to their metal pets in confusion.

Without warning they fell from the sky as fast as rain, exploding as they crashed into the pavement. He looked at Jason, who flashed him a bright smile, his eyes beaming out rays of hope to everyone the man looked at. He was truly Tyler's light in a time when all other lights were out. He gave them all a direction to head towards. He felt a feeling he had never felt before.

He couldn't help but smile.

"Come on, kid it's time to go! We've caught them in a tight spot! Now is our chance!" Monty shouted as the rest of the soldiers began sprinting toward the end of the runway. The TOC soldiers seemed to be retreating.

"I don't see our ride yet!" Tyler yelled.

"It's there!" Jason yelled.

Tyler looked everywhere, but there was no ship. It was beginning to rain.

As if reading his mind, out of thin air a plane emerged right before his eyes. He felt like a kid again as he thought about the fact that this was one of the coolest 'planes' he had ever seen. It was black; with a sleek, fast design that looked military and yet was unlike anything he had ever seen in the military. They were almost home!

It was as if it was something not meant for everyone to see, let alone be in.

"Jason…how?"

"We have the best cloaking systems in the world right there!" Jason screamed over the roar of the shouting and explosions.

Monty jumped on the ramp and began getting soldiers in, one by one in strategic formation.

An explosion rocketed right in the middle of their formation throwing Tyler and Jason off his feet along with the rest of the soldiers.

He thought he could hear a faint voice.

There it was again.

And again.

The world seemed to be shaking. Why was it so dark?

"Tyler! Tyler, wake up!"

He slowly forced his eyes open.

Jason was staring him in the face.

"Get up, Ty!"

"What….what happened?" He muffled as best as he could. There was a grim pounding in his head, and his ears had never screamed so loud. Gunshots and shouts rang throughout the runway as a massive gun battle ensued. The smell of burnt flesh made him sick. He looked around to see bits of fire and blackened bodies littering the runway.

"A rocket." Jason gasped as he scanned the area. Tyler had never seen him with such a frantic look on his face. It truly ripped his heart to shreds. The plane was on the other side of the runway turned battlefield, shooting everything it could, but the TOC presence was far too strong for them to handle and they would have to leave soon. The blackened, burning mess of bodies had become the kill zone. Both sides had bullets and rockets flying at each other through this area. And that was the same area they had to get through to get on the ride home to freedom.

He put his hand on Jason's shoulder.

"We will make it out of here, Jason." He coughed, a tear sliding down his cheek. "I know we will."

"I know, Ty. We just have to find a way."

"Can't our plane just shoot the soldiers and building as a distraction?"

Jason looked as though Tyler had insulted him. "Those buildings have innocents in them! People who have no idea what's going on. We will not sacrifice them in order to seek gain. We are *not* Venom!"

"Jason…"

"Whatever happens right now, Tyler, I have no regrets and I wouldn't change a damn thing. I love you like a son, Tyler. You are going to do great things."

"Jason…why are you—

"Don't worry, Tyler. We can talk another time. Right now we—

"Hey…thank you for believing in me when no one else would."

Jason smiled. "Alright kid, lets do this!"

Tyler watched as the firefight continued and more and more of their soldiers fell lifeless on the ground.

He took a deep breath, preparing to run for his life.

"Lester!" Jason yelled into his earpiece. "What can we do? NO! Do not shoot the building!"

Tyler turned to see a mass of enemy soldiers charging toward the two of them.

"DAMN! JASON! Forget about me, what about them?" He pointed at the enclosing soldiers.

"Tyler, we aren't going to make it yet!"

"What about them, Jay!" He pointed at the bodies littering the runway. "What about them?"

"Tyler...

"Jason, we need to go *now*! Or their sacrifice will be for nothing" Hesitantly, Jason shook his head. The enemy was closing in. They couldn't wait to do this cleanly.

"Alright Monty, we are leaving. Time to pull the rabbit out of our hat!"

"We aren't ready! It is too much of a risk! Ten more minutes and—

"No. Monty, Monty.... NOW!"

Tyler could see a grim look overtake Lester Monty's face as he guided a wounded soldier on board the ship. He reluctantly nodded. "If you say so, my friend."

They exchanged frightened glances, as if each knew what the other was thinking.

Jason grabbed Tyler's arm and pulled him to his feet.

"When I give the signal, you are going to run as fast as you can to the plane. Do you understand me? Do not stop for anything. It is up to you, now. You need to do what I could never do."

"What? What are you talking about?" Tyler begged, pleading with the bravest man he ever knew.

"Okay Monty, on my go" Jason commanded as signaled the other soldiers to brace themselves for immediate departure. "One.... two.........three!"

The next thing Tyler knew, they were on their feet sprinting as fast as they could. Jason grabbed his arm and threw Tyler forward, ahead of him. The ship was getting closer and closer!

*   *   *

He opened his searing eyes. He felt a burning sensation rising from the pit of his stomach. It was not a burning from his burnt back, his sizzling arm, or his searing face.

Oh no.

This one was much more stronger. The flames of hatred inside of the second most powerful man in the world were more molten than the burning and collapsed building he stood so confidently on just moments before. He looked around as the remainder of his metallic beasts fell from the sky, resulting in a last few violent explosions.

His army was in disarray from the lethal shower.

The rats had taken his generosity and opted to use it against him. He struggled to move, wincing in pain as his injuries rebelled at every bit of effort he made. Stumbling on the broken concrete and glass, slowly, he made his way to his feet.

He tried to throw off his suit jacket, but the material was burnt into his arm. He grabbed his face in pain, only to stop in shock. It felt as though it was clay someone had just rearranged on the left side...

He tapped his ear. His earpiece had survived...along with him.

The man smiled. Perhaps it was fate.

He peered at their pathetic plane. They almost made it. He commended them. Perhaps in the future, he should rule out mercy altogether. It was...such a weakness.

Very well. He would let them escape. He couldn't possibly stop all of them at this point.

But he didn't need to stop *all* of them.

As if the odds continued to stack in his favor, he found the instrument of his revenge right at his feet. Ignoring the ripples of pain throughout his body, he grasped the .905 shell plasma backed sniper rifle.

It took him a minute, but he was able to concentrate while looking through the backup scope. The computerized one of course, had been blown by the same EMP that took out his birds.

Where were those rats? He could smell their filth from here! Ignoring the burning of his face he searched, and searched, and searched. Frustration began to take its toll.

He felt his will leaving him as the pain continued to get worse. They were probably...*wait*! What was *that*? The rat he was looking for graced the scope of the world's most deadly sniper rifle.

Alfredo Lopezzi smiled as he took aim.

*   *   *

Tyler had never heard a sound so piercing in his entire life. Not since earlier that night anyway, when Dei had been shot. Panic overtook him as he frantically searched the environment. He stumbled and crashed onto the concrete as his attention continued to divert toward the air, listening for another piercing sound.

There it was again…like a raging shard of steel cutting through sheets.

"TYLER! WHAT ARE YOU DOING?" He turned to see Jason charging at him, signaling him to get up.

He heard another devastating piercing sound rip through the air…and felt his heart turn to ice seconds later as blood spattered out of Jason, who collapsed in front of him.

The world seemed to go completely silent of everything but the ringing in his ears and the noises that escaped his throat.

"No… no… Jason! NO! NOOOOO!" Tyler yelled, tears streaming down his face. "I. I am…g-g-going t-t-to…g-g-get you…uh-out of…h-h-here J-J-J-Jason."

He felt powerful hands grab ahold of him and drag him to his feet. Men in black surrounded him. "I don't care what our rules are. I don't care about that right now!" He heard Monty furiously shriek. "Shoot those buildings now!"

Balls of flames erupted as missiles from their escape plane hit their targets, laying waste to the airport. Their troopers picked up Jason's limp body, while others continued dragging a struggling Tyler back to the ship.

He tugged at the grip of the soldiers; straining to break free! *He* needed to be the one to make sure Jason got on the ship! It was his fault, all of it! The soldiers carrying Jason stumbled as one collapsed after being hit.

They couldn't leave him. They couldn't!

"ARRGH!" He broke free, running to Jason, his arms shaking as he grabbed ahold of him from one of the soldiers.

"Jason, I am s-s-so s-s-s-sorry!" He whaled, hoping Jason would reply.

Another piercing sound ripped through the night, launching Tyler backwards. He was suddenly aware of an excruciating pain in the left part of his upper body. He lay gazing at the stars. Slowly, they became more and more distant from him.

A sort of peace began to overtake him.

The last thing he knew was that the grip was back.

Slowly, the darkness began to lift.

The sound of roaring engines could be heard along with voices as people yelled around him. The people were right next to him, but he couldn't understand them. They seemed so...distant. He had never felt such a pain before.

But it didn't bother him.

His eyes searched the table next to him. Jason lay silent.

I'm sorry I did this to you, Jason. I'm sorry.

Tyler.

It was...Jason.

You need to do what I could never do. Jason's voice echoed in his head. *I'm not asking you to do it because it is easy, I am asking you to do it because it is right.*

They had done it though, hadn't they?

They had accomplished their mission for coming to Lanstark City! He had defied Casper! His last act on the mat was an act of sportsmanship and love, potentially crushing the hostilities between the people of the United States and China. What would Casper put between the two superpowers now? He had taken Casper's biggest weapon away from him!

The pawns had broken the chessboard!

Tyler strained a smile; the voices in the distance broke into a frantic and excited chatter.

The feeling he had...he had never felt something so...pure. It felt far better than the fame, VIP treatment, even better than flying a Dragon Fly X!

The urge to go back to the dark slowly began to suck him back.

Was this the end?

He felt no distraught in his heart if it was. He had found a joy unlike anything he had ever felt. His dream of changing the world had come true. The men who had come before him had left the world a bad place, and wanted to make it worse. He had given it his all to make it a better place. Casper's plan now had a huge wedge driven into it. The boy with a heart no longer felt like a weight drowning him to the bottom of the ocean.

It now lifted him!

It became clear to him that life was not about the destination…being champion. Rather, the journey, and the experience along the way. That is where the real difference was made.

The power of a simple act of kindness, that's where true greatness could be found.

He stood up for what he believed in, the freedom of choice was something bigger than one person. And that was something worth fighting for.

If this truly was the end, he had never been more at peace.

Thank you for reading

SIX MINUTES

I look forward to continuing the journey with you by my side. Please share your thoughts with me!

@brandonmattinen

See you soon...☺